AUNT BESSIE ENJOYS
AN ISLE OF MAN COZY MYSTERY

DIANA XARISSA

Text Copyright © 2015 Diana Xarissa
Cover Photo Copyright © 2015 Kevin Moughtin

All Rights Reserved
ISBN: 1505596653
ISBN-13: 978-1505596656

❧ Created with Vellum

For all of Bessie's fans throughout the world.

ACKNOWLEDGMENTS

I am, as always, grateful to my editor, Denise, for all of her hard work and to Kevin for his stunning photos.

My beta readers, Janice, Charlene, Ruth and Margaret, do so much to make Bessie better and I am thankful for their continued assistance.

Mostly, I'm thankful for you, my readers. I love hearing from you and finding out what you like (or dislike) about Bessie and her friends. My contact information is available in the back of the book and I'd love it if you got in touch.

AUTHOR'S NOTE

Welcome to book five in the Aunt Bessie Cozy Mystery series. I'm sure everyone now knows that this series began with a character in my Isle of Man Romance, *Island Inheritance*. Of course, Bessie, in that book, was recently deceased, so I had to set the cozy mystery series about fifteen years before the romance. This series began, therefore, in March 1998 and continues at a steady one book per month (Bessie's time) pace.

Some characters appear in both series, as both younger (in Bessie) and older (in the romances) versions of themselves. If you read both series, I hope you will enjoy seeing these characters reappearing from time to time. There is no need to read both series to enjoy Aunt Bessie, though.

I've tried hard to stick to British and Manx terminologies and spellings throughout the book, but one or two American words or spellings might have snuck in. The usual glossary of translations and explanations, mostly for readers outside of the United Kingdom, appears at the end of the book.

What else can I tell you about the Isle of Man? It is a small island in the Irish Sea that is part of the British Isles, but is a country in its own right. This means it has its own currency, stamps, language and government. It is home to around eighty-five thousand lucky people, with the population concentrated in Douglas (and Onchan), Ramsey, and Peel. Port Erin and Port St. Mary are smaller villages in the south of the island.

This is a work of fiction. All of the characters are a product of the author's imagination. Any resemblance to actual persons, living or dead, is entirely coincidental. Similarly, the names of the restaurants and shops and other businesses on the island are fictional.

Tynwald Day and Tynwald Hill are both quite real (and Tynwald Hill graces the cover), but the events in this story that take place there are fictional. (There may not have been fireworks at Tynwald Day in 1998, but I thought Bessie and her friends deserved them!)

I feel I should apologise to the very real Isle of Man Constabulary, as I'm sure I make their fictional representatives here behave in ways they never actually would!

My contact details are in the back of the book as well. I'd love to hear what you think of Bessie and her friends.

CHAPTER 1

The sun was already shining when Bessie opened her eyes at six o'clock on Tynwald Day morning. She stretched and looked at her clock. There was no rush. Getting up slowly, she took a shower and then dressed and headed out for her usual morning stroll on the beach. It was going to be a long day, so she didn't want to overdo it, but she walked slowly past the new cottages that were now packed full of summer visitors. No one seemed to be awake yet in any of the cottages.

Back at home, feeling invigorated by the fresh air, Bessie made herself some toast with orange marmalade and a cup of tea. She carried them out to the large rock that sat in the middle of the beach behind her cottage. Sitting on the rock, she watched the waves and felt herself relaxing. Her life had been full of all sorts of unusual stress lately, and this sort of quiet time was exactly what she needed.

When she began to hear excited voices from the small children in the cottages, she decided it was time to head indoors. It wouldn't be long before her friend Doona arrived. Bessie and several of her friends were spending the day at Tynwald Hill in St. John's, celebrating the Manx National Day. They needed to get there fairly early, as it would be a long walk from wherever they could park to the ceremony that marked the beginning of the festivities.

Doona arrived a short time later and Bessie was, as always, happy to see her good friend.

"I'm so happy to see the sun today," Doona told Bessie as Bessie climbed into her friend's car. "I was afraid the festivities would get rained out."

"The forecast has been going back and forth," Bessie told her. "But I was sure it would be nice. We all deserve a bit of fun."

"We certainly do," Doona replied stoutly. "Now I'm worried about it getting too hot, though."

Bessie laughed. "I know what you mean. It does seem as if we are never happy, though. It is July; it should be hot, anyway."

Doona nodded. "I know, and hot is better than rain."

The pair chatted about nothing much as they made their way into Douglas and then across the island. Doona turned into the first temporary car park that they came to and pulled into a spot.

"I thought we might as well park here and catch the shuttle," she told Bessie. "No matter how close we get, it will be too far to walk, so why not take advantage of the free shuttle service?"

"That sounds good to me," Bessie told her. Bessie had never learned to drive, so she was quite used to various types of public transportation. In recent years she'd been fortunate to have friends like Doona, who were happy to take her places, but she often relied on a small taxi company as well. When she was younger, and money was more of an issue, she'd regularly taken buses and trains to get places as well. A short shuttle bus ride was no problem.

It only took a few minutes for the bus to take them to the centre of St. John's, where everything was happening. Doona had arranged for their group to meet across the street from the Royal Chapel, where the religious service that marked the beginning of the official events was about to get underway.

John Rockwell was already there when Doona and Bessie arrived. He didn't notice their approach, and Bessie wondered if she would have had the nerve to speak to him if she didn't know him. He was somewhere in his forties and very handsome, being over six feet tall, with dark hair and stunning green eyes, but there was something almost unnerving about the way he was surveying the crowd. Of course, he was a CID inspector with the Isle of Man Constabulary, so even though he was officially off-duty, he was always watching for trouble.

"Hello, Bessie and Doona," he smiled warmly at them, when they reached his side. "I have no idea what's going on, but it all feels very exciting."

Bessie smiled back. "You would insist on growing up across, wouldn't you?" she teased.

John had only moved to the island in the last year, and this was his first Tynwald Day. His family was finding the adjustment to life on a small island difficult. His wife rarely stayed on the island when she had an opportunity to leave. Most weekends she took their two children and headed back to Manchester to spend time with her ailing mother. This weekend was no exception; she'd taken advantage of the extra day off that Tynwald Day afforded to have an even longer visit with her mum.

"Ah, if only my parents had had the good sense to settle here," he said with a chuckle.

"You won't be the only one that's clueless," Doona told him. "I know a lot of natives who never bother coming to Tynwald Day."

Bessie frowned. "I've missed a few over the years," she admitted. "But it's such an important tradition, and they've made it such good fun as well."

"So remind me what's going to happen," John said.

"First there's a religious ceremony in the Royal Chapel," Bessie replied. "Then there will be a procession of dignitaries to Tynwald Hill, where they will take their seats."

Bessie pointed and her friends turned to look at the hill. Where there was normally just grass, now the hill was covered by a canopy and all along its tiers were rows of chairs.

"You mean the members of the House of Keys and other government officials, right?" John checked.

"Exactly, they'll do two really important things. One is read out all of the new laws that have been passed on the island in the past year. They'll be read in both English and Manx. And then there will be an opportunity for the public to bring forward petitions for redress. Any resident of the island is allowed to present a petition to the government." Bessie said.

"Anyone can complain directly to the government?" John asked.

"Yes, well, anyone who's followed the instructions for doing so. There are lots of rules, apparently, but if you have a problem, it's one way to make sure you get some attention for it," Bessie told him.

Before they could continue, the last two members of their group arrived.

"Parking was a nightmare," Hugh Watterson grumbled as he gave Bessie a hug. "I hope you didn't have to walk as far as we did."

Bessie smiled. "We took the shuttle bus," she replied.

"I told you there was a bus," Hugh's girlfriend, Grace, said with a giggle. She stepped forward to hug Bessie as well.

As the church bells began to ring, everyone focussed their attention on the chapel, and Bessie took a moment to consider her friends. They seemed an unlikely group, really, although maybe it was just she who didn't appear to belong.

Hugh was a police constable in Laxey, working directly under John Rockwell. He was in his mid-twenties, with brown hair and eyes, although he looked no more than fifteen to Bessie. Perhaps he seemed a bit older these days as he grew into his relationship with the pretty blonde school teacher, Grace Christian, though. He put his arm around her now, his lanky frame towering over the petite woman.

Doona also worked for the Laxey Constabulary, but she was a civilian employee. She manned their front desk and answered their phones. Doona was in her mid-forties, with highlighted brown hair and green eyes that were courtesy of coloured contact lenses. Doona was a couple of inches taller than Bessie's five feet, three inches, but she carried several pounds more than her slender friend. Twice divorced, Doona was currently telling everyone who would listen that she was done with men for good. Bessie didn't believe her.

Bessie shook her head. She supposed she really was the one who didn't belong. She was considerably older than her friends, although she didn't like to think just how much older. Her grey hair was cut short and it was an almost perfect match for her eyes. She'd never held a paying job, let alone one with the police, although the past several months had given her the chance to be something of an amateur detective, whether she'd wanted to be or not.

"Maybe we should move closer to the hill?" Doona suggested.

"That's not a bad idea," Bessie replied. "We definitely want to hear the new laws read in Manx."

Doona laughed. "You may want to hear them read in Manx," she said. "I know I won't understand a word of it."

"Sadly, I won't understand a word of it either," Bessie replied. "But I still really enjoy hearing it. It's an important part of our island's heritage."

Bessie and Doona had actually first met in a Manx language class some two and a half years earlier. Neither one of them had had much luck in learning the difficult Celtic tongue, however, in spite of taking the class together multiple times.

Now the little group moved across the road and into the huge green space between the chapel and the hill. All around them groups, large and small, were spread out on the grass enjoying picnics and waiting for things to get properly underway. Bessie and her friends found a small space as close to the hill as they could get and Doona pulled a large blanket from her bag.

"I meant to get you a folding chair for today," she told Bessie as the group settled in on the ground.

"I wouldn't have wanted to carry it all this way, anyway," Bessie told her. "I don't mind sitting on the ground. You'll all just have to help me get back up."

A few minutes later the procession started and everyone watched as the various government officials marched past.

"Oooh, look at all the lovely hats," Grace exclaimed.

Bessie smiled at her. "When I was younger, ladies wore hats regularly. Now you never see them, except at very fancy occasions."

"That's such a shame," Grace sighed. "They look so elegant."

"But they're itchy and they ruin your hairstyle," Bessie told her. "I don't miss them. As soon as they started going out of style, I cleared mine out."

"All of them?" Grace asked.

Bessie laughed. "There might be a few, inside dusty old boxes, in the back if one of my wardrobes. You must come by one day and help me dig them out. You're welcome to any or all of them, if we find any."

Grace flushed. "Oh, I didn't mean to suggest, I mean, thank you, but I couldn't possibly...."

Bessie held up a hand. "I have no use for them," she told Grace. "If I have any left, they'll be forty or fifty years old, I should think. If you don't want them, maybe the museum will."

Grace laughed. "But what if you suddenly get invited to an occasion where you need to wear a hat?" she asked, casting a coy look at Hugh.

Bessie smiled. "If I were invited somewhere, maybe a wedding or something like that, I'd buy a new hat anyway," she told the girl. "But I don't know of any event like that coming up in a hurry. Do you?"

Grace blushed bright red and quickly shook her head. "No, nothing," she mumbled, glancing at Hugh, who didn't seem to have been paying attention to the conversation.

Bessie smiled. She really shouldn't tease the girl; she really ought to be pestering Hugh to propose. Grace was perfect for him and she didn't even seem to mind the long hours and stress that his job included. It would be a shame if he let her get away.

In spite of her insistence on hearing the laws in Manx, Bessie didn't really pay attention to them. Instead, she let the sound wash over her, feeling an affinity for the many generations of island residents who'd met here over the years. Once the official part of the day was over, Bessie was as excited as anyone for the festivities that followed.

"What should we do first?" Doona asked as they all stood up.

"Well, we need to get out of the way," Bessie replied. "They'll be starting bands and dancing and other things on the green space once the crowd clears off of it."

"How about lunch?" Hugh asked.

Grace grinned at him. "How can you always be hungry?" she asked in an affectionate voice.

"I don't know," Hugh shrugged. "But I am."

"Lunch does sound good," John said. "I'm pretty hungry as well. I wanted to get out here early, so I skipped breakfast."

Bessie frowned at him. "Breakfast is very important," she told him. "You should have at least grabbed an apple or something."

John shrugged. "I'll try to do better from now on," he said.

The group made their way towards the long row of food vendors that had set up along the road.

"There's a little bit of everything, isn't there?" John remarked.

"Indeed, and they're here all day, so you'll have time to try something from everyone," Bessie told him. "I like to make sure I get something at every stall. I like to spread my pounds out over as many local traders as possible."

She stopped at the first food stall and studied the menu. Everyone joined her and they all ordered something off its varied menu. There were a few picnic tables set up to accommodate people who were eating, and Bessie and her friends were happy to take advantage of them.

"We're lucky we headed straight here," Doona remarked after a few minutes. "Look at the queues for food now."

The crowds were slowly making their way off the green as the first band began to set up. Many headed for the tents that were set up on the far side of Tynwald Hill, but it now seemed that at least as many people were hungry. Within minutes, another small group had joined Bessie and her friends at their small table. When a third group tried to squeeze in as well, Bessie crumbled up her napkin and stood up.

"I've finished," she told the others. "I'm going to have a walk around."

"I've certainly had enough," Grace told her. "I'll come with you."

The others decided that, even if they hadn't finished eating, they'd had quite enough of being squished together on a hard picnic bench, so they all joined Bessie and Grace.

"So what's in all the tents?" John asked.

"One is full of various non-profit groups who are selling crafts or car boot items to raise funds for their organisation. That's where groups like Manx National Heritage have their table. We'll have to visit and see who got stuck staffing it this year," Bessie told him.

"I bet it gets hot inside the tents," Hugh said.

"It certainly does," Bessie agreed. "That's why MNH sometimes has trouble finding people to sit behind their table all day. There were quite a few years, back when MNH was a much smaller concern, that I helped out."

"What's in the blue tent?" Grace asked.

"More food vendors," Bessie replied.

Hugh's face lit up. "Really? We should check it out."

Everyone laughed.

"We will," Bessie promised. "And the third tent is full of Manx businesses. They'll be passing out promotional materials like refrigerator magnets and pens with their names on them. It's a good chance to find out what our local businesses are getting up to, as well. Sometimes it can be quite impressive to see what's actually made on the island."

"Like what?" John asked.

"Oh, cheese is the first thing that pops into mind," Bessie told him. "There are a few farmers around the island who are making some wonderful cheeses. There will be samples to try and opportunities to purchase as well."

"Cheese samples?" Hugh looked even happier. "I don't know why I never come to Tynwald Day," he said, shaking his head. "It's wonderful."

Everyone laughed again, and then the group made their way towards the first tent in the row, the one full of Manx companies. In the entrance, Bessie was stopped.

"There you are. I knew you'd be here somewhere," a loud voice boomed.

Bessie held back a small sigh and forced herself to smile brightly. "George Quayle, how are you?" she asked the large man who now enveloped her in a hug.

"I'm fine, but how are you? I do hope you're all recovered from the recent nastiness?"

"Oh, I'm very well, thanks," Bessie told him. She quickly changed the subject. "I had lunch with Mary last week," she said, referring to his wife. "She told me you're expecting another grandchild, congratulations."

"Oh, thank you," the man replied. "That's much more of her concern than mine, of course. She quite dotes on the little beasties. I find them so very loud."

Bessie bit her tongue, thinking how ironic that was from the loudest man she'd ever met. George had spent his entire, very successful, career in sales and he still had the loud overconfidence that some good salesmen seem to possess.

"Anyway, I'm glad to see you here," George continued. "I was hoping we might have you for dinner one day next week. I've a few things I'd like to discuss with you."

Bessie nodded. "I'm sure we can work something out," she answered as vaguely as she could. "Have Mary ring me."

"I will do," George promised. He lumbered off, shouting a greeting to someone on the other side of the tent as he did so. Bessie just managed to hold back a sigh as she smiled at her friends.

"Sorry, I should have included all of you in that," she said.

They all shook their heads. "I don't mind not talking to him," Doona muttered as they began to make their way through the tent. There were several neat rows of tables, and Bessie made a point of stopping at each to chat with whomever was behind it. Hugh enjoyed several cheese samples and ended up purchasing a packet of nearly everything he tried.

They were about halfway through when they caught up to another of Bessie's friends. "Bahey Corlett, how nice to see you," Bessie said, genuinely pleased to see the woman she'd known for many years.

Bahey, a somewhat plump and plain woman with grey hair cut in a short bob, flushed and gave Bessie a strange look. "Oh, aye, I didn't get to Tynwald all those years I was working across for the Pierces," she replied. "I try to get here every year now. It's interesting to see how it's changed, like."

Bessie nodded. "It is very different, from when we were young," she said.

"Oh, aye." Bahey glanced around as if nervous.

"Aren't you going to introduce me to your friend?" a tall man standing next to Bahey asked in a slightly amused voice.

Bahey turned an even brighter shade of red and then sighed. "Yeah, of course," she muttered. She turned to Bessie. "This is my, um, friend, Howard Mayer," she told Bessie.

Bessie performed the required introductions of her own group, while she studied the man. He was probably around Bahey's age, somewhere past retirement. What little hair he had left was grey, and while he had probably been taller in his youth, he still had an advantage of several inches over Bahey and Bessie. He was trim and elegantly dressed and Bessie found herself approving of his old-fashioned manners as he shook hands with each of her friends in turn.

"Howard lives next door to me," Bahey told Bessie. "In my building in Douglas."

Bessie grinned. She knew that Bahey had just started a relationship for the first time in her life; clearly this was the man in the question. "Well, it's very nice to meet you," she told Howard.

The pair began to walk away and then Bahey rushed back over to Bessie. "I've been wanting to talk to you," she told her. "There's something strange going on and I want your opinion."

"Give me a ring," Bessie told her. "We can get together later this week or early next," she promised.

"It might have to wait a bit," Bahey replied. "But I'll ring you."

"What was that about?" Rockwell asked, always the policeman.

Bessie shook her head. "You know as much as I do," she replied. "But when I find out, I'll let you know."

"I'd appreciate that," he replied.

A few tables later, Bessie was surprised to run into Finlo Quayle, behind a table full of brochures advertising "Quayle Airways – the Isle of Man's most exclusive and affordable charter air service – launching soon."

"Won't it be the island's only charter air service?" Bessie asked the gorgeous young man.

He beamed at her. "Well, yeah," he admitted. "But that didn't sound as good on the signs."

Bessie chuckled. "Your cousin William told me you wanted to start your own charter service," she told him. "I didn't realise you were this far along in getting it going."

"Our first flights start in a month," he told her confidently. "We're still looking for a few silent investors, though, if you want to make a lot of money."

Bessie laughed. "Thanks, but I think I'll pass on this particular opportunity."

"You'll be sorry," Finlo replied. "I'm going to be a huge success."

Bessie didn't doubt it. Bessie had known Finlo, and all the Quayle cousins, for many generations. The man was not only gorgeous, but he was smart, and when he was determined to do something, he could be ruthless. His only problem was staying motivated. Bessie worried that if a pretty girl came along at the wrong time, he'd forget all about his fledgling business and spend all of his time pursuing pleasure.

"I wish you the very best of luck," she told him. "If I have to fly anywhere, I'm sure I'll keep you in mind."

Finlo pressed brochures on all of them. "Throw it in a drawer and the next time you decide to fly anywhere, ring me. I can't beat the commercial airlines on their prices for their everyday scheduled flights, but if you are wanting to fly somewhere that they don't go or you're looking for a much higher standard of service that's significantly more convenient, I'm your man."

Having visited every stall, the group made their way back out into the open air.

"It was stuffy in there," Grace said, fanning herself with her hand.

"It's warm out here as well," Doona answered.

A Manx dance troupe had just finished setting up and the group watched as they began to dance to the music provided by their small band.

"I took a class in Manx dancing once," Doona told everyone. "I thought I might meet a nice guy, but it was all couples and single women. I never did master even the simplest of patterns, either."

"They're a good deal harder than they appear," Bessie said. "They'll be looking for people who want to give it a try in a bit."

Grace looked at Hugh and then down at the ground. "Maybe we could try," she said softly.

Hugh's jaw dropped and then he gave Bessie an anxious look. "Oh, but, I mean, I've rather got my hands full."

Bessie laughed. Hugh was telling the truth. He was now carrying several bags full of Manx cheeses, jams and honey that he'd purchased.

"I can hold all of that for you," John told him. "You don't want to disappoint Grace."

The dancers finished a pattern and then spread out into the crowd, coaxing people to come and join them. Hugh handed his bags to John and then, with one last desperate look at Bessie, took Grace's hand and followed her into the middle of the green.

Bessie and her friends watched as the dancers taught their newest recruits a very simple folk dance pattern. After a few minutes of instruction, the band began again. Several minutes later, Grace and Hugh rejoined their friends, both slightly out of breath from the unusual exercise.

"You did very well," Bessie told them both. "Hugh, I was surprised at how quickly you caught on, and Grace, you certainly lived up to your name."

They both flushed with pleasure at the compliments. Doona and John were quick to add their own praise, as well.

"Gee, thanks," Hugh said. "It was almost kinda fun. But now I've worked up quite an appetite."

As they laughed, the group headed for the second tent, full of food stands. They would get back to the outside food vendors later. Bessie wasn't all that hungry, so she searched for a table while the others queued for their food.

"Ah, Bessie, come and sit with me," a voice called across the crowded tent.

Bessie headed towards the voice, uncertain exactly where it had come from or who was calling her name.

"Over here, Bessie," the voice called again.

Bessie looked around and smiled as she spotted Henry Costain, one of her favourite Manx National Heritage's employees, who had also taken one of her Manx language classes with her. She quickly crossed over to him and sank down into a chair.

"Thanks," she said. "It's pretty busy in here."

"You aren't here on your own, are you?" Henry asked.

"No, Doona and the others are getting food. I said I'd get us a table," she explained. "Are you working at the MNH table?"

"Nope, I got a day off today," he told her. "Actually, I have a whole week off. I'm planning on taking my nephew's kids to the wildlife park tomorrow and I'm hoping to do a lot of reading as well."

"Good for you," Bessie replied. "You've earned a holiday."

"I have at that," Henry said firmly. Henry had been caught up in many of the recent murder investigations that seemed to be plaguing Bessie. He was a kind and sensitive man and he deserved a chance to relax and forget about all of the bad things that can happen in life.

Doona and the others soon joined them. Doona brought Bessie a huge cup filled with sweet, milky tea and a sandwich.

"I said I wasn't hungry," Bessie argued as she unwrapped the sandwich.

"Hugh will eat it if you don't want it," Doona replied.

Bessie laughed. "Well, now that you're all here, eating, I am a bit peckish," she admitted. The sandwich disappeared almost as quickly as Hugh's very full plate of food did.

The afternoon was rapidly turning into early evening as they made their way back outside. A group of martial artists was just getting started, demonstrating impressive-looking kicks and breaking wooden boards with flying fists and feet.

Bessie spotted another friend in the crowd. "Hello, Liz," she said once she'd made her way through the audience.

"Ah, Bessie, so good to see you," Liz Martin, another friend from a Manx language class said, giving Bessie a quick hug.

"You can't be here on your own?" Bessie asked.

Liz laughed. "No way, hubby has the kids up as close as they could get. Jackson is desperate to have a go."

"How old is he?" Bessie asked.

"Nearly three," Liz sighed. "I'm just afraid he's going to try kicking his way through everything in our house when we get him home. Our coffee table probably isn't safe."

Bessie and her friends watched the demonstration for a while.

"That was exciting," Doona remarked as the group finished. "Did you see the man in charge? He was very impressive."

"Maybe I should try some taekwondo," John said in a thoughtful voice. "I wonder if we could add that to the fitness classes we're already providing at the station."

"If you can get that guy to teach them, I'd give it a try," Doona laughed.

John frowned. "Maybe not," he muttered.

After a stop at a couple more food vendors, the group made their way towards the third tent.

"So how many people are you going to know in here?" Doona teased Bessie.

"Probably a lot," Bessie said with a grin. "Whoever's working for MNH, plus a lot of other people from the various organisations in Laxey that will be here. There's probably a dozen other groups around the island that I've been involved with at some point in my life as well, and most of them will probably have a table."

"So we'll be in here until the fireworks start," Doona concluded.

Bessie laughed. "You'll all have to pop out for food once in a while. I'd hate to see Hugh starve."

"Actually, if no one minds, Grace and I thought we might go and see the next band," Hugh told them. "The Screamin' Manxmen are really good and Grace has been wanting to see them again."

"You go," Bessie told them. "We'll catch up with you guys later."

Noble's Hospital had one of the first tables. Bessie smiled at her friend Helen, who was behind it.

"Helen, I didn't realise they drafted nurses to work at these things," she exclaimed.

"They normally don't," Helen explained. "But the woman who was going to do it managed to break her leg yesterday. Since I was planning on coming anyway, I offered to step in for some of the day."

"That was kind of you," Bessie replied.

A moment later, another familiar face came into view. Bessie held her tongue as the tall, forty-something man handed Helen a bag.

"Here you go," he said to her. "I think I got exactly what you ordered."

"I'm sure it will be fine," Helen assured him.

"Inspector Corkill? I wasn't expecting to see you here," Bessie interrupted.

The man spun towards her and then turned back towards Helen. When she didn't say anything, he looked back at Bessie. "Miss Cubbon, I didn't see you there," he said. "I was just, um, bringing some food to Hel, er, Ms. Baxter."

"Hey, Pete, how are you?" John jumped in, slapping his Douglas counterpart on the back.

"Oh, I'm fine," the man replied, clearly unsettled by something. "I was just, that is, I haven't been to Tynwald in years, but I thought it might make a nice change."

"You were lucky to get the day off," John remarked. "But I suppose St. John's is out of your jurisdiction."

"Yeah, although we help out with security and the like, but there isn't usually much for CID to worry about."

The two men chatted about police business for a moment while Bessie caught up with Helen.

"So, what's going on with you and the inspector?" she couldn't help but ask in a very low voice.

Helen shrugged. "We're seeing each other, I suppose," she replied. "But very slowly. He isn't really totally over his ex-wife and I'm not rushing in. I think I've finally found a good guy, and I intend to take it at whatever pace he feels comfortable with. We were meant to spend the day together, before I got tapped to do this."

"What a shame," Bessie said.

"It's okay," Helen answered. "I'm done in another hour or so. We'll get to watch the fireworks together."

Bessie's group moved on, and Bessie was correct; she knew people at several of the tables. Marjorie Stevens, the Manx Museum librarian and archivist, who also taught the Manx language courses that Bessie and Doona had taken, was behind the MNH table.

Bessie gave her a big hug. "Fastyr mie, kys t'ou?" she greeted her in Manx.

"Ta mee braew," Marjorie answered with a grin. "And it's good to hear that you're still working on your Manx."

"Well, a little bit, anyway," Bessie laughed. "I thought you'd have your most junior staff member handle today," she added.

"I wish," Marjorie laughed. "Seriously, though, I volunteered. I love the atmosphere out here and I love what the day represents. The island might just be my adopted home, but I couldn't love it more if I'd been born here."

Two tables further along, Bessie found herself engulfed in a flurry of hugs. "The Raspberry Jam Ladies," she laughed. "I didn't know you were still meeting."

"Every Tuesday afternoon, from one until three," Agnes Faragher answered. "We've been doing it for fifty-odd years and we'll be doing it for another fifty." Agnes was a plump widow with grey hair and thick glasses.

Bessie laughed and then introduced the five ladies to her friends. "I think they're Laxey's longest-running women's group," she told the others. "They started meeting when they were young newlyweds and they've been meeting ever since."

"Why the 'Raspberry Jam Ladies?'" Doona asked.

Nancy King, a petite woman with reading glasses perched on the end of her nose, laughed.

"We started out rather informally," she explained. "Just any of us getting together whenever we had a chance. One day we met at

Elinor's house and made a big batch of raspberry jam with wild raspberries. The war was on or not long over, so we pooled our sugar ration to make it and then we shared the results. My husband stopped complaining about me meeting up with my lady friends after that. He wasn't going to complain if there was a possibility of jam coming home with me. The name sort of became a joke between us girls, but it stuck."

"Bessie, you must buy something to help us out," Elinor Lewis said firmly. Elinor still looked much the same as ever: tall, slender and no-nonsense.

Bessie looked over their table, which was full of the sort of merchandise you would normally get at a car boot sale. Mismatched cups and plates jockeyed for space with old board games and jigsaw puzzles.

"It looks as if you emptied one of my cupboards," she told the ladies.

"We all thought we'd have a go at clearing out a few things," Margaret Gelling said quietly. "Any money we raise is going to a charity; I forget which one, though." Margaret was the quietest member of the small group, often fading into the background where other, stronger personalities dominated. She, too, was grey-haired and tended towards plump.

Bessie found a stack of old paperbacks on the table and managed to find a few books in the pile that she thought she might enjoy. She paid for her purchases while the others moved on to the next table.

"Thank you kindly," she told Agnes as she took the bag of books from her.

"The children's ward at Noble's will appreciate your kindness as well," Joan Carr said. Joan was perched on the edge of her chair, her fingers bent from years of suffering with arthritis, but she gave Bessie a huge smile. "You know that's a favourite cause of mine."

Bessie nodded. "It's a favourite cause of mine, as well," she told the other woman.

"Hang on," Agnes told her. Agnes looked back and forth and then winked at Bessie. "Have a jar of raspberry jam," she whispered, slipping the jar into Bessie's bag. "It may well be the Raspberry Jam Ladies' last-ever batch. We're all getting too old for that sort of thing."

Bessie smiled. "We're all getting older," she replied, conscious that she was at least a few years older than the ladies in the group. "But I've always loved your jam. Can I pay you for it?"

"Oh, no," Agnes grinned. "It's a gift. We're only sharing it with a few very select friends."

Bessie caught up with her friends and they finished visiting the tables in the tent. Outside it was getting dark and the crowds were thinner as families with very small children headed for home. They easily found Hugh and Grace, and Hugh, once more, had food on his mind. Things were fairly quiet at the food stalls, so everyone ordered a last treat for the day. Then they sat together at one of the tables, watching the crowds.

At long last, it was time for the fireworks and Bessie and her friends enjoyed the colourful display that was set to live music by one of the local bands. After it was over, there were, of course, long queues for the shuttle buses back to the car parks.

"My car's in the first lot," John told the others. "I can give you all rides to your cars."

They all followed him the very short distance to the VIP lot.

"Should I ask how you managed to get a space in here?" Doona asked.

John laughed. "I was here nice and early and the man on the gate recognised me. He insisted that I park in here. I suspect it was just in case something came up and they needed someone from CID in a hurry."

"But nothing did come up," Bessie said reflectively. "We got through the entire day without anything going wrong. I can't tell you all how much I enjoyed it."

CHAPTER 2

The skies were cloudy the next morning, a Tuesday, when Bessie woke. It was somewhat later than six, after her late evening the night before. With nothing on her schedule for the day, she took her time getting up and dressed. The rain hadn't actually started yet, so she took her usual walk, keeping one eye on the skies as she went. She didn't bother with an umbrella, but she did wear her raincoat.

She was back at home before she needed it, though. As she waited for her toast to pop, she looked longingly at the jar of raspberry jam her friends had given her the day before. She thought about opening it, but she had only just started on the jar of orange marmalade and she didn't want the marmalade to spoil while she ate raspberry jam instead. The jam would wait.

After breakfast, anticipating rain later, she took a second, shorter walk. Then she curled up in her sitting room in her most comfortable chair, a cup of tea to hand, and lost herself in one of her favourite books. When she heard a car going past, she didn't even look up. During the summer months, her normally quiet road became quite busy. She couldn't ignore the sudden loud banging on her door, however.

Bessie felt a flutter of nerves when she reached the door. It was quite unusual for anyone to be knocking on her door this early in the morning, and this sort of frantic pounding was even more worrying. She took a deep breath and opened the door, sighing with relief when she recognised Hugh on the other side.

"You didn't eat the jam, did you?" he demanded.

Bessie stared at him. "Pardon?"

"The jam, you know, that you were given yesterday by your friends," Hugh said, speaking so quickly that Bessie could barely understand him. "You haven't had any, have you?"

Bessie shook her head. Hugh gave her a quick hug.

"Thank goodness," he said with a sigh, suddenly looking exhausted.

"What's going on?" Bessie demanded.

"I'm sorry to be the one to tell you, but one of your Raspberry Jam Ladies was found dead this morning," he replied. "At the moment, it looks as if her jar of jam was poisoned."

Bessie felt the colour drain from her face. Hugh took her arm and led her to the table, where he helped her into a chair.

"I'm sorry," he said sheepishly. "That came out rather more bluntly than I'd intended."

"But who died?" Bessie asked, feeling confused. "And why do you think the jam killed her?"

Hugh took a deep breath. "Hang on," he told Bessie. He pulled out his mobile phone and punched in some numbers. With the phone held up to his ear, he paced around Bessie's kitchen. When he spotted the jam jar on the counter, he spun around. Before he could speak, however, it seemed his call was answered.

"Ah, yes, Inspector Rockwell, I'm here with Bessie Cubbon. She hadn't opened the jam yet, so I'll bring her jar back with me. Obviously, she has several questions, though."

Hugh was silent for several minutes, nodding pointlessly with the phone in hand. Finally, he spoke again. "Yes, sir, that's fine. I'll see you soon."

He pressed a button on the phone and then turned and smiled at

Bessie. "The inspector suggests that you save your questions for now," he told Bessie. "He would like to interview you as soon as possible and he'll answer whatever questions he can at that time."

"Can't you at least tell me who died?" Bessie asked.

Hugh nodded. "That'll be common knowledge by now, anyway," he told her. "Mrs. Nancy King was found unresponsive this morning by her daughter. The daughter called the emergency services, but, sadly, Mrs. King was pronounced dead at the scene."

Bessie sighed deeply. Nancy hadn't been a close friend, but she was something more than simply an acquaintance. "How very sad," she said softly.

Hugh bent down and gave her an awkward hug. "I'm sorry," he said. "I wish I could stay with you, but I need to get back. We have a list of folks who were given jars of jam and I've got to help track them all down."

He took a large plastic bag out of his pocket and, after putting on gloves, put Bessie's jam into the bag and sealed it. "I was really worried about you," he told her as he did so.

"But why didn't you just ring me?" Bessie asked.

"We did," Hugh answered. "You didn't answer your phone."

Two pairs of eyes went to the answering machine sitting on Bessie's counter. Bessie flushed as she spotted the blinking red light. She hadn't noticed it after her second walk. She'd been so intent on tea and her book that she hadn't given it a thought.

"I was out walking," she told Hugh. "I should have checked the machine when I got back, though. Sorry."

"It's fine," he assured her. "I would have had to come and collect the jam jar anyway."

Bessie followed Hugh to her door and let him out. "Is the inspector coming here or am I supposed to go into the station?" she asked him in the doorway.

"He said to tell you that he'll be here around midday," Hugh replied.

"I think I'll make some coronation chicken," Bessie said, as much to herself as to Hugh. "I have some leftover chicken from the weekend. No doubt the inspector will be hungry."

Hugh grinned. "Maybe I'll find a way to convince him to bring me as well," he teased.

Once he'd left, Bessie started working on her lunch plans. She wanted to ring Doona to find out what was happening, but there was no doubt her friend was busy at the station. It would be rude to bother her under the circumstances.

With the chicken salad safely tucked up in her fridge, Bessie settled back in with her book. Shortly before midday, Bessie filled three bowls with salad greens and added a generous spoonful of the chicken salad to each. She pulled out a loaf of crusty bread and cut it into thick slices. John Rockwell pulled up as she was arranging things on her kitchen table.

"Bessie, it's so good to see you," he told her, giving her a quick hug as he walked into the kitchen.

"It's good to see you as well," Bessie told him. "No Hugh?"

"He's still tracking down jars of jam," the inspector replied. "The ladies were quite generous with it, it seems."

"But what's going on?" Bessie asked.

John sighed. "At this point, I'm not even sure," he told her.

"But where are my manners?" Bessie said, shaking her head. "Sit down and have something to eat," she suggested, gesturing towards the table.

Bessie poured iced tea into glasses and then joined him at the table.

"This is delicious," John said after several bites. "I didn't realise how hungry I was."

"You always forget to eat when you're working," Bessie told him. "I thought that the least I could do is feed you."

John smiled. "It is much appreciated, but more than food, I need information from you."

Bessie nodded. "I expected as much," she told him. "And I expect there isn't much you're going to be able to tell me, as well."

"Unfortunately not," John told her. "We're trying to keep as much back as we can. We've had to admit that we suspect something was in the jam, because we're rushing all over the island collecting every jar we can find and warning people not to eat it, but that's about all I can share at this point."

"Does that mean you can't tell me which of the ladies made the jam, then?" Bessie asked.

He shrugged. "That's part of the problem," he said. "No one seems to know where the jam came from."

Bessie frowned. "What do you mean, no one knows?" she demanded.

John shook his head. "Can we do this my way?" he asked. "I have a lot of questions for you and I'd really like to go through them. I'll try to answer yours as well, but this is a police investigation. Please keep that in mind."

Bessie flushed. "Sorry, I think I'm just in shock," she muttered.

The inspector nodded back. "I really need your help," he told her. "I need a lot of background and I need it quickly and concisely. As you can imagine, the rest of the ladies from the group are both shocked and upset. None of them were able to tell me much of anything. I'm counting on you to fill in a lot of blanks."

"What do you need to know?" Bessie asked.

"Let's start with a brief history of the Raspberry Jam Ladies, please," John said.

Bessie sighed. "I think the group started in the early forties," she began. "I was never a part of it, so I'm a little fuzzy on the details."

"Why weren't you a part of it?" John asked. "You're about the right age, aren't you?"

Bessie shook her head. "I think most of the ladies are a few years younger than I am," she told him. "Besides, they first met when they all shared a midwife, I believe. They all became new mothers at the same sort of time. I simply didn't fit into their group."

"And did you mind?" John asked.

Bessie frowned. "There isn't an easy answer to that one," she admitted. "There were times when I would have liked to feel more a part of the community, especially in those days, when the village felt smaller and more close-knit. But they didn't deliberately exclude me; I just had nothing in common with them. They were married with children and I was single and lived on my own."

John made a few notes in his notebook and then moved on. "Can you give me a brief rundown of the members of the group, then?" he asked.

"Hugh said Nancy King was the victim," Bessie replied. "She was probably the woman I knew the least well in the group. She had four or five children and the last I knew, they were scattered around the world. At least one is still on the island, though, but I think in the south somewhere."

"Yes, her daughter lives in Port Erin. She's the one who found the body," John told her. "There are three other children, but two are across and one is in Australia."

"From what I can remember, none of them were particularly close to Nancy," Bessie continued. "There must be grandchildren and even great-grandchildren, as well."

"Indeed, but as you say, none of them were close to Mrs. King."

"I'm not sure what else you want to know," Bessie said. "Her husband worked in Laxey at one of the banks, but he died in the late sixties and she never remarried. If you're looking for motives for murder, I can't even begin to imagine why anyone would want to kill her. As far as I knew, she was a harmless and ordinary woman."

"Let's run through the rest of the group, please," John said.

"I think there were originally seven of them," Bessie replied, struggling to remember. "I know Peggy Cannon passed away about five years ago. Nancy had a sister or a sister-in-law or maybe it was a cousin. Anyway, she was called Elizabeth, and she was one of the ladies for a while. She passed away in the seventies, though, after a car accident. I've quite forgotten her surname."

John flipped through his notebook. "She was Elizabeth Porter and she was a cousin to Nancy King. You're right; she died in a car accident in the seventies. Her husband was driving and he lost his life as well. They had two children, who were both living across by that time."

"It seems like you already know everything," Bessie said.

"I have some facts," he replied. "But I'm more interested in personalities."

Bessie nodded. "I hate to speak ill of the dead, but Nancy and I never hit it off. She wasn't always the most pleasant person to spend time with, especially after Elizabeth died. I can't see that as a motive for murder, though."

"So let's talk about the rest of the jam ladies who are still alive," John said.

"Elinor Lewis is the driving force behind the group," Bessie said. "If you're looking for personality, she has some to spare. She was a schoolteacher before she married and she's very smart. I think, if she'd stayed single, she could have had a brilliant career. Of course, in the nineteen-forties, women didn't work after they married."

"I've met Mrs. Lewis," John said. "She struck me as a very intelligent woman, in spite of her upset."

"She's a few years older than some of the others," Bessie continued. "And I've no doubt the group would have broken up many years ago if it wasn't for her. Her husband learned all about cars and trucks during the war and when he came home he opened a garage in Ramsey. They only had the one child, a boy called Nathan. He wasn't very bright; in fact he had learning difficulties, and I don't think he ever held a proper job. Elinor's husband, Nicholas, passed away, oh, goodness, maybe twenty years ago. The son died just last year, having lived with his mother for his entire life. It was tragic, really, because he drowned in the bath one afternoon while his mother was out."

The inspector made a few notes and then nodded. "I've asked Doona to pull the files on his passing," he told Bessie.

Bessie gasped. "You don't suspect...."

"I don't suspect anything," he assured her. "I'm just trying to understand the people involved."

Bessie hesitated. She had a dozen questions running through her mind. "Margaret Gelling has two children, but I think they're both across. As far as I know, she doesn't really keep in touch with them," Bessie said, after a moment's thought and the last bite of her lunch.

The inspector wasn't going to answer her questions and she needed to do what she could to help him. "Her husband was a teacher at the school here in Laxey, and he passed away in the sixties or seventies, I forget."

"Right, what's she like?" John asked.

Bessie shrugged. "Quiet and mousy," she replied. "I can't imagine her saying boo to a goose, really. I always thought her husband dominated her, but she hasn't changed since she's been widowed."

"Who else do we have, then?"

"Agnes Faragher," Bessie replied. "Her husband was an electrician. They only had one child, a son called Matthew, but he moved across as soon as he finished school. I recall hearing that he'd passed away, but I could be wrong about that."

"You're not," John said after checking his notes.

Bessie nodded. "Agnes didn't talk about him often. There have been all sorts of rumours over the years, but I don't know anything definite."

"What sort of rumours?"

Bessie sighed. "I hate talking about this sort of thing," she complained. "I think people should be able to live their lives without being gossiped about."

"But someone murdered Nancy King," John reminded her.

"Whether Matthew Faragher was gay or not can not possibly have anything to do with that," Bessie replied.

John just made another note in his notebook. "That just leaves Joan Carr, according to my notes."

"Joan's lovely," Bessie said. "She's in quite a bad way from arthritis now, but she used to be very active. Her husband, Michael, owned a small landscaping company that he inherited from his father. Joan always insisted on his coming over and looking after the little bit of landscaping my cottage needs." Bessie sighed. "Their son took over the company and ran it out of business in less than a year."

"I understand they had three children?" he asked.

"They did," Bessie agreed. "They lost their youngest, a little girl, to some childhood cancer that was untreatable in those days. She must have been about three when she passed. Their other daughter lost her life to breast cancer in the seventies. The last I heard about their son, he was serving time in gaol across for some sort of fraud."

"We're checking on his whereabouts now," was all that John would tell her.

"That's all the ladies," Bessie told him. "Their lives all seem rather tragic now that we've discussed them like this, but I never really thought about them that way."

"They certainly seemed like a happy enough group yesterday," John said.

"They did," Bessie agreed. "They were always like that, though. Growing up in the twenties and thirties meant they'd seen a lot of difficult times. Getting through the Second World War was tough, as well. Some of their husbands or future husbands were sent to serve." Bessie shook her head. "They were raised to just keep carrying on, no matter what life brings," she told the inspector.

"Now I just have to work out who stopped Nancy King from carrying on," the inspector said with a frown.

He politely refused Bessie's offer of tea and biscuits as she cleared away the lunch dishes. "I need to get back to the office. The ladies are all coming in, one at a time, to talk to me this afternoon," he told her.

Bessie shook her head. "I just can't get my head around it," she replied. "I can't imagine why anyone would murder Nancy King, or any of the Raspberry Jam Ladies for that matter."

"Thank you for the background," the inspector said, as he stood up to leave. "I expect it to be very helpful when I talk to the ladies."

"I wish I could do more," Bessie said. A thought suddenly occurred to her. "Nancy King might not have been the target, though," she said slowly. "You're collecting all the jam jars. They might all have been poisoned, mightn't they?"

John gave Bessie a quick hug. "At this point, it's too soon to say anything for certain. We aren't even sure Mrs. King's jar was poisoned. It's just a strong possibility at this point."

"But if all the jars were poisoned, someone could have killed dozens of people," Bessie said worriedly.

"But they didn't," John told her. "We've managed to track down every single jar of jam and no one else has had so much as a stomachache from it."

"So some people did eat their jam?" Bessie asked.

"Some people did eat some of the jam," John said, seemingly reluctantly. "And there haven't been any negative reactions anywhere else."

"Maybe the jam that killed Nancy was from a totally different place, then?" Bessie asked.

"Anything is possible," John told her. "For now, we're collecting all of the jars and having them all tested. We won't have any results until Friday at the earliest. Until then we don't know what killed Nancy King and we don't know if anyone else was in any danger."

Bessie frowned. "I don't understand any of this," she complained. "If no one knows where the jam came from, and all the jars are identical, then anyone could have been given the jar with the poison in it."

"You're making assumptions that I can't confirm or deny," John told her. "Just try to put it all out of your mind for now. I'll tell you what I can, when I can."

"In the meantime, I suppose I shouldn't accept jam from strangers," Bessie said wryly.

"I would suggest you don't accept anything from strangers," John told her. "Not until we get this mess worked out."

Bessie locked up behind the inspector and paced around her small kitchen. She had dishes to wash, but her mind was racing and she couldn't concentrate, even on as small a task as that. It was raining lightly, but she threw on a raincoat and headed out for a walk. She couldn't think of a better way to let her mind work.

The beach was deserted and Bessie felt as if a million eyes were on her as she stomped through the rain past the row of rental cottages down the beach from her home. She glanced over at children and adults who all seemed to be staring out at the rain with sad expressions on their faces. When she couldn't stand their bored scrutiny any longer, she turned and headed for home.

The walk had at least partially cleared her head, so she settled in and washed up the dishes. Her answering machine light was blinking, so after she'd tidied the kitchen, she pressed play on it. Several messages from concerned friends and nosy gossips played, one after another. Only the final message held any interest for Bessie.

"Ah, Bessie, it's Agnes, Agnes Faragher. I'm sure you've heard about poor Nancy. We, that is the Raspberry Jam Ladies, we're all ever so upset. Anyway, we're getting together tomorrow afternoon for tea to remember Nancy and we wanted to invite you come along and share your memories of her with us. Her daughter will be planning the formal services and whatnot. This is just a chance for us, um, older ladies to meet up and remember. We'll be at our usual place at two if you can join us. You don't need to ring me back. And feel free to bring a friend, as well if you'd like."

Bessie played the message a second time and then nodded. She'd be there, and if possible, with a friend.

CHAPTER 3

The next morning it was already raining when Bessie got up. She sighed and tried hard to convince herself that a walk in the rain would feel good. Not convinced, she nevertheless walked for a good hour, past the holiday cottages and along the long stretch of sand. When she reached the beach below Thie yn Traie, which she still thought of as the Pierce mansion, she glanced up at the huge house. She was surprised to see lights on inside some of the rooms. Perhaps the house had finally been sold. She'd have to ring her advocate and ask.

Back at home, she dried off and then read for a short time before making herself an early lunch. She'd rung Doona yesterday, after she'd listened to Agnes's invitation, and Doona had agreed to accompany Bessie to the gathering.

"I'm sure John won't mind, if I can get someone to cover for me," she'd told Bessie. "I just hope he doesn't think I'm snooping. There's something strange about this case and he's already feeling tense about it."

After lunch Bessie changed into a black skirt and short-sleeved grey blouse. She brushed her hair and added an unaccustomed touch of makeup.

Now, as Bessie paced around her kitchen waiting for Doona to pick her up, she couldn't help but think that John wasn't the only one who was feeling tense about this particular murder. The short car ride was a fairly silent one. After initial greetings, Bessie was quickly lost in her own thoughts again.

The small hall where the ladies always met was little more than an old cottage that had been converted for community use. Doona parked her car in the small car park and the two friends made their way inside.

As they entered the meeting room, Bessie noted that all of the Raspberry Jam Ladies were already there. She felt a bit out of place, as she and Doona were the only other people in the room. She smiled and nodded at them in a vague way as she crossed the room. It wasn't a large space and it was fairly sparsely furnished with a few couches and chairs. Several boxes of toys in one corner seemed out of place under the circumstances, but the group of mums and children that had use of the space several days a week had nowhere else to store things in the small building.

The ladies were scattered around the room, presumably each lost in her own private contemplation. Bessie headed towards Agnes, as she was the one who'd invited her.

"Agnes, how are you?" she asked as she squeezed the other woman's hand.

"Horrible, so about what you'd expect," Agnes answered. Bessie could see tears forming in her friend's eyes that were already red-rimmed.

"I'm so sorry about Nancy," Bessie told her. "I can't imagine how shocked you all must be."

"Of course we are," Elinor Lewis told her as she joined Bessie and Agnes. Elinor looked the same as ever, with her severely cut grey hair and dark eyes that seemed to miss nothing.

Doona had stayed a few steps behind Bessie; now she stepped forward.

"I'm so sorry about your friend," she told the two ladies.

"We're like sisters," Agnes said sadly. "We've been there for one another through all sorts of almost unspeakable things. I'm sure we'll miss Nancy much more than her family will."

"Especially that daughter of hers," Elinor added. "All she was interested in was her mother's money. She hadn't been up from Port Erin to visit Nancy in nearly a year. Suddenly, when Nancy mentioned on the phone that she might be changing her will, Sarah is on her doorstep before the sun's even up."

"Was Mrs. King changing her will?" Doona asked.

"She wanted to," Elinor said. "She wanted to leave everything to the Raspberry Jam Ladies. She said she wanted us to have a holiday or do something extravagant with her money. Unfortunately, she didn't manage to get a new will written before she died."

"Have you told the police about this?" Doona asked.

Elinor gave her a strange look. "Of course I have, dear," she answered. "But aren't you with the police? I'm sure I saw you at the station yesterday. I assume you're here with Bessie to investigate."

Doona flushed. "I'm just civilian front desk staff," she said. "I just came with Bessie as a friend."

"Of course, you still don't drive, do you?" Elinor smiled at Bessie. "It's never too late to learn, you know."

"I'm more interested in learning where the jam came from," Bessie told her.

Elinor shook her head. "If we knew that, we'd all be sleeping better," she replied. "As it is, we're all convinced that any one of us could have been the target."

"The jars weren't labeled with any names or anything?" Bessie asked.

Agnes sighed. "I can't bear to go through this again," she said plaintively. "I'm going to go and start the kettle."

They watched her go. "Agnes is taking Nancy's death very hard," Elinor told Bessie and Doona. "They were very close."

"It's always hard to lose old friends," Bessie said, thinking briefly of some of the people she had lost in her own life, beginning with Matthew Saunders, the man she would have married, had he lived.

Elinor passed a hand in front of her eyes. When they met Bessie's, they were quite dry, however.

"You were asking about the jam," Elinor said. "When I arrived at the tent on Tynwald Day morning, there was a box on our table with twenty-four identical jars of jam on it. Well, at the time I assumed they were identical. Agnes and Nancy were already there, and when I asked them who had brought the jam, they both just shrugged. I assumed it was one of them, but I didn't give it much thought."

"Wasn't that a bit unusual?" Bessie asked. "A box full of jam turning up out of the blue?"

Elinor shook her head. "It was and it wasn't," she said. "Years ago, when we were a younger and more energetic group, we'd often bring jars of jam or marmalade or some such thing to gatherings. We'd usually try to slip them on to the table unnoticed. That way, if our efforts were, well, not terribly successful, we could deny all knowledge of the runny marmalade or the slightly scorched jam. If everyone loved our offering, we'd take full credit, of course."

Bessie nodded. "I remember being gifted with many jars of various preserves by the Raspberry Jam Ladies over the years," she said softly. "They were nearly always delicious, as well."

Elinor laughed. "Some of us were more successful than others," she said. "I don't think anyone would disagree that Peggy was probably the worst of our little bunch. She just didn't have the patience to do things properly. She was forever undercooking things or forgetting about them and letting them burn."

Bessie laughed. "I remember opening a few jars and finding runny jam or jam that had a rather peculiarly burnt flavour, but, as I wasn't about to fuss with making it myself, I never complained."

"Yes, well, over the last several years the tradition has rather died out," Elinor continued. "I'm afraid age has begun to catch up with us, and making homemade jam just seems like too much bother. I simply assumed that someone had decided to make the effort again, probably for one last time."

"But no one has come forward to admit to making it?" Doona asked.

"Everyone in the group has denied any knowledge of where the jam came from," Elinor said. "Agnes says the box was there when she arrived, and she assumed it came from Nancy, who was the only one at the table at that point."

Bessie nodded; she'd make a point of asking Agnes about it later. "So everyone in the group took a jar and then you gave the rest to other friends?" Bessie asked.

"Some of the ladies took more than one jar," Elinor replied. "As I'm all alone, I only took one, but Nancy took a second jar for her daughter, because she knew she was coming to see her, and Margaret took an extra jar to share with her neighbour who hasn't been well. The rest we passed out to people we knew as we saw them in the crowd."

"Do we know why the police think the jam was poisoned?" Bessie asked Doona.

Doona shook her head. "The inspector has his reasons, but he certainly isn't sharing them with me," she replied.

"And we don't know if all twenty-four jars were poisoned or just some of them," Bessie mused.

"They weren't all poisoned," Elinor told her. "I opened my jar and had some on my breakfast toast before the police rang me. It was fine. It was delicious, in fact. I know at least a few others jars were opened and eaten from before the police started ringing around."

"I don't suppose you could work out who made the jam from the taste?" Bessie asked.

Elinor shook her head. "Years ago I could have tried, but my sense of taste has dulled with age. It was very good, though, and perfectly set. If I had to guess, I would say Nancy. Though I hate to admit it, she was always better at making jam than anyone else."

"Why would Nancy put poison in her own jam?" Doona asked.

"Maybe she wanted to die," a morose voice came from behind Bessie. "I can certainly sympathise."

Bessie turned and then embraced the woman who had joined them.

"Joan Carr, this is Doona Moore," Bessie said. "I don't think I introduced you yesterday."

Joan's husband had been a gardener, and Joan had often helped out. Her many wrinkles reflected the years she'd spent out in the sun. She was shorter than Bessie, with a slight stoop that probably came from time spent bent over weeds and plants.

"Perhaps that's where we've gone wrong," Joan said now. "Us jam ladies have stayed friends for years. Perhaps we should have made friends with younger people instead, like Bessie has. That might have been better than staying stuck in the past."

Bessie smiled. "I do think my young friends are good for me," she replied. "But I also enjoy spending time with my old friends, like you."

Joan nodded. "We were like sisters for so many years, the Jam Ladies were. We've been there for each other through so many of life's tragedies. It was sad when Elizabeth died, and we all still talk about Peggy as if she's just missed an odd meeting or two. But losing Nancy feels much more difficult somehow."

"And I'm sure the possibility that it might have been murder makes it even more difficult," Bessie said.

Elinor drew a sharp breath. "The police must have it wrong," she said firmly. "No one would murder Nancy or anyone else I know. Nancy must have accidently added the wrong thing to her tea or something. Or maybe she just had a heart attack and your friend the police inspector is simply overreacting."

"Anything's possible," Bessie said, determined not to argue with the woman. Clearly Elinor was very upset and Bessie could understand her not wanting to consider that her friend had been murdered.

"The tea's ready," Agnes called from the doorway.

The small group made their way from the small sitting room into the kitchen area. Agnes was busy pouring cups of tea. She'd set out several small plates with biscuits on them. The ladies each helped themselves to tea, adding milk and sugar as they preferred, before taking seats around the round table.

Bessie sat down next to Margaret Gelling and patted her hand. "I'm so sorry about Nancy," she told her.

"Thanks," Margaret whispered, staring into her teacup.

"I hadn't really talked to Nancy lately; was she doing okay?"

Margaret shrugged. "She seemed okay to me," she said. "She's the only one who had children still on the island and I know she was having trouble with her daughter, but that wasn't unusual."

"How are your two children?" Bessie asked. "The last I knew, they were both in the Manchester area."

"Hazel's still there. Her husband had to take early retirement due to his health, I understand. Jack moved to Rugby a few years ago. I don't really hear from them very often."

Bessie nodded. "Of course, they're adults with their own lives."

"Indeed." Margaret picked up a digestive from the plate of biscuits in front of her and took a tentative nibble.

Bessie helped herself to a chocolate digestive and ate it slowly, washing it down with her tea. She didn't want to upset anyone by asking about motives for murder directly, but that's what she was fishing for.

"Was there a lot of money for Nancy to leave her children?" Bessie asked Margaret after a moment.

"She was comfortably off," Elinor said from across the table. "Perhaps more so than most of us."

Bessie nodded. "And the children are all over the world, aren't they?"

"Sarah lives in Port Erin, of course," Elinor replied. "But she wouldn't have crossed the street to help her mother. She only happened to find her mother's body because she was worried about her inheritance."

"And the other children?"

"Fred is in London. He followed in his father's footsteps and does something in banking. He went to university in London and I don't think he's been back on the island since," Elinor said.

"I remember Fred vaguely," Bessie said, thoughtfully. "He was very bright and not very friendly. Nancy's second son, James, was always my favourite."

"James used to come and visit Nancy once in a while, after his father died," Agnes spoke up. "Once he got married, however, the visits stopped. I don't think his wife was fond of Nancy."

"She wasn't," Elinor confirmed. "And Nancy wasn't about to chase after them, begging for them to stay in touch."

"Nancy told me she had a card from them last Christmas and they've settled in Cornwall now," Margaret added.

"That's where the wife was from originally," Elinor said.

"And the third son?" Bessie asked.

"Adam?" Elinor laughed harshly. "He moved to Australia on his eighteenth birthday. I don't think Nancy ever heard from him again."

"How very sad," Doona said.

"He was nothing but trouble, that one," Elinor said tartly. "He caused his mother nothing but grief when he was at home. She was lucky he left when he did."

Bessie exchanged looks with Doona, but neither responded to Elinor's comment.

"If she didn't have time to change her will, who inherits the estate?" Doona asked.

Elinor shrugged. "Nancy didn't say. She told me she wanted to change her will in favour of the group, but she didn't talk about who she might be disinheriting."

"As far as you know, though, she never changed her will?" Bessie asked

"As far as I know, she didn't have time," Elinor said with a sigh.

"A holiday would have been nice," Margaret said softly.

"Well, if everyone's done with their tea, let's move back across the hall, shall we?" Elinor announced.

"I'll just tidy up," Agnes told her.

"I'll give you a hand," Bessie said.

The others headed back across the short hallway, while Bessie donned an apron and began washing the teacups.

"Ah, Bessie, I'm just not myself today," Agnes said as she dropped a plate of biscuits.

Bessie picked up the broken plate and biscuit pieces as Agnes stood and sobbed. Once the mess was cleared away, Bessie gave her friend a hug.

"Come on, Nancy wouldn't want you crying over her like this," she told Agnes firmly.

"I know," Agnes said, wiping her eyes with a dishcloth. "But I can't seem to stop myself. I just can't believe she's gone."

Bessie patted Agnes's back, and waited patiently for the woman to calm down. "I am very sorry," she murmured. "It must have been such a huge shock."

"It was," Agnes agreed. "We had such fun on Tynwald Day. It was almost like old times, you know? Someone brought jam and we were laughing about whether we were going to share it or not. Nancy was worried about the meeting with her daughter, but she tried hard to act like it wasn't bothering her."

"And you don't have any idea where the jam came from?" Bessie asked.

Agnes shook her head. "It was there when I arrived," she told Bessie, wiping more tears from her eyes. "I thanked Nancy for it, but she told me the box had been there when she'd arrived as well."

"So who could have left it for you?"

"I haven't any idea," Agnes shrugged.

"What did you think at the time?" Bessie pressed her.

"I didn't think much of anything," Agnes said, tears running down her face. "I suppose, if I had thought about it, I would have thought that one of the others brought the jam and left it there and then snuck away so no one would know for sure who'd brought it."

"Elinor said you all used to do that," Bessie told her, patting Agnes's back, as the tears didn't seem to be stopping.

"We did," Agnes agreed. "But no one had fussed with homemade preserves in years now. We just haven't the energy to bother, not when shop-bought is nearly as good, anyway."

"And all of the jars looked the same?"

"Exactly the same," Agnes said. "I didn't look real closely, though. It simply wasn't a big deal at the time."

"Did you see Nancy pick out a jar?"

Agnes shrugged. "We just left them in the box at first. We had the table to get set up, you know? Then, later, someone asked what we were doing with the jam, so we all took out a jar or two for ourselves before we started passing them out to other friends."

"Did you try your jar of jam?" Bessie asked, more out of curiosity than anything else.

"I did. It was really good, and I was not happy when the police took it away, I can tell you."

Bessie smiled. "I don't suppose you could tell who'd made it?" she asked.

"That's clever," Agnes replied. "I didn't think of that." She frowned and Bessie could almost see her thinking hard. After a few moments, Agnes shook her head.

"Sorry, I don't know. The jam was good, but there wasn't anything special about it. I think, if Peggy had made it, I might have been able to tell. She was terrible at making jam. But she's been dead for what, five years now? The others all make good jam. We all used the same recipe, you know, ever since the first time we made jam as a group."

"Was Nancy upset about anything?" Bessie asked. "Was there any reason why she might have taken her own life?"

"I don't know," Agnes replied sadly. "Like I said, she was worried about the meeting with her daughter. They met for tea once every six months or so in Douglas, but other than that, they only spoke on the phone once a month or so. Sarah insisted that they meet, but Nancy said that Sarah was coming for lunch, not first thing in the morning. I'm not sure if Nancy got it wrong or Sarah changed her plans."

"If it was murder, who will benefit from Nancy's death?" Bessie couldn't stop herself from asking.

"Just Nancy's children, I think," Agnes said sadly. "But even if the jam was poisoned, I can't see how the murderer made sure that Nancy got the poisoned jar." She shook her head. "It's all muddled up in my head," she told Bessie. "It's like the plot of a murder mystery or something, not real life."

"Maybe the jar at Nancy's house wasn't from the box at Tynwald," Bessie suggested. "Maybe Nancy got it somewhere else."

"Or maybe she made it for herself," Agnes said with a sigh. "I hate the thought of her killing herself, but nothing makes sense anymore."

Bessie helped Agnes into a chair and made her another cup of tea. "You relax for a few minutes while I get the washing-up done," she told the other woman.

It only took a couple of minutes for Bessie to tidy away the biscuits and wash the teapot and the cups. Once she'd finished everything else, she collected the now empty cup from Agnes and washed it quickly. She was just drying that last cup when Elinor swept in.

"What on earth is keeping you two?" Elinor demanded, her eyes moving from Bessie to Agnes and back again. "You've been ages."

"Sorry," Agnes said softly. "I couldn't stop crying and Bessie had to step in and do all of the work herself."

"You must get yourself under control," Elinor told Agnes sternly. "Now, we're all going to say a few words about Nancy. If you aren't up to joining in, I suggest you head for home."

"I think I might just do that," Agnes said. "I don't think I can talk about Nancy right now."

"Didn't you say your doctor gave you some tablets?" Elinor asked. "Maybe you should take one and have a rest. I'll come by and check on you before tea time."

Agnes nodded. "You're right, of course," she said. "I'll do just that."

Bessie gave Agnes a hug and watched silently as she headed towards the front of the building. Elinor had taken Agnes's arm and Bessie could see the pair having a whispered conversation as Elinor walked Agnes to the door.

Bessie rejoined the others in the small sitting room, and a few moments later Elinor strode in.

"Agnes has gone home to have a nap," she announced to the group. "She's taking Nancy's death incredibly badly. I suggest we set up a rota and make sure someone is checking in with her regularly for the next few days."

Joan walked over to an ancient filing cabinet in one corner and opened the top drawer. She pulled out a sheet of paper and carried it back over to where the group had assembled in a small circle in the centre of the room.

"I'll check on her tonight," Elinor said.

Joan nodded and then wrote something on the paper.

"I'll check on her after breakfast tomorrow," Joan told the others, adding her name to a space on the sheet.

"I can take her some lunch tomorrow," Margaret said quietly.

"That brings it back to me, then," Elinor said.

"I can help," Bessie interrupted. "I'll take her something for tea tomorrow night."

"Oh, no, we can't impose on you like that," Elinor objected. "We've been looking after one another for many years. Agnes is our responsibility."

"If you can do tomorrow evening, I'll see if she wants a day out on Friday," Joan suggested. "Maybe we can go into Douglas and do some shopping and have lunch there."

"That might cheer her up," Elinor agreed. "And then Margaret can check on her some time before bedtime on Friday."

"I can," Margaret agreed.

"I'll check on her at breakfast time on Saturday and then I'll ring you all. We can discuss whether we need to keep visiting or not after I see how she is on Saturday," Elinor said.

Joan made a few more notes on the sheet. "I'll just copy this for everyone," she said. There was a small office in one room of the building that housed a typewriter and a small photocopier. Joan was only gone for a few moments.

"Did you leave twenty pence?" Elinor asked as Joan handed each of the other ladies a copy of the schedule.

"I did," Joan assured her. "I'm sure it's the mums' group who use the machine and never pay."

"Undoubtedly," Elinor agreed. "Now, we were all going to share memories of Nancy, so let's get started."

Bessie smiled at Doona, who was looking quite uncomfortable. Of course, Bessie's friend hadn't known Nancy at all. Undoubtedly she felt out of place at the gathering. Aware that she herself hadn't really known the woman well, Bessie wondered if she and Doona should take their leave.

"Would you prefer us to leave you alone now?" Bessie asked Elinor as an uneasy silence descended on the group.

"Oh, good heavens, no," Elinor said. "It's bad enough there's only five of us here. I can't imagine how grim it would be with just the three of us. I'm sure you can come up with some remembrance of Nancy, can't you?"

Bessie smiled. "Of course I can," she said. "I have many fond memories of Nancy."

"You may start, then," Elinor told her.

"Many of my memories are from when I first met her," Bessie said, casting her mind back over the decades. "Nancy used to bring her children to the beach near my cottage nearly every day when the weather permitted. She used to tell me that those three little boys of hers needed lots of exercise. Sarah used to sit quietly and build sandcastles while the three boys would run up and down the beach shouting and bashing one another." Bessie smiled. "Nancy would come over to my cottage for a quick cuppa some days, when the boys were especially rambunctious."

"I remember when my husband died, Nancy came over that night and stayed with me for over a week. She helped me get through the worst days of my life," Margaret told the others.

"She was there for me when I lost Michelle just before her fourth birthday. I thought I'd never get over it, but Nancy stayed with me. She kept reminding me to be strong for my other children," Joan said. "Neither of us expected that she'd have to be there for me again when Mary got sick, but she was. Nancy was very special."

"She was indeed," Elinor said briskly. "She offered to help me when I lost Nicholas and again when Nathan passed."

The room fell quiet again.

"She seemed very lively and fun at Tynwald Day," Doona offered after a bit.

"She loved life and she loved helping her friends," Margaret whispered. "If she were here, she'd know what to say and how to help us get through this."

"Well, now, if no one else has anything to add, maybe we should wrap up for today," Elinor said.

Bessie and Doona exchanged glances, but neither spoke.

After a moment, Joan sighed. "I suppose that's it, though it doesn't seem much after fifty years of friendship," she said.

"We'll all remember Nancy in our own ways, of course," Elinor said. "But we haven't all day to sit around talking about her."

"They'll be some sort of service as well, won't there?" Bessie asked.

"You'd have to ask Sarah about that," Elinor replied. "She'll be handing such things."

"And she'll be having the service in Port Erin, knowing her," Joan added. "Especially if she thinks that might keep us away."

"You were her mother's closest friends," Bessie said. "Of course she'll want you at the service."

"She won't," Elinor said sharply. "She hated us, especially once Nancy started talking about changing her will in our favour. I wouldn't be surprised if she didn't have a service at all."

Bessie and Doona gathered up their handbags and walked out of the building with the other ladies. Bessie hugged each one briefly before climbing into Doona's car.

"Well, that was interesting," Doona remarked as she pulled out of the car park.

"It was sad," Bessie replied. "I'm sure Agnes has lots of lovely memories of Nancy. It's a shame she left early."

"It was kind of them to sort out a schedule for checking on her, though," Doona pointed out.

"It was," Bessie agreed. "But I think I might just check in on her myself in a day or two. She was very upset while we were tidying up."

"I think we need to talk to John about everything that was said," Doona suggested. "Maybe he's free tonight."

"I could make something for everyone," Bessie offered. "Assuming young Hugh comes along as well, I think I can make just about enough food for all of us."

Doona laughed. "I'll talk to John. I'm sure he'll want to include Hugh if he's available. I'm not sure what you'll make to feed us all, though."

Bessie grinned. "I have a couple of chickens in the fridge," she told

Doona. "I was going to boil them up and make several batches of soup, but I can roast them instead with some vegetables."

"It's too hot for soup anyway," Doona replied.

"It is rather," Bessie agreed. "Chickens were on special at ShopFast and I grabbed them without thinking. It's almost too hot to roast them as well, but it sounds good and we have to eat."

When they arrived at Bessie's cottage, Doona pulled out her mobile and made a few quick phone calls.

"Okay, we're all set," she told Bessie when she was finished. "John and Hugh will be here at seven. John said he'd bring something for pudding, and he gave me the rest of the day off. I suppose that means I should help you with the chickens."

Bessie laughed. "And don't you sound thrilled at the prospect," she said. "Come on in and I'll get the birds ready and in the oven. Then we can take a walk on the beach and let our minds settle."

"That sounds like a plan," Doona agreed.

CHAPTER 4

*B*essie wasn't sure how Doona felt after their walk, but she was refreshed. The sea breeze seemed to blow away a lot of the disquiet she had been feeling since she'd first heard about Nancy's death. Now back at her little cottage, she worked through the final preparations for the evening meal.

"Do you mind mashing the potatoes?" she asked Doona as she checked on the Brussels sprouts.

"Not at all," Doona answered.

A knock on the door a moment later interrupted their work. Bessie rushed over to let John and Hugh in. Both men gave Bessie quick hugs as they entered.

"I brought a rhubarb crumble," Hugh announced, handing a warm tin to Bessie. "I thought you might pop it in the oven when the chickens come out so it can stay warm."

Bessie grinned at him. "You're becoming quite domestic, aren't you?" she teased.

Hugh flushed. "Grace and I have a deal, like. She cooks most evenings, but I make pudding. I'm learning to make all sorts of things."

"Where can I find a man that can make puddings?" Doona demanded.

"Is there anything I can do to help?" John asked Bessie.

"I think we're just about ready," Bessie answered. "You can start carving the birds if you like, while Doona mashes the potatoes and I start putting out the veggies."

A few minutes later the foursome were settled in at Bessie's kitchen table with heaping plates of food in front of them. No one spoke for several minutes as chicken, potatoes, stuffing, sprouts, carrots and peas disappeared quickly.

"That was a big meal for a Wedneday night," Doona said as she pushed her empty plate away. "But it was delicious."

"It's great," Hugh agreed, helping himself to another scoop of potatoes. "I should have you teach me how to make this. It would impress Grace for sure."

Bessie laughed. "It's really quite simple," she told the young man. "Come over some Sunday afternoon and I'll walk you through the whole thing."

Hugh nodded, his mouth full of peas.

"It was very nice," John said politely, pushing his own plate away. Bessie noticed that he'd actually eaten only about half of the small portion he'd taken.

"Is everything okay?" she asked the man, catching his eye.

"Everything's fine," he said, looking away. "The Nancy King case is complicated, that's all."

"Having spent the afternoon with the Raspberry Jam Ladies, I'm hoping I may be able to help," Bessie told him. "They're an interesting group of friends."

"They are," John agreed. "And there's no doubt in my mind that they'd lie to protect one another."

"You think one of them gave Mrs. King the poisoned jam?" Doona asked.

"At this point, I suspect everyone," John replied tiredly. "I find it strange that no one seems to know where the jam came from, but everyone was prepared to eat it anyway."

"It might seem strange now, but years ago I'd often come home and find a few eggs or a bag of potatoes on my doorstep," Bessie said.

"Sometimes there would be a note, but a lot of times it was just someone being kind and sharing their extra with their neighbours. The Raspberry Jam Ladies were well known, in the fifties and sixties at least, for leaving little jars of jam and preserves all over Laxey. Even if they'd known none of them had made the jam, they'd have probably thought it was just a small gift from someone who remembers them from that time."

John shook his head. "Accepting gifts from strangers is dangerous."

"Maybe," Bessie shrugged. "But there's no way any of the ladies could have suspected that there was poison in the jam. Who would want to kill one of them?"

"Which brings us to our first question," John said with a sigh. "Who was meant to be the victim?"

"Agnes says Nancy just grabbed a jar at random," Bessie said.

"So if the poison was in the jar at that point, it was just random bad luck that Nancy was the one that got it," Doona said.

"Was it the only jar that had poison in it?" Bessie asked.

John shrugged. "We won't have lab results on any of the jars until early next week. Until then it's pointless to speculate."

"So at this point we don't know if there was a single target or multiple ones," Bessie said. "Who could possibly have wanted to kill all of the Raspberry Jam Ladies and their friends?"

"I've been studying terror attacks and serial killers," Hugh said. "Sometimes a terrorist will target a group of people when he or she doesn't agree with their beliefs or politics."

"So someone really hates raspberry jam?" Doona asked.

Hugh shook his head. "I reckon if it was a terrorist thing, the idea was to disrupt Tynwald Day. Maybe the killer thought someone would try the jam right away and that would make them cancel the ceremony or something."

"Who would want to ruin Tywald Day?" Bessie asked.

Hugh shrugged. "Take your choice between the people who argue for more independence from the United Kingdom, those that argue for closer ties with them, people with a grudge against the current administration on the island, or, of course, there's always random crazies."

"It seems far-fetched to me," Bessie said. "Besides, we know all of the jars weren't poisoned. Some of the ladies told me they'd tried their jars before the police contacted them."

"If only one jar was poisoned, though, was Nancy the target?" Doona asked.

"I think better with crumble," Hugh announced.

"I forgot about pudding," Bessie exclaimed. She got up and pulled the crumble from the oven. Hugh pulled the tub of vanilla ice cream he'd also brought from the freezer, and he and Bessie served generous helpings of crumble to everyone. The group went back to eating for several minutes.

"If only one jar was deadly, then there are two possibilities," Hugh said after he'd scraped up the last of his ice cream. "It's possible that the killer didn't care who got the poisoned jam. He or she just wanted someone to die."

"Are you still thinking of a terrorist attack in that case?" Doona asked.

"It's possible, but less likely. Terror attacks tend to be about maximum impact. This strikes me as something else," Hugh said. "Either we have a killer who's happy with taking out anyone just for the thrill of it or we have a killer who is targeting someone specific, but trying to hide their intentions."

"I don't think the island has ever had to deal with a serial killer," Bessie said. "How do you even start looking if the target was completely random?"

"It's certainly a challenge," Hugh said with a sigh.

"What did you mean when you said they might be targeting someone but hiding their intentions?" Doona asked.

"There have been cases where someone decides to kill a family member or friend and they kill a few others, almost at random, to confuse motive," Hugh explained.

"If that's the case, the other Jam Ladies could be in danger," Bessie said.

"They've all been warned to be extra careful until we have Mrs. King's killer behind bars," John said quietly.

"I can't imagine anyone wanting to kill any of the ladies," Bessie said.

"Having spent time with them all today, I'm not so sure about Elinor Lewis," Doona said. "She's bossy and overbearing and I could just about imagine one of the other ladies deciding to get rid of her."

"Surely the killer isn't one of the ladies," Bessie protested. "They're all in their seventies and I doubt any of them have ever had so much as a parking ticket."

"We're taking a close look at all of their families," Hugh said. "But none of them seem to be close to their children. Nearly all of the kids have moved away."

"I think the ladies themselves would pick Sarah, Nancy's daughter, as the most likely murderer," Bessie said. "Is it possible that she switched the jars of jam when she arrived to visit her mother, and then rang the police after her mother died?"

"A neighbour saw her going into the house and heard her screaming about ten seconds later," Doona told Bessie.

"That's classified information," John snapped.

"I didn't get it from the police report," Doona told him. "I live in the same neighbourhood, remember? I bumped into Ted, the man who lives next door to Nancy, last night on a walk around the neighbourhood. He told me that he'd seen Sarah going in and heard her screams. From what I could tell, he's been telling everyone he meets. It's the first bit of excitement he's had in years."

Bessie chuckled. "Ted needs to get out more," she said. "Since Betty died he just sits around the house and watches the neighbours. I can't imagine there's all that much to see in that neighbourhood."

"I love that it's a nice quiet area," Doona said. "This is first time we've had the police there since I moved in. Well, other than when John picks me up or drops me off or whatever."

"Sarah wasn't meant to visit until later in the day," Bessie said. "At least that's what Agnes was told. Did she give a reason for why she turned up when she did?"

John shook his head at Doona, who opened her mouth and then snapped it shut. "I'm sorry, Bessie," he said, sounding exhausted. "We're keeping everything we can as quiet as we can at this point. And I think, in this instance, it would be best if you stayed as far away from the investigation as possible. I'd rather you didn't spend any more time with the Raspberry Jam Ladies until Nancy King's killer is behind bars."

Bessie drew a deep breath and forced herself to count to ten before she replied. "I'm sorry, John, truly I am," she said eventually. "But Nancy was my friend. I've known her and the other Raspberry Jam Ladies for too many years to stay away from them now. I'll try hard not to interfere with your investigation, but I don't intend to avoid my friends, not when they need me."

John nodded. "I knew I was wasting my breath," he said. He stood up. "I really need to get home," he told the others.

Bessie followed the inspector to the door, uncertain of what she should say to try to defuse the strain between them.

"I'll let you know if I hear anything that I think might be relevant," she said as she pulled her front door open for him.

"I'd appreciate that," he replied tightly. John stepped through the door and then stopped and turned back towards Bessie. "I'm sorry. I have too much going on right now and I'm taking all my problems out on you. Please be very careful if you do spend time with the ladies. I worry about you."

Bessie gave him a hug. "I worry about you as well," she said. "If you need to talk about anything, you know where I am."

John nodded. "I might just take you up on that," he said with a small smile that looked only slightly forced.

Bessie shut the door behind him and returned to the table.

"That was weird," Hugh said. "I mean, I know we aren't supposed to talk about stuff we learn in interviews and whatever, but the inspector has never really worried about that with you, Bessie."

Bessie shook her head. "Maybe I'm too close to this one," she suggested. "I was given one of the jars of jam, remember? And I've been friends with the Raspberry Jam Ladies for as long as they've been meeting."

"I'm sure John doesn't think you're involved," Doona said stoutly.

"But there's a good chance someone I know is," Bessie replied sadly. "What possible motive is there for Nancy's death?"

"Money," Hugh said. "It's at the root of a lot of murders."

"And Elinor said Nancy was thinking of changing her will. Surely that gives her daughter a strong motive," Doona added.

"What about opportunity, though?" Bessie asked. "When could she have given her mother the jam?"

"She might have given her the jar weeks ago," Hugh said. "Maybe the jam at Tynwald was all absolutely fine, and the jar that killed Nancy came from somewhere else altogether."

"It's possible, I suppose," Bessie said slowly.

"Anything seems possible at this point," Doona said, frustration evident in her voice. "The more we talk, the more confusing it all gets."

"Maybe we should call it a night," Bessie suggested. "I'm going to ring a few people tomorrow and see what I can find out."

"Please be careful," Hugh said as he stood up to go. "I don't want anything to happen to you."

Bessie gave him a hug and then let him out. Doona was clearing away the pudding dishes when Bessie turned back into the kitchen. Bessie ran a sink full of hot water while Doona dumped John's barely touched pudding into Bessie's bin.

"It isn't like John to leave food," Bessie commented.

"He's been working out in the gym almost every day," Doona told her. "Maybe he's worried about his weight."

"He could do with adding a few pounds, in my opinion," Bessie replied. "He looks thinner lately."

"He does," Doona agreed. "I don't know if it's this case or something else that's bothering him. He seemed okay on Tynwald Day."

"I'm sure Nancy's death has him working very hard," Bessie said. "Once her killer is found, he'll probably get right back to his old self."

Doona nodded slowly, but didn't look convinced. "I hope so," she muttered as she dried the last of the dishes. Doona left after that and Bessie headed straight to bed.

At breakfast the next morning Bessie sighed deeply as she spread marmalade on her toast. She had a sudden craving for raspberry jam that she knew was just her mind being contrary. "There isn't any raspberry jam," she told herself loudly. "Stop thinking about it."

After a short walk in the early morning July sunshine, she sat down in the kitchen and flipped through the island's telephone directory. It took her several minutes to remember Nancy's daughter's married surname. She dialed slowly, mentally rehearsing everything she wanted to say to the woman. The phone rang several times before an answering machine picked up.

"This is Mike and Sarah; leave a message after the tone."

"Hello, Sarah, this is Bessie Cubbon. I was just ringing to tell you how very sorry I was to hear about your mother's passing. I don't know if you remember me, but I certainly remember you and your brothers playing on Laxey Beach as children. Anyway, I would very much like to pay my respects to you and your family and attend whatever service you decide to hold for Nancy. If you can find the time to ring me back, I would appreciate it very much. I understand how difficult this time must be for you. Please accept my deepest sympathies."

Bessie disconnected and frowned at the phone. She wasn't sure she'd said the right things and she wished now that she could do it all over again. She shook her head at her own foolishness and then got up to make a cup of tea. Before she could switch on the kettle, however, her phone rang.

"Hello?"

"Ah, Ms. Cubbon? It's, um, it's Sarah Combe, just ringing you back."

"Hello, Sarah, how are you, darling?" Bessie asked in her most sympathetic voice. To her surprise, it sounded as if Sarah burst into tears.

"I'm not very well," Sarah said tearfully. "I mean, mum and I didn't really get along well, but I'm ever so sorry that she's gone. I can't believe how much I miss her."

"I find that's often the case," Bessie said soothingly. "I was estranged from my parents for many years, but when they passed I still felt as if a hole had suddenly opened up in my life."

"That's it, exactly," Sarah said. "I can't seem to stop crying."

"Perhaps you'd like to come over for a visit?" Bessie suggested. "I can offer you tea and sympathy."

Sarah managed a small chuckle. "That's very kind of you," she replied. "But I've so much to do, I'm not sure I could manage it. I'm off to mum's this morning to start sorting out her things, you see."

"Would you like a hand with that?" Bessie asked. She was shocked at how quickly the woman was acting, but that didn't make her any less willing to help.

"Oh, I couldn't impose," Sarah began.

"It's no imposition," Bessie told her. "I can meet you at your mum's whenever it's convenient for you. You may find the job quite emotionally challenging."

"I might at that," Sarah said with a sigh. "Can you meet me there in about an hour? I have to run a few errands on my way up, but I expect I should get there around ten."

"Of course I can," Bessie assured her. "It's a lovely day, so please don't worry if you get held up. I can happily sit on your mother's garden bench and wait for you."

"Ah, yes, I love that bench," Sarah said. "I must remember to grab that at some point."

With that she disconnected, leaving Bessie with the impression that Sarah was more concerned about collecting what she liked from the house than sorting through her mother's things. Presumably Nancy's other children would soon be on their way to the island. Sarah was making sure she got in first.

With an hour to waste, Bessie decided to walk to Nancy's house. The neighbourhood was almost entirely made up of small detached bungalows built in the nineteen-thirties and forties on tiny lots. A few had been extended or remodeled over the years, but most looked exactly the same as they had for the last forty or fifty years. Bessie found herself strolling past some of the other Raspberry Jam Ladies' homes as she went. When she walked past Agnes's house, she decided to check on the woman.

"Ah, Bessie, what brings you here?" Agnes greeted her at the door.

Bessie forced herself to smile at the other woman, even though Agnes's appearance surprised her. The other woman looked as if she hadn't slept since Bessie had seen her last. She was wearing crumpled clothing and her hair obviously hadn't been brushed in some time.

"I just wanted to make sure you were okay," Bessie told her. "You were quite upset yesterday."

"I still am," Agnes admitted. "I still can't believe that Nancy is gone."

"That's only natural," Bessie said reassuringly. "She was a good friend for many years."

"She was my best friend," Agnes said, almost angrily. "She was always there for me, no matter what, and I'll never find another friend like her."

"It's good you have Margaret and Joan and Elinor," Bessie said. "I'm sure they're being supportive."

Agnes shrugged. "They're trying, but they don't understand," she said, tears filling her eyes. "They weren't as close to Nancy as I was. She was just one of the group to them."

Bessie patted her friend's arm. "Maybe you should go and stay with one of them for a few days?" she suggested. "You don't have any family on the island, do you?"

"No," Agnes said softly. "All I ever had was my Matthew, and he moved away from me as soon as he could."

"I'm sure you must have missed him," Bessie said, feeling quite lost as to what to say.

"My husband, he was the one that drove him away," Agnes said. "He didn't want a son that wasn't, well, like other men. He told Matthew to leave, he did. I never forgave him for that. When he died, I hoped that Matthew and I might get another chance, but Matthew was already sick by then."

Agnes shook her head. "Too much sadness," she said, tears flowing freely now. "I don't think I can take any more sadness."

"Bessie? What brings you here?" The voice came from behind her and Bessie turned slowly to greet Eliinor.

"I was just walking past and I wanted to check on poor Agnes," Bessie said, feeling as if she'd been caught doing something she shouldn't.

"Oh, that is kind of you," Elinor said briskly. "But, as I told you yesterday, there's no need. We're looking after poor Agnes quite well. Aren't we Agnes?"

Agnes nodded slowly. "They've all been very kind," she said softly.

"But we mustn't keep you, Bessie," Elinor said. "I'm sure you have many better things to do."

Bessie nodded. "Actually, I'm just off to Nancy's house. I told Sarah that I would give her a hand as she starts going through Nancy's things."

Agnes gasped, and even Elinor looked shocked.

"Trying to grab the valuables before her brothers arrive, no doubt," Elinor said scathingly.

"She'll be wanting to get the house on the market," Agnes whispered. "She'd been nagging her mother for years to sell it. Now, with the market going higher and higher every day, she'll be even more eager to get it listed."

"Nancy didn't want to move?" Bessie asked.

"Nancy loved that house," Agnes answered. "She moved in right after she and Frederick got married and all four of her children were born in their bedroom. There was no way she was ever going to sell it."

"I feel the same way about my cottage," Bessie said. "It's home and it always will be."

"There's a time and a place for sentiment," Elinor said coolly. "But I don't think bricks and mortar deserve such devotion. I made a good profit when I sold my house last year and my new little flat has all the modern conveniences."

"Of course, your house had bad memories in it," Agnes said.

Elinor bristled. "I wouldn't agree," she said sharply. "And I don't want to discuss it."

"Where is your new flat?" Bessie asked, anxious to change the subject.

"I'm just a few streets over from here," Elinor told her, rattling off the address. "I'm in number 608, which is the top floor. I have wonderful views."

"It sounds lovely," Bessie said. "Although I love my cottage, I wouldn't mind a few modern conveniences."

Elinor laughed condescendingly. "Yes, well, I have to say I love the covered parking, the grocery delivery service, the unlimited hot water, the built-in microwave…." She waved a hand. "I could go on, but I suspect you don't have any intention of moving, do you?"

Bessie shook her head. "I don't, but it all sounds very nice."

"Yes, well, we won't keep you," Elinor said. "I'm sure you've things to do, and I'm going to make Agnes some nice breakfast."

"I had breakfast," Agnes said.

"I'm sure you did," Elinor said, patting the woman's arm. "But I think you probably could do with a little bit more to eat, couldn't you? I thought you might like a nice bowl of oatmeal."

"I don't like oatmeal," Agnes said in a petulant voice. "I'm fine anyway, and I think you should go away."

Elinor shook her head. "Now, now, darling, that isn't any way to talk to me. I've made a special effort to come to see you. The least you can do is invite me in for a chat."

Agnes opened and then closed her mouth. After an awkward moment, she finally sighed. "Sure, come on in. Bessie, why don't you come in as well?"

Bessie hesitated for a moment, but as she was certain that Elinor wanted her to refuse, she couldn't resist the invitation. "I can only stay for a few minutes," she said as she walked into the house.

As soon as she was across the threshold she wrinkled her nose. The house had a musty smell that suggested it hadn't been cleaned in a while.

"Agnes, when did you last vacuum?" Elinor demanded as she strode into the house.

"Oh, it's been a few days," Agnes admitted sheepishly.

"A few days?" Elinor asked, looking around pointedly.

Bessie did her own looking around and sighed. The front door opened right into a small sitting room and it didn't appear as if it had been cleaned in weeks or even months. There were plates with half-eaten biscuits on them piled haphazardly on tables and Bessie counted four teacups balanced on top of the piles of books and magazines that were scattered around the room.

"I should have insisted on coming inside last night, shouldn't I?" Elinor asked. "I can't believe the state of this room."

"I haven't been feeling well for a few weeks," Agnes said. "I just haven't had the energy to clean."

"You should have rung me," Elinor told her. "I would have come and helped you."

"I hate to bother people," Agnes said, looking at the floor.

"I'm surprised Nancy didn't do something," Elinor said as she began collecting dishes and cups.

"She hadn't been here in a while," Agnes said quietly. "She was quite busy lately with her own life."

A knock on the door startled them all. Agnes crossed over to it and opened it.

"Joan? What brings you here?" she asked.

"It's my turn to check on you," Joan replied.

"Join the club," Agnes muttered as she pulled the door open. "Come on in then, you may as well."

Bessie smiled at Joan as she took a few steps into the room. "We've all been checking on Agnes today," she said.

"I see that," Joan answered, looking from Bessie to Elinor and back again. She frowned. "But what's that smell?" she asked.

"Our Agnes hasn't been keeping up with her housework," Elinor said. "I think we're all going to have to lend a hand."

Bessie glanced at her watch. "I only have a few minutes before I'm meant to be meeting Sarah," she said. "What can I do that will be the most help in the least amount of time?"

"Oh, no, dear, I didn't mean you," Elinor said. "I meant Joan and myself. We'll have to ring Margaret as well, of course. And Agnes, you'll have to help."

"Of course," Agnes said. "Or you all could just go and leave it with me. I'm sure I can handle a bit of cleaning on my own."

"It will do us all good to help," Elinor said firmly. "And you're clearly not up to it, anyway."

"I'm happy to help out as much as I can," Bessie tried again.

"That is kind of you," Elinor replied. "But really, you go and help Sarah. That can be your good deed for the day."

Bessie opened her mouth to protest, but Agnes caught her eye and shook her head.

"I'll walk you out," she told Bessie, taking her arm.

Bessie said quick goodbyes to Elinor and Joan and then let Agnes lead her to the door. Once Bessie was through it, Agnes followed her and shut the door behind them.

"It's no use arguing with Elinor," she told Bessie.

"But you shouldn't have to put up with her," Bessie argued.

"She means well," Agnes insisted. "And besides, the house is a mess. If she wants to spend her day cleaning my house, why should I stop her?"

Bessie grinned. "I suppose you have a point there."

Agnes sighed. "I haven't been at all well," she told Bessie. "I simply haven't had the energy to clean. If Elinor and the others can get the house back into shape, I'll be really grateful."

"Are you okay, though?" Bessie asked, looking into Agnes's eyes.

"Not really," Agnes sighed. "But there are some things in life that simply can't be repaired."

Before Bessie could reply, the front door swung open.

"Now, Agnes," Elinor said brightly, "we aren't going to do all of the work. In you come."

Agnes gave Bessie a hug and then dashed back inside her home.

"Thank you so much for coming to check on Agnes," Elinor told

Bessie. "But really, she's our problem, not yours. I think the fewer people bothering her the better at the moment."

She turned and was back inside the house, pushing the door firmly shut before Bessie could choke out a reply. Bessie considered knocking on the door and telling Elinor a thing or two, but she decided against it. All of the ladies were under considerable stress at the moment. She'd have to try to be extra patient with them until the murderer was caught.

CHAPTER 5

Bessie headed back down to the pavement and turned towards Nancy King's house, which was further down the same street. As she walked, she spotted Sarah Combe's car as it drove slowly past her. Bessie felt a sudden knot in her stomach as she headed towards the woman.

As Bessie approached Sarah's car, she gave herself a mental shake. She'd recognised the woman driving, but she'd been surprised at how old she looked. Sarah had to be getting close to fifty, but Bessie had somehow still been thinking of her as the young woman she'd last seen some thirty years earlier. By the time Bessie reached the car, Sarah had parked and was getting out.

"Ah, Bessie, you haven't changed a bit," Sarah said as she shut the car door behind her. "I can still remember sneaking over to your cottage for a biscuit while my brothers chased each other up and down the beach."

Bessie smiled. "You've changed a lot," she said honestly. "I still think of you as a little girl."

Sarah grinned and then gave Bessie an awkward hug. When she moved away, Bessie took a moment to study the other woman. Sarah hadn't been a small child and she wasn't a small adult. At least three or four inches taller than Bessie, she carried more weight on her sturdy frame than was healthy for her.

Her hair was shoulder-length and cut in a bob that was expertly coloured so Sarah appeared to have not yet begun to go grey. She was expensively dressed in carefully casual clothes that Bessie recognised as coming from the island's premier fashion boutique. Bessie didn't shop there herself, but she often window-shopped there with Doona, who also couldn't afford to buy more than an odd item when they had their annual sale.

"I hope I don't look too much older," Sarah said with a frown.

Bessie shook her head. "I was thinking of you as a teenager, or even as a small child," she told her. "You're definitely older, but you don't look anywhere near your age."

Sarah smiled and seemed satisfied with that. "Let's get inside and see what needs doing, shall we?" she asked.

"I didn't realise the police were done with the house," Bessie remarked as the pair walked slowly up the short path to the large bungalow.

"They've told me I can't go in the kitchen," Sarah said. "But I'm more interested in mum's bedroom. I want to make sure everything of value is safe. I've heard about burglars who break into houses where they know someone has just died to steal all the valuables."

Bessie nodded. It was as good an excuse as any she'd heard for clearing out someone's home. Bessie just hoped Sarah's brothers would believe it when they arrived.

Sarah pulled out a key and let them into the house. She switched on a light and Bessie stood blinking in the entryway. The curtains were drawn, and the room was fairly dark, even with a light on.

"Mum had the curtains drawn when I arrived Tuesday morning," Sarah said. "I thought it was probably best to leave them that way. I'm hoping it discourages the nosy neighbours."

As her eyes slowly became more accustomed to the light, Bessie looked around the room. If she'd thought Agnes's home was a mess, she had no words to describe what she now saw.

"Was your mother unwell?" Bessie asked before she could stop herself.

Sarah frowned. "I can't believe she was living like this," she said. "I didn't really notice the mess on Tuesday, because I was really just looking for mum. This is terrible."

Bessie looked at used cups and plates and even a dirty pan that were scattered across nearly every flat surface. There were newspapers spread across the floor and piles of books in every corner. Bessie could see a layer of dust seemingly everywhere.

"Maybe she didn't have as much energy for cleaning so she only cleaned the rooms she used most," Sarah suggested.

It certainly looks as if she used this room a lot, Bessie thought but didn't say.

Bessie glanced towards the back of the house. She could see crime scene tape blocking the entrance to the small kitchen.

"Let's see what her bedroom looks like," Sarah continued.

Bessie followed Sarah down the short hallway to the bedrooms. She couldn't stop herself from glancing into each one. The first one they passed, apparently a guest room, looked as if it hadn't been used in many years. There was a thick layer of dust covering everything from the bed to the small desk in one corner.

"This was my room," Sarah said, stopping and flipping on the light. The room wasn't large, but it looked like it would have been comfortable if it had been clean. "The boys had to share a room, since the house only has four bedrooms, but as I was the only girl, I had my own space."

"Did all three boys share?"

"They did," Sarah said. "They were in here."

She opened the door to the next room along the corridor and flipped on the light. Bessie glanced around the nearly empty space.

Sarah frowned. "Mum got rid of most of the furniture in here a long time ago," she told Bessie. "There used to be three beds, all crammed together for the boys."

"It isn't a very large room," Bessie commented. "It must have been a tight fit."

Sarah laughed. "I was always jealous because they got to share and always had someone to talk to when they couldn't sleep and someone else there if they had a bad dream. Of course, they were always jealous because I had my own room. Nothing makes children happy."

Bessie smiled at her. "What did your parents use the fourth bedroom for?" she asked curiously.

"My father insisted that he needed an office at home," Sarah told her. "I don't ever remember him actually using it. He wasn't home enough to actually need it. But no matter how much my brothers begged, he wouldn't let them use the room."

She opened the next door off the hall, again switching on the light. Bessie glanced inside at the completely empty and windowless room. It was by far the smallest of the rooms she'd seen with only carpeting and bare walls to look at.

Sarah shook her head. "I didn't realise mum got rid of everything in here as well," she said. "I wonder when she did that."

"It looks as if there is some water damage in that corner," Bessie commented, pointing to the ceiling. There was a large wet patch on the ceiling and part of the way down the wall beneath it.

Sarah walked over to take a closer look. "It looks as if the roof might be leaking," she said. "I'd better get someone to come and take a look at that. I want to get the house on the market as quickly as I can. People won't be interested in buying it if the roof leaks."

"From what I've heard about the property market at the moment, I'm not sure people will care," Bessie said.

Sarah shrugged. "I need to talk to my brothers and see what they want to do, I suppose."

The last bedroom was the largest. Sarah opened the door and switched on the lights. The curtains were drawn and the room felt dark and dreary, even with the lights on. This room, at least, was fairly clean and tidy.

"The police have been all through here, of course," she told Bessie as they waited for their eyes to become accustomed to the dim lighting. "They took mum's appointment diary and a few other papers that were on her desk. I imagine I'll get them back one day."

Bessie looked around the large room. There was a large bed in the centre of the space, with small bedside tables on either side of it. A large wardrobe took up most of one wall and opposite it was a small desk with a chair. There were a few sheets of paper and a handful of pens on the desk, but nothing else.

"Did your mother have a computer?" Bessie asked.

"Mum? No way," Sarah laughed. "She couldn't work out how to use a mobile phone. She wasn't interested in technology."

Sarah walked over to the small desk and opened the top drawer. Bessie tried to wander over to join her in a casual manner. She didn't want to appear too nosy, but she was curious what Nancy kept in her desk.

The top drawer looked exactly like the one in Bessie's desk in her cottage. It was full of pens, pencils, scraps of paper with seemingly random numbers scribbled on them, pads of sticky notes, rubber bands and what looked to be hundreds of paper clips. Sarah ran her hand through the junk, as if rummaging around for something. After a minute, she shook her head.

"It's all the same junk I have in my desk at home," she told Bessie.

"Me, too," Bessie admitted.

Sarah sat down in the small chair and pulled open the top drawer of the three that ran down one side of the desk. Inside were sheets of stationery and matching envelopes. Bessie felt a pang as she recognised the uniquely coloured sea green paper. She'd never really thought about it, but all of the Raspberry Jam Ladies used different coloured stationery. Bessie probably had notes from every one of them tucked up in boxes at home. She loved to keep written correspondence, and Nancy's notes would take on new meaning for Bessie now that she had passed away.

Sarah sighed. "I have hundreds of notes from mum over the years," she told Bessie. "Even though we didn't really get along for much of the time, she often wrote me notes. I don't know what to do with this stationery. There's no way I can use it."

"I don't think you need to worry about that for today," Bessie said soothingly. "No one is going to break in and steal stationery. Maybe one of your brothers would be able to find a use for it."

Sarah shuddered. "I would hate to get a letter from them on this paper," she told Bessie. "It would feel like something from beyond the grave."

Bessie leaned over and pushed the drawer shut gently. "You mustn't let yourself get upset by such things," she told Sarah. "There's going to be a lot to go through in the days to come."

"I know," Sarah sighed. "But for today, I just want to make sure nothing of value has been left lying around. I think I'll make Fred and James do the actual clearing out of the house. Neither of them will see any sentimental value in anything."

"What about Adam?" Bessie asked.

"What about him?" Sarah shrugged. "We haven't heard from him since he left at eighteen," she told Bessie. "That's another thing I was hoping to find in mum's desk. An address for my baby brother."

She took a deep breath and then pulled out the middle drawer. Inside were a few folders that Sarah took out and laid on the desk. The first was labelled "banking," and as Sarah flipped through it Bessie could see what must have been several months worth of bank statements.

Sarah studied the top one for a moment and then put it back in the folder and flipped the folder shut. "Nothing unexpected there," she muttered. The second folder was labelled "bills" and it was exactly what Bessie expected from the label. Months of utility bills were hastily shuffled through by Sarah.

Another folder, "savings," had bank savings books inside. Sarah glanced at each one briefly and then put the books into her large handbag. "Don't want to leave these lying around," she told Bessie.

The final folder said "correspondence," and Bessie recognised some of its contents. The various coloured sheets had to be letters from the other Raspberry Jam Ladies. Sarah simply glanced at each sheet quickly and then returned the folder to the drawer with the others.

"Last drawer," she said.

Bessie could hear the tension in the other woman's voice and she wondered what Sarah was expecting to find.

The bottom drawer was the largest and Sarah pulled it open and then frowned. After a moment, she reached in and took out a shoebox that had taken up nearly all of the space in the drawer.

When she opened the box, Bessie could see that it held the sorts of family mementoes that nearly everyone possessed. There were stacks of old photographs, postcards and letters, and what looked like a very small and very misshapen cuddly toy.

Sarah stared into the box for a moment and then slammed the lid back down on it. She put it down on the desk and walked quickly to the opposite side of the room.

"I think mum must have kept her jewellery in her bedside table," she said curtly, pulling open its small drawer. "Ah, yes, here it is."

Sarah held up a small jewellery box and then opened it. Bessie watched as she looked through it very carefully.

"I think everything is here," Sarah said after a moment. "I can't remember anything else she had."

Bessie shrugged. "I don't remember your mum wearing much jewellery," she told the other woman.

"She didn't wear it often," Sarah said. "But she had some lovely pieces. Dad did quite well in the fifties and sixties and he liked to bring mum little surprises. I doubt she ever bought herself anything, though, after dad died."

Bessie nodded. "Is there anything else of value that you want to take with you?" she asked.

Sarah checked the rest of the drawers in both bedside tables and then moved on to the wardrobe. It was only about half-full and a large portion of the clothes inside looked like they must have belonged to Sarah's father.

"Your mother kept your father's things?" Bessie asked in surprise.

Sarah nodded. "She, well, she had a hard time letting him go. Keeping his things was what she did to keep his memory alive. At least that's what she told me whenever I suggested she get rid of them. They weren't causing any real harm, I suppose. She wasn't all that interested in clothes herself. I bet everything in here is at least ten years old, and I'm sure I remember some of these outfits from my childhood."

Bessie glanced into the wardrobe and turned to Sarah. "I remember seeing your mum in some of those things," she told her. "From when you and your brothers were still quite small."

"I doubt the charity shops will take them," Sarah sighed. "Maybe a museum might be interested, though."

Bessie stayed where she was while Sarah did a quick check of the house's only bathroom, making sure the medicine chest wasn't hiding any secrets.

"I think we can go now," she told Bessie, glancing one more time around what had been her parents' bedroom.

Bessie turned towards the door.

"Oh, can you just grab that shoebox?" Sarah asked. She sounded as if she was trying to sound casual, but Bessie could hear all sorts of repressed emotions in the request.

"Sure," Bessie replied, picking up the box from where Sarah had left it on the desk.

"Maybe I could invite myself over for a cuppa?" Sarah asked as they walked towards the front door.

"Of course you can," Bessie replied. Outside it had begun to rain lightly. Bessie climbed into Sarah's car and the pair made their way to Bessie's cottage, with Bessie still carrying the shoebox.

In Bessie's small kitchen, Bessie put the kettle on while Sarah sat looking out the window at the rain.

"It doesn't rain as much in the south of the island as it does here," she told Bessie.

"Really?" Bessie asked.

"No," Sarah sighed. "I should have said it doesn't feel as if it rains as much in the south. Every time I come up to Laxey it rains. It doesn't matter if it's spring, summer, winter or autumn. It just always rains."

Bessie took out a couple of boxes of biscuits and arranged several varieties on a plate, passing Sarah a small plate to use for her selections.

"Oh dear," Bessie said as she noticed the clock. "It's really time for lunch, not just biscuits." She opened her fridge and frowned. There wasn't a lot in it. Friday was her regular shopping day and she really needed a trip to the grocery shop. She opened her cupboards and inspected the contents.

"I can make some tomato soup, but it will have to come from a tin," she told Sarah. "And I have a loaf of stale bread. How about cheesy garlic bread with it?"

"That sounds wonderful," Sarah told her. "I haven't had much of an appetite since mum, well, in the last few days."

Bessie got busy with the preparations while Sarah picked listlessly at a biscuit. When the kettle boiled, Bessie made a pot of tea and poured out a cup for Sarah.

"Add extra sugar," Bessie suggested. "It will help."

Sarah nodded and did as she was told. After a few sips of tea, while Bessie carried on with making the soup, she sighed deeply.

"Have you seen the Raspberry Jam Ladies since mum, well, since Tuesday?" she asked Bessie.

"I saw them yesterday. They had a gathering for some of your mother's friends so we could share our memories of her."

Sarah sighed again. "I suppose they told you I killed her," she said softly. "Mum was threating to change her will again. People seem to think that would motivate me to kill her."

"Did she tell you she was changing her will?" Bessie asked.

"Yes," Sarah nodded. "But then, we rarely spoke, and just about every time we did she told me she was changing her will. I sort of assumed years ago that I wasn't going to inherit anything from her. My husband and I don't really need the money. Anyway, she never liked me."

Bessie stared at the woman, wondering what she could possibly say to that. The oven buzzed, which gave her a welcome minute to think.

"I'm sure your mother loved you very much," she said eventually, the words sounding inadequate even as she said them.

"Oh, I suppose she loved me, in her own way," Sarah replied. "But I also know she didn't much like me. Mum didn't like children, you see. It wasn't just me. She didn't enjoy spending time with any of us."

Bessie slid the bread, now smothered in garlic butter, into the oven. Again, she was uncertain of how to reply. She was used to spending time with younger children who were easily reassured as to their mothers' devotion. Sarah, in her early fifties, was a rather different case.

"What makes you think that?" Bessie finally asked.

"Mum was absolutely devoted to dad," Sarah told her. "I mean, I love my husband, I really do, but that doesn't mean I don't think for myself or ever disagree with him. Mum almost stopped being a separate person when she married dad, or certainly by the time I came along. I never saw them argue, never saw my mother express an opinion that was different to his. She was almost obsessed with him or something. He was her reason for existing and when he died, I thought she might give up on life."

"Women in those days were expected to be submissive and obedient to their husbands," Bessie told her. "That's one of the reasons I never married."

Sarah nodded. "It was more than that, though. I think mum actually believed that dad was truly the smartest and most handsome man in the world. I think she always felt like she didn't quite deserve him and she was constantly trying to find ways to make him happier. And he wasn't all that fond of children, either."

"Men weren't involved in childrearing in those days," Bessie pointed out.

Sarah shrugged. "I know things have changed," she said. "But I also know things were different in other families. I would go and spend an afternoon with a friend and her mum would want to hear about our school day or would play a game with us or show us how to cook something. My mother simply didn't enjoy my company, not when I was small and not even as I got older."

"What about your brothers?"

"If it's possible, I think she had even less time for them. Fred and James were better at finding things to do away from home than I was.

They'd go to school and then do sports or hang out with friends. Mum never minded where we were as long as we weren't underfoot."

"What about Adam?"

Sarah laughed bitterly. "I always felt sorriest for him," she told Bessie. "At least I was a girl. Dad always wanted a girl; that's why they kept having children after Fred and James. Poor dad thought that he'd get a little dainty thing, tiny like mum was, who he could show off to his work colleagues. Unfortunately, he ended up with me, an outsized tomboy who hated frilly dresses and despised being dragged out for show. But poor Adam, well, mum and dad made no secret of the fact that they wanted to stop after they had me. Adam was an unwelcome surprise and they didn't make any effort to hide that fact."

"No wonder he left as soon as he could," Bessie remarked.

Sarah sighed. "I still miss him," she said sadly. "I still can't believe he left and never even sent me so much as a postcard."

"Did he keep in touch with your mother?"

Sarah shrugged. "She never said. I think she would have told me if she heard from him, but it's possible she wouldn't have bothered. I'm sure she couldn't imagine that I would care."

Bessie gave her a surprised look and then poured soup into bowls. She took the garlic bread out of the oven and slid it onto a serving plate. After slicing it into several pieces she put the bread in the centre of the table. While she'd been doing that, Sarah had carried the soup bowls across and now the pair sat down to eat.

"Your mother always seemed like a very kind woman," Bessie told Sarah as they ate.

"She was kind to strangers and to her very close friends," Sarah said. "But she had a very limited capacity for love, I think. She loved dad with a fierce intensity that just didn't seem to leave any room for anyone else in her heart."

"The times were so different, though," Bessie said thoughtfully. "Maybe she was a bit too reserved. In my day, being reserved was seen as a very good thing."

"When I was in my late twenties and my husband and I were struggling with infertility, I came to visit her. In those days, there weren't any test tube babies or anything and I went to mum, sobbing almost hysterically, because I wanted a baby so badly it physically hurt. I still remember exactly what she said to me. She said 'Children are nothing but hard work. You don't really want one.'"

Sarah's eyes filled with tears. "My husband and I really wanted children and I would have been a better mum to them than my mother was to me."

Bessie patted her hand. "I'm so sorry," she said simply.

After a moment Sarah swallowed hard and then began to eat her soup. Bessie ate her own lunch, quietly watching the other woman.

"I'm sorry," Sarah said eventually. "You're just such a good listener. Anyway, I was lucky, because my mother-in-law is nothing like my mother. She spent hours crying with me when I realised I wouldn't be able to have children and then she helped me pick up the pieces and find other ways to share myself with future generations. I just want you to understand why I wasn't close to my mother, that's all."

Bessie nodded. "I do understand," she told the other woman. "When I lost my Matthew, I thought my world had ended. My mother told me to stop being silly and pretending to be upset. She didn't think I'd known him long enough or well enough to be as devastated as I felt. I never forgave her for not understanding or at least accepting my emotions."

"Anyway, that's why I never really visited mum. I don't think she cared anyway. I thought, for a long time, that if I gave her grandchildren she'd want to be a part of my life, but Fred and James both have children and mum never bothered to go across to see them."

"Did they visit her here?" Bessie asked.

Sarah shrugged. "James used to come across once a year or so, usually for mum's birthday. Once he and his wife had three kids, though, it got to be too much work to drag them all here. James told me that he offered to fly mum across to see them every year and mum always found excuses for not going. I'm sure Fred invited mum to come and visit him as well, but I don't think he's been back on the island since he finished uni."

"So if you weren't worried about the will, why did you come to see your mother on Tuesday?" Bessie asked.

"Mum broke her hip a few years ago. When she was in hospital, they made her give them contact information in case anything happened. Obviously, since I'm the closest, she gave them my details. Apparently, they kept them in her file. I was rung last week and told that mum's latest test results showed malignancies in several areas. She didn't have more than six months left and they wanted me to help make arrangements for hospice care."

Sarah brushed tears from her eyes. Bessie quickly got up and found a box of tissues.

"I'm sorry," Bessie said softly.

"I don't know why I'm crying," Sarah said after a moment. "Mum didn't even want me to know. She was furious that the doctors had rung me about it. She said I should mind my own business. I told her I was coming up to see her on Tuesday afternoon, but I didn't sleep on Monday night, so once I got up, I thought I might as well just get it over with. I thought maybe if I turned up early she'd be so surprised she'd actually speak with me."

"But instead you found her," Bessie said solemnly.

"I was sure she'd killed herself," Sarah replied. "I thought she decided she didn't want to suffer so she'd taken too many pain pills or something. Murder never crossed my mind, not until the police started asking questions."

"They seem pretty sure it was murder," Bessie said "Who would have wanted to kill your mother?"

Sarah shook her head. "No one," she replied with a sigh. "I can't believe there was anyone that would have wanted to kill her. She was dying anyway and even if she wasn't, she was just a harmless old woman."

"Surely there were people she argued with?" Bessie asked tentatively. She wasn't sure how far she should push the other woman. The topic had be painful.

"Not that I know of," Sarah told her. "Maybe she had a disagreement with one of her precious Raspberry Jam Ladies and they got rid of her." She held up a hand. "I'm not serious. As far as I know the ladies all got along brilliantly well for the last fifty years. They were as close as sisters. Mum would have done anything for them and I'm sure they felt the same way about her."

Bessie bit back a sigh. She'd been hoping Sarah would be able to offer some suspects for the seemingly random murder.

"Anyway, thank you for lunch," Sarah said now. "I suppose I should be going."

Bessie cleared away the soup and bread plates and put the biscuits back on the table. "Have a biscuit before you go," she suggested.

Sarah took one and nibbled on it slowly, staring at the shoebox that they'd brought from her mother's house as she did. "Maybe it will be easier to take a look here," she said under her breath.

Bessie got up and handed her the box from where she'd left it on the counter. Sarah took several deep breaths and then opened it again. She carefully removed the small cuddly toy and then began to look through the other items in the box. After several minutes, while Bessie felt as if she were holding her breath, Sarah sighed and pushed the box away.

"As far as I can tell, it's all notes, postcards and letters from my father," she told Bessie. "Look at this."

Sarah held out a postcard and Bessie took it from her.

It was postmarked the third of June 1957, and the front of the card was a picture of Tower Bridge in London. Bessie read the note on the back.

"My darling, I miss you more than words can say. Only two more days and I shall be with you again. I may even be back before you receive this card. Much love, Frederick."

"He obviously cared a great deal for your mother," Bessie observed.

"Yeah, he did," Sarah said bitterly. "I was six years old when he sent that and the boys were ten, eight, and four. You'd think he might have thought to mention us as well, wouldn't you?"

Bessie opened her mouth to reply, but she wasn't sure what she was going to say. Sarah held up a hand.

"Please don't try to defend him, or her, for that matter. Take a look." She pushed the box towards Bessie, who couldn't stop herself from glancing inside. She flipped through several dozen postcards, mostly with pictures of London sites on them. Every one had a similar declaration of undying love on it, and not a single one mentioned the children.

"Not one single scrap from anything my brothers or I ever gave her," Sarah said with a catch in her voice. "She never saved our art or our schoolwork, but I've sent her hundreds of letters and cards over the years and she doesn't seem to have saved a single one."

"I'm sorry," Bessie said, feeling as if the words were totally inadequate.

Sarah shrugged. "I shouldn't be surprised," she said grimly. "Although this is a surprise."

She held up the tiny cuddly toy, turning it over and over in her hands.

"What is it?" Bessie asked.

Sarah laughed, a strangely hollow sound. "It's Mr. Hiccup," she told Bessie. "When I was about ten I decided that Adam needed a friend. I slept with two or three cuddly toys and he didn't have any. Mum wouldn't consider buying him one, even though I begged her to, so I used some scrap fabric and made Mr. Hiccup for him. He's supposed to be a monster of some sort. I thought a boy wouldn't want a teddy or a bunny, so I made a monster and I stuffed him with feathers that I pulled out of my pillow. Mum was angry about that, but she soon forgot all about it."

"What did Adam think?" Bessie couldn't help but ask.

"Adam was kind enough to at least pretend to love him," Sarah said with a teary-eyed smile. "Of course Fred and James teased him, but he always told them he just slept with Mr. Hiccup to make me happy. They were so much older that they didn't really care what he did, anyway. I always thought, that is, I always assumed that Adam took Mr. Hiccup with him when he left."

Bessie could hear repressed tears in Sarah's voice. She patted the woman's arm and pushed the tissue box towards her. After several minutes and more than a few tears, Sarah shook her head and looked at Bessie.

"I'm sorry. It's just a cuddly toy, and an ugly one at that, but it's brought back so many memories." She shook her head again. "I really should be going," she said again. "Thank you for lunch and for everything."

Sarah stood up and turned to leave, Mr. Hiccup clenched tightly in her hand. Bessie closed up the shoebox and offered it to her.

"I don't really want that," Sarah said harshly. "Though maybe it would make me feel better if I burned the lot."

"Maybe I should hang on to it for now," Bessie said hastily. "Your brothers might like a look at everything, if nothing else."

Sarah looked as if she might argue, but then sighed. "That's probably best," she agreed. "Thank you again."

When she'd gone, Bessie climbed her stairs and went into her bedroom. Her bed was nearly completely covered with cuddly toys. Without children of her own, she'd become something of an honourary auntie over the years to most of the children who grew up in Laxey. And many of those children insisted on gifting Bessie with cuddly toys. She had so many now that she couldn't really remember where most of them had come from.

She picked up a random teddy and hugged it tightly. Poor Sarah and her brothers had grown up too long ago to take advantage of running away to Bessie's house to get a break from their parents. In those days, when Bessie had been younger, she'd been an oddity. Women simply didn't live on their own in the forties and fifties. It wasn't until she'd reached a somewhat more respectable middle age that the community had begun to appreciate her.

CHAPTER 6

Friday was dull and overcast, but Bessie had a standing arrangement with her taxi service. Dave, her usual driver, was at her door not long after she'd had her walk and breakfast.

"Did you get your walk in this morning?" he asked Bessie as she settled into the taxi.

"I did, but I didn't go very far," Bessie replied. "It looks ever so much like rain."

"It does indeed," Dave agreed.

He left Bessie at her favourite bookshop in Ramsey. She spent a happy half hour browsing the shelves. Unusually for her, she didn't find anything new to add to her enormous book collection.

There were a handful of charity shops between the bookshop and the supermarket, and she couldn't resist popping into each one to look over their collections of second-hand books. She didn't find anything until she got to the last shop in the row. There she ended up with three paperbacks, two from authors she knew well and the third from one she'd never tried before.

"These should keep me out of trouble," she said cheerfully to the young woman at the till.

The girl shrugged and took Bessie's money without comment.

Bessie left the shop shaking her head at the manners of some young people.

At ShopFast she quickly ran through her list, adding a few little treats to her shopping trolley as they caught her eye. She'd always kept herself slim and she thought that her daily walks were a big part of that. Worrying about calories was not something she'd ever had to do.

In nearly every aisle, she ran into someone she knew, and everyone wanted to talk about Nancy King's murder.

"It's terrible," one woman said. "I had a jar of that jam from them ladies and I could tell there was something not quite right about it. I wasn't the least bit surprised when the police came and took the jar away."

Bessie murmured an appropriate response.

"To think I could have been killed right in my own kitchen," the woman had said, shaking her head as she wandered away. "In my own kitchen...."

"I heard her daughter wanted to get rid of her," an elderly man whispered to Bessie in the produce aisle. "That house of hers is a gold mine, worth an absolute fortune it is. That daughter of hers just wanted to get her hands on it, that's what I heard."

Bessie didn't bother to argue with the man, even though it was hard not to try to defend Sarah Combe. For all she knew, he could be right.

"It's a government conspiracy to get rid of the old folks," an elderly widow hissed in Bessie's ear at the bakery. As the woman had been seeing government conspiracies behind every island happening for at least fifty years, Bessie didn't worry too much about her words.

"One of us will be next," the woman told her as Bessie selected a baguette. "Mark my words, they're trying to save money by getting rid of everyone who's old."

Bessie patted her hand. "I'll keep that in mind," she told her gently.

"It's a serial killer," another acquaintance announced, ironically enough in the breakfast aisle. Bessie reached for her usual cereal as the woman continued.

"I've been saying for years that we're going to have one and now we do. Imagine poisoning one jar of jam and then giving away two dozen jars full. The randomness of it must be part of what makes it fun for them, wouldn't you think?"

"I'd rather not think about it," Bessie said firmly as she steered her shopping cart away.

She'd nearly finished her shopping when she ran into Maggie Shimmin. She and her husband, Thomas, owned the row of holiday cottages just down the beach from Bessie.

"Hello, Bessie," Maggie said. "I've been meaning to drop in to say hello for ages, but I'm so busy this time of year."

Bessie smiled at the plump fifty-something woman whose long brown hair was caught up in a messy plait. "I'm glad business is good," she said.

"It's almost too good," Maggie laughed. "I'm here every day shopping for the good folks who want to self-cater but don't want to have to find a grocery shop."

"I hope you charge them for the service," Bessie said as she looked at Maggie's trolley. It was full to overflowing with everything from loo rolls to fruit to bottles of wine.

"Oh, we do," Maggie told her. "And I'm thinking of raising the charge. No one seems to object to what we've been asking, so I think we should ask for more."

"I assume you're all booked up for the rest of the summer?"

"Oh, aye, and then some," Maggie said. "The school holidays will be starting soon and we've never had trouble filling the cottages when the kids are off. We've a waiting list with dozens of names on it, as well, if we do get any last minute cancellations."

"Good for you, although I'm sure it's awfully hard work."

"It is, aye, although it's harder on Thomas than it is on me. He's got to deal with the good folks. I just deliver the shopping, like. He's the one that has to go and help them when they've managed to lose their keys or break something."

"And he loves every minute of it," Bessie suggested. "I've never seen him as happy as he is during the summer, even when he has to deal with horribly demanding guests."

"You're right," Maggie chuckled. "He worked for too many years in banking, always dreaming of doing something like this. He's never happier than when he's soothing some unhappy guest."

"Well, I hope you have a wonderful summer," Bessie told her, preparing to move on.

"Oh, but Bessie, what about your raspberry jam friends?" Maggie asked. "I mean, I heard about Nancy King. How are the others holding up?"

"As far as I know, they're all fine," Bessie assured her. "They're all quite sad, of course, but they have each other for support."

"Any idea who might have killed her, though?" Maggie asked. "It's quite scary to think there's a murderer running around Laxey."

Bessie shook her head. "I'm sure the police are doing everything they can to work out what happened to Nancy," she said. "You needn't worry."

"Oh, I'm much too busy to worry," Maggie laughed. "But speaking of those jam ladies, you'll never guess who I saw the other day."

"Who?"

"Spencer Cannon; do you remember him?"

Bessie thought for a minute. "Peggy's son? He moved away, what, fifteen or so years ago. What's brought him back?"

Maggie shrugged. "He's actually staying in one of the cottages," she told Bessie. "He booked it nearly a year ago for a two-month stay. I reckon he's doing some job hunting. Maybe he got tired of living across and decided to come home."

"The last time I saw him was his mother's funeral, five years ago," Bessie recalled. "He actually mentioned moving back to me then, but the job market wasn't great. I remember him saying that he never felt properly settled in the UK. He only left the island because he was transferred for work and I know he didn't like being so far from his mum."

"She was a sweetheart, Peggy was," Maggie said with a sigh. "Not like some of the others."

Bessie smiled. "They've all been wonderful friends to one another over the years," she pointed out.

"They have at that," Maggie agreed. "Too bad some of them didn't spend a bit more effort on their children."

Bessie pressed her lips together. She wasn't going to repeat anything Sarah had told her. "Raising children is not a subject I know anything about," she said eventually.

Maggie grinned. "You've done a lot for the kids in Laxey over the years," she said. "Including my two. But if you look at those jam ladies, not one of them had a good relationship with their children. Too busy spending time with each other, I reckon."

Bessie shrugged. "I know Elinor was devoted to her Nathan."

"Oh, she was at that," Maggie agreed. "That was what broke up her marriage, of course."

"I didn't realise she and Nicholas had problems," Bessie said, surprised at the information.

"Oh, aye, I went with Fred King for a little while when we were both in our late teens, and all the kids knew about Nathan. He was, well, slow, I think is the best way to put it. He never went to school, but Elinor was a teacher and I imagine she taught him as best she could. Anyway, Elinor's husband was really into cars and he ended up getting a job across with one of the big car manufacturers, remember?"

Bessie nodded. "It's all coming back now," she said. "I remember him going across. Elinor said it was a once in a lifetime opportunity for him, but he used to come home on weekends and for holidays."

"I know he came to visit Nathan once in a while," Maggie told her. "But he and Elinor could only just barely stand each other. He'd wanted to put Nathan in a special school, you see, and Elinor wouldn't hear of it."

Bessie shook her head. "It's all so sad," she said.

"It is, aye," Maggie agreed. "I used to go over and play with Nathan once in a while, when he was younger. A special school might have been good for him. He might have had a chance to have something like a normal life. But Elinor was sure she knew what was best for him. I thought she might, well, that is, I wondered how she'd do once he passed away."

"She seems to be doing fine," Bessie said.

"Yeah, last time I saw her she was just as pushy and demanding as ever," Maggie said with a grin. "Well, I'd love to stand here and chat all day, but I've ever so much to do."

With that, Maggie walked away, struggling to control the overstuffed shopping trolley. Bessie shook her head and continued towards the tills. Her brain felt almost overloaded with everything that had been said.

Dave was waiting patiently for her when she finally got back outside.

"I'm ever so sorry," she told him. "I ran into a friend and we got to talking."

"It's quite all right," he assured her. "I turned off the meter and took part of my lunch break."

"You shouldn't have done that," Bessie tutted. "I should have to pay for wasting your time."

"I have to eat lunch," he told her with a grin. Back at her cottage, he insisted on helping her carry her shopping inside. She made sure she gave him a generous tip and a few biscuits before he left.

With the shopping put away, she made herself a light lunch and then settled in with one of her new books.

Friday evening, Bessie and Doona took a taxi into Douglas for dinner.

"We should do this more often," Bessie said as she looked over the menu. The restaurant they'd chosen had only opened a few months earlier and neither of the women had tried it yet.

Doona ordered a glass of wine and, after a moment's hesitation, Bessie joined her.

"We're not driving," Doona said.

"No, but then I never am," Bessie pointed out.

Doona laughed. "I need wine," she said. "I know Nancy King's murder is causing him all sorts of grief, but John is really hard to work with at the moment."

"Oh, dear," Bessie said. "He's usually so even-tempered."

"Yeah, and I usually love my job," Doona told her. "But right now, I'm not enjoying it one little bit."

"What is it about this case that's bothering him so much?" Bessie asked.

Doona shook her head. "You know I can't talk about the case," she replied.

The waiter arrived and took their order and then disappeared again before Bessie could reply. Once he was gone, she took a sip of wine and then smiled at her friend.

"If it were me, I'd be frustrated by how random it all seems," she said, almost conversationally. "I mean, if all of the jars seem to be the same, then it looks as if Nancy got the poisoned one entirely by chance."

Doona smiled at her. "I haven't seen all of the jars," she told Bessie. "But that's certainly one theory."

"I simply can't imagine anyone wanting to kill Nancy," Bessie replied. "Sarah, her daughter, told me that she only had six months to live anyway."

"Really?" Doona said. "I didn't know that. I wonder if John does."

Bessie shrugged. "I assume he spoke to Sarah. I can't see why she'd tell me anything different to what she told him."

"It would be easy enough to verify," Doona mused. "One call to Nancy's doctor would confirm it, if it's true."

"Perhaps I should ring John and tell him what Sarah said," Bessie suggested. "I've heard a lot of skeet lately that he might be interested in as well."

"I bet everyone in Laxey has an opinion on what happened to Nancy," Doona said. "I've been fielding dozens of phone calls from people who are sure it's a serial killer, or Sarah, or aliens."

Bessie laughed. "I hadn't heard aliens, but I've heard all the rest. I've also heard more about the Raspberry Jam Ladies than I ever wanted to know."

"They're an interesting group," Doona said. She was interrupted by the starters and for a few moments the pair concentrated on eating.

With the first course out of the way, Doona picked up where she'd left off.

"I don't actually know any of them, but they sort of came across as creepy old ladies. None of them seemed like the sweet grandmotherly type."

"I suppose they probably aren't," Bessie told her. "I don't think most of them were particularly close to their children, although Elinor was devoted to her son, Nathan."

"Everyone says that in the same tone of voice," Doona said. "What's the story with Nathan?"

"I forget that you haven't lived in Laxey your whole life," Bessie told her. "Nathan was, well, I think slow or simple is the word that people used in those days. I don't know what his proper diagnosis was, but it was whispered that Elinor had had a difficult labour and he'd suffered from lack of oxygen for a time. All I know for sure is that physically he seemed perfectly normal, but his mind never developed much past that of a small child."

"Could it have been something chromosomal?" Doona asked.

"I suppose it could have been anything, but I do know that Elinor never had any more children. Again, it was just whispers, but it was said that she'd had to have an emergency caesarean, and that it left her unable to have any more."

"Why is it always just whispers?" Doona complained as she finished her glass of wine.

"Women didn't talk about such things in those days," Bessie told her. "Not even with other women, at least not as much as they do now. It simply wasn't polite to talk about things like reproduction."

Doona laughed and waved at the waiter, who rushed over. "We need another round of drinks," she told the man.

Their drinks arrived with their main courses, and Bessie was delighted with her grilled chicken with vegetables and roast potatoes. Doona was equally pleased with her lamb chops served with the same sides.

"Let's just take a peek at the pudding menu," Doona suggested as the waiter cleared their plates a short time later.

"I can never just peek," Bessie laughed.

"Yeah, me either," Doona said.

Everything on the menu sounded delicious, and eventually they both settled on the sticky toffee pudding. Bessie ordered hers with cream, while Doona decided on custard.

"So, are any of the other Raspberry Jam Ladies close to their children?" Doona asked while they waited for their final course.

"Peggy Cannon was very close to her son, Spencer. He moved across about fifteen years ago, but not by choice. His company transferred him to a site in the UK."

"I don't remember meeting anyone called Peggy Cannon," Doona said.

"Oh, she passed away about five years ago," Bessie told her. "She was a lovely woman but she couldn't make jam to save her life. The other ladies often poked fun at her for belonging to their group in spite of that."

"I suppose all of the others make perfect jam," Doona said. "Especially Elinor."

Bessie laughed. "They all make good jam, certainly, but they've had a lot of years to practice. The other woman I always thought was close to her children was Elizabeth Porter. She died in the seventies, though, and both her kids were already living across when she had her car accident."

"At least with all the new tax regulations more companies are moving over to the island," Doona said. "More kids can come back here after university instead of having to stay across to find jobs."

"Elizabeth had two boys, and they were both really smart. I think the elder went to Oxford and the younger one went to Cambridge. I might have them backwards. Anyway, they both found work across after university, but they both used to visit their mum often, even after they married. The older one had a couple of kids, and Elizabeth loved being a grandmother." Bessie sighed as she thought about the woman who had been her friend.

"Are you okay?" Doona asked, taking Bessie's hand and giving it a squeeze.

"This thing with Nancy is churning up all sorts of memories," Bessie told her. "For me and for everyone involved."

"And maybe buried in someone's memory somewhere, there's a clue to who killed her," Doona suggested.

The waiter delivered their puddings and Bessie sighed happily as she took her first bite.

"Agnes was close to her son, Matthew," Bessie said after she'd scraped up the last bite from her plate. "It nearly broke her heart when he left the island."

"Why did he go?"

"Again, we're back to whispers," Bessie replied. "Agnes would never talk about it, but everyone thought he was gay. What I heard was that her husband found out and kicked him out."

"Poor Agnes," Doona gasped.

Bessie smiled. "Even though she'd never admit why he left, she sometimes talked to me about him. She used to go across to see him at least twice a year. I gather he paid for it. I can't see Agnes's husband being willing to do so. He was a hard-working electrician, Agnes's husband was, but he was always very careful with money. Their son, though, he was a very successful interior designer, so he could afford to pay for his mother's visits."

"What happened to him?"

"He died a couple of years ago. The skeet was that he had AIDS, but, of course, Agnes never talked about it."

"None of them seem to have had very good lives," Doona said.

"They grew up in difficult times," Bessie replied. "They met and started their married lives in the war years. Bringing up small children during the lean years that followed the war wouldn't have been easy. And in those days you married for life, no matter how things turned out after the wedding."

Doona shook her head. "If I'd have had to stay married to my second husband, I'd be in gaol for murder myself," she told Bessie. "I do sometimes wonder if I didn't give up too easily on my first marriage, but as he's very happily married to someone else now, it's no use speculating."

Their waiter cleared the pudding dishes and offered them coffee, which they both declined.

"Maybe we should have another drink in the bar?" Doona suggested.

Bessie looked at her watch. "We haven't time," she replied. "Dave should be here in a few minutes to take us home. You're welcome to come back to my cottage for a drink, of course."

"Hmm, maybe," Doona said.

A sudden buzzing noise, very close by, made them both jump.

"What on earth is that?" Bessie demanded.

"I think it might be your mobile," Doona suggested.

"Oh, good heavens," Bessie laughed. "I was playing around with the settings," she told Doona as she dug around in her bag.

"I never seem to hear it, so I was trying to find something louder. This is definitely loud, but it isn't very pleasant."

She finally found the phone and answered it.

"That was Dave," she told Doona after a brief chat. "He's stuck on the mountain. Apparently there was a bad accident and they've stopped traffic both ways to let the emergency services through. He said he could try to get someone else sent for us, or, if we don't mind a wait, he'll be here as soon as he can."

"Let's wait," Doona said. "I know he's your favourite and I quite like him as well. If they send someone else, it might be Mark"

Bessie made a face. She didn't like Mark any more than Doona did. "I told Dave we'd wait," she told Doona.

"Let's grab that drink in the bar, then," Doona suggested.

The bar area was quiet. A young couple was sitting together in one corner, staring into each other's eyes and barely speaking. A couple of middle-aged businessmen were scattered across the long row of bars stools. Bessie and Doona settled in at one of the small tables.

"Do you suppose there's table service?" Doona whispered.

"I doubt it," Bessie replied. "I'll go to the bar. What would you like?"

"Just another glass of wine will do. Do you mind?" Doona asked.

"It's just that both those guys at the bar gave me the once-over as we came in and I'm not in the mood to get chatted up."

Bessie laughed. "I'm in no danger there, at least."

While she waited at the bar for their drinks, Bessie watched one of the men. He was staring at Doona and after a moment he got up and wandered towards her. Bessie quickly grabbed their drinks, arriving back at the table just in time to hear Doona's response to whatever the man had said.

"I'm sorry, I don't speak English," Doona told him, smiling sweetly.

"Oh, sorry, I didn't realise." The man nodded at Bessie as she put the drinks down and then ambled back to the bar.

Bessie swallowed her laughter with a sip of wine.

"If he'd been even a little bit sober, that wouldn't have worked," Doona told her. "But then, even a little bit sober he probably wouldn't have come near me."

"None of that," Bessie scolded. "You're a beautiful woman and there are lots of men who'd jump at a chance to go out with you."

"If only they were queuing up," Doona sighed. "I'm not really looking, but it would be nice to be asked once a while."

Bessie laughed. "You just were asked," she reminded her friend.

"Oh, yeah," Doona laughed. The pair chatted about nothing much as they waited for their ride. Dave appeared in the doorway just as they were discussing whether or not to order another round of drinks.

"I'm so sorry, Bessie, Doona," he said when he reached their table. "I ended up having to take someone from the sea terminal to Ramsey and then I got caught on the mountain."

"Was it a very bad accident?" Bessie asked.

"From what I've heard, it was just the one car. It went off the road near Kate's Cottage. Apparently it was travelling at a pretty high speed, because it rolled a few times. They were lucky nothing exploded or caught fire," Dave told them.

"Fatalities?" Doona asked.

"They're saying the driver was alone in the car. He or she didn't make it."

Bessie blinked back tears. "How sad," she said with a sigh.

"It is, aye," Dave agreed.

The threesome made their way out of the restaurant. Dave held the passenger door of his taxi open for Bessie while Doona climbed into the back. They made their way out of Douglas towards the coast road that would take them back to Laxey.

Before they'd reached the outskirts of Douglas, they had to stop as a police car blocked the road.

"They're bringing the crash car down from the mountain," Dave said as they waited.

After a few minutes the flatbed lorry with the badly mangled car made its way slowly past.

Bessie gasped. "That looks like Agnes Faragher's car," she said in a shaky voice.

CHAPTER 7

"Oh, Bessie, are you sure?" Doona asked.

Bessie couldn't take her eyes off the wreck that was now past them. "No," she admitted. "I'm not sure. But it certainly looked like it. It was such an old car, there can't be many like it on the island, not any more. Her husband was very careful with his money and he bought that car second-hand probably twenty years ago. I was always amazed it was still running."

"It did look like a very old car," Dave said. "But it was in such bad shape, it's hard to say exactly what it was. I'm very sorry, if it was your friend's car, though."

"Thank you," Bessie murmured dazedly.

In the back, Doona had her phone out and was speaking to someone. Bessie's brain couldn't make sense of the words. She'd just seen Agnes; it couldn't possibly have been her.

Dave made his way along the coast road as Bessie stared out towards the sea. It was too dark to see the water, but Bessie's eyes weren't focussed anyway. After a few minutes, Doona dropped her phone in her bag.

Bessie knew, when Doona didn't speak, that she was right about the car. She felt too numb to ask questions, though.

At Bessie's cottage, Dave helped Bessie from the car and Doona opened the cottage door with the set of keys Bessie had given her a while ago. She helped Bessie into a chair at the kitchen table. A few minutes later, Bessie took the cup of tea Doona offered her, with muttered thanks.

"It was Agnes, then?" she asked, although she knew the answer.

"It was," Doona said, patting her hand.

"I don't understand," Bessie said.

"No, neither do I," Doona told her. "Right now it just looks like an unfortunate accident."

Bessie shook her head. "I don't believe in coincidences," she said softly.

"Neither does John," Doona said. "He's going to be here in the morning to talk to you about this."

"I should sleep, then," Bessie said.

"Yes, you really should," Doona agreed.

"I don't think I can."

"Come on, you can at least get ready for bed," Doona said soothingly. She pulled Bessie gently to her feet.

Doona helped Bessie up the stairs and for once Bessie didn't object to her friend's fussing over her.

"I feel as if I'm in shock," Bessie said as she changed into her nightgown.

"You probably are. I don't suppose you have any brandy?"

"I don't want brandy," Bessie said with a faint smile.

Doona helped her climb into bed and tucked the covers around her. "Get some sleep. I'll be in the spare room if you need anything."

Bessie's eyes filled with tears. "Thank you," she whispered, immensely grateful for her friend.

While it was a badly shaken Bessie who struggled to get to sleep that night, it was an angry and determined Bessie who woke up the next morning. She got up and showered and dressed, patting on her favourite rose-scented dusting powder purposefully. Downstairs, she boiled the kettle and made herself a cup of tea before setting out for a long walk along the beach.

At the base of the steps that led up to Thie yn Traie, Bessie took a few deep breaths. She'd walked fast and furiously to here and now she rested and watched the waves.

Someone had once pushed her down these steps, trying to kill her, and now she glared up at the wooden planks.

"I'm not that easy to get rid of," she said in a loud voice. "And I won't stand by and watch my friends die, either."

She marched back past the rental cottages, ignoring the handful of holidaymakers who were slowly straggling out of them. Inside her cottage, she slid some bread into the toaster and turned the kettle back on. A few moments later, she could hear Doona moving around upstairs.

"Toast and tea?" Bessie asked her friend as a blurry-eyed Doona wandered into the kitchen a few moments later.

"Coffee might be better," Doona said with a sigh. "I didn't sleep well."

Bessie filled the coffee pot and switched it on. A moment later the room filled with the delicious aroma of freshly brewed coffee.

"I didn't sleep well, either," Bessie admitted. "Coffee sounds wonderful. I should have thought of it."

"You seem incredibly wide awake and full of energy, all things considered," Doona said.

"I'm wide awake and I'm angry," Bessie told her. "I don't know what's going on, but I intend to find out."

Doona nodded. "I talked to John when I first woke up. He'll be here in about an hour. He's hoping you might have some ideas for him."

"I hope he's going to share some information with me," Bessie said. "I can't help if I don't know what's going on."

"I'm sure he'll share all that he can," Doona replied.

Bessie rolled her eyes. "Hmph, what's the use of being friends with a police inspector if he won't give you inside information?" she grumbled.

Doona just laughed and poured herself a cup of coffee. After a quick sip, she gave Bessie a hug. "This is wonderful," she said. "But I need to get through the shower and get out of here. I don't want to be in the way when John gets here."

"What's that supposed to mean?" Bessie asked. "Since when would you be in the way? You and John are friends and you work together as well."

"Yeah, well, as Saturday is my day off. Let's just say I'd rather not spend time with my boss."

Bessie stared at her friend. "What's going on?" she demanded.

"Nothing," Doona said, staring at the ground. "John's just being difficult right now and I'd rather not get caught up in another of his bad moods, that's all. I'm being cowardly and getting out of here and leaving you to deal with him."

Bessie shook her head. "I'm not worried about John," she said stoutly. "I'm just hoping he can help me work out what's going on. No one targets my friends and gets away with it."

Doona looked as if she wanted to say something, but then she shook her head. "I'm going to grab a shower," she told Bessie, heading for the stairs.

Bessie poured her own cup of coffee and then made herself some more toast. She tried to settle in with a book, but her mind was racing and she couldn't concentrate. After several frustrated minutes, she took her coffee out to the large rock behind her house. Sitting down on the rock, she sipped the hot drink and watched the waves as they came closer and closer.

She listened to the children playing and people calling back and forth, watching them at least as much as she watched the water. They were all so carefree and happy, while she felt so sad and shocked.

Doona found her on the rock a short time later and gave her a big hug. "I'll ring you this afternoon," she promised Bessie. "I'll bring something for tea and stay over again tonight."

"You don't have to do that," Bessie replied. "I'm fine."

"I know you are, but I haven't anything better to do," Doona said with a grin. "I'll bring dinner and a couple of bottles of wine and we'll get silly drunk and talk about everyone we know."

Bessie smiled. "I hate when you make a fuss over me," she

reminded Doona. "But I won't say no to tonight. I think I'd like the company."

Doona had only just gone when Bessie saw the inspector's car pull into the small parking area beside her cottage. She climbed down off her rock and headed back towards the cottage, intercepting the inspector before he had time to get to the front door.

"Hello, John," she called. "I'm just here. Why don't you come around to the back door?"

The man quickly walked around to join Bessie and the pair made their way inside.

"I have coffee," Bessie told him after they'd exchanged greetings.

"I could use some," John said with a sigh. "I had a very late night."

Bessie filled a cup for him and then refilled her own mug. She glanced at the clock and then made up a plate full of biscuits that she sat in the middle of the table. Handing John a small plate, she piled a few biscuits on a plate of her own.

"Thanks," he said as he grabbed a handful. "I didn't get breakfast and I'm not sure if I got dinner last night or not."

Bessie shook her head. "You need to look after yourself," she said sternly.

John waved a hand. "Let's not worry about me. How are you?"

"I'm okay," Bessie said. John stared hard at her and Bessie felt herself flushing under the gaze. "I'm not okay," she admitted. "I'm confused and bewildered and a little bit frightened, but mostly I'm angry at whoever is doing this to my friends."

"As far as we can tell, Mrs. Faragher's accident was just that, an unfortunate accident," John told her.

"I don't believe it," Bessie said firmly.

"I don't really believe it, either," John told her. "It seems too great a coincidence, coming so soon after Nancy King's death."

"She was so upset by Nancy's death," Bessie said slowly. "Could she have, that is, can you tell if she might have done it on purpose?"

John shook his head. "While anything is possible, we have firm evidence that her brakes failed."

"So she was murdered," Bessie said grimly.

"There's no definite evidence that her brakes were tampered with," John said. "The car was over twenty years old and it wasn't particularly well-maintained. Our police mechanic went over it meticulously and, at least in his preliminary examination, he can't say for certain whether the brakes failed on their own or if the failure had outside assistance."

"Why was she on the mountain road last night?" Bessie asked.

"I don't know," John replied. "No one I've spoken to seems to know, but I haven't been able to see any of the jam ladies."

"Why not?"

"All three have said they're too upset to talk to me," John said in a disgusted voice. "I can't push it at this point. I'm just hoping, after the initial shock wears off, that they'll be able to help."

Bessie sighed. "I'm devastated," she told him. "I can't imagine how they must be feeling. When I saw them on Thursday, they set up a rota for visiting Agnes, to keep an eye on her. They must all be overcome."

"Assuming they didn't have anything to do with it, of course," John said.

Bessie frowned. "I can't imagine why any of the ladies would want to harm Nancy or Agnes," she said sadly. "There simply isn't any motive."

"Maybe one of them decided she wanted to be the best jam maker in Laxey and she's eliminating the competition."

Bessie shook her head. "I'm sure you meant that a joke, but nothing is funny at the moment," she told him.

"Sorry," John said. "But there simply doesn't seem to be any motive for anyone to kill either Nancy or Agnes."

"Who inherits Agnes's estate?" Bessie asked.

John shrugged. "I'm sure it will be common knowledge soon enough," he said with a sigh. "I spoke to Doncan Quayle, her advocate, this morning. She left a few charitable bequests and the rest gets split between her late sister's children. They live in Leeds and as far as I can tell, Agnes barely knew them."

Bessie nodded. "I remember her telling me, when her son died, that the only family she had left were some nieces in the north of

England. She and her sister never got along, apparently, and she said she had no interest in meeting her sister's children."

"Well, apparently she made them her heirs in spite of that," John said. "Unless a later will turns up, of course. We will be checking on the two women, just to make sure they didn't decide to get their inheritance early, but as of now we have no reason to believe that they even knew they were in line for anything."

"It just doesn't make sense," Bessie said. "Nancy and Agnes were just ordinary people. I hate the idea that there might be a random serial killer on the island who is, what, targeting the Raspberry Jam Ladies? None of this makes sense."

"I don't know what to think," John told her. "I'm trying to consider every possibility. Do you know of anyone who might have had a grudge against the Raspberry Jam Ladies?"

Bessie started to laugh and then stopped abruptly. "You can't be serious," she said. "They're just a group of old widowed women who get together once a week for tea and to complain about their dead husbands and their kids. Some of them probably have a bit of money, but none of them are rich, by any means."

"What about their homes?" John asked. "Do they all own their own homes? Is there anything special about any of them?"

Bessie shrugged. "I think they all own their homes, and with the cost of housing where it is, all of the houses are probably worth quite a bit, as well. But I don't think there's anything special about any of them. Nancy and Agnes both needed to clean more, and I don't think either of them ever modernised anything."

"Could someone be wanting to buy them all up to tear them down for a new development?"

"Agnes and Nancy lived near each other, but there are at least a half a dozen houses between the two. I haven't heard that any developers are poking around in Laxey, at least not in that neighbourhood. Doona might know more, though. She lives in that area, too."

The inspector made a note and then drained his cup. Bessie quickly refilled it, which earned her a smile.

"As do I," he reminded Bessie. "Although I'm only renting, so I probably wouldn't hear about such things."

"Margaret lives nearby as well, on the next street, but Joan lives on the other side of Laxey. Elinor lived on the same street as Margaret, but when her son died she sold her home and bought a little flat in that new building on the south side of the village."

John nodded. "Any idea how she likes it?" he asked. "I think I'd like to buy a place up here. It looks as if I'm going to be stationed here for a while and the rental is great for just crashing, but I'd like something more permanent."

What about your wife and kids? Bessie bit her tongue and asked the question silently. "Elinor says she loves it," she told him instead. "Apparently they have all the modern conveniences as well as a grocery delivery service and covered parking."

"Grocery delivery sounds handy," John said. "Maybe I'll take a look."

"Anyway, I can't see what's happening being tied to where the ladies live," Bessie said, dragging the conversation back to murder. "Not unless it's like Hugh said and only one victim is specific."

John grinned. "Hugh's been studying all sorts of interesting and unusual cases, and he's proposed a number of very creative solutions to our latest case."

"Agnes's murder wasn't random, anyway," Bessie said. "Assuming it was murder, of course, whoever tampered with her brakes had to know whose car it was."

"Which is making us take a long look at possible motives," John told her. "Thus far, though, we haven't found anything. That's why I was asking about a possible grudge against the ladies as a group. The poisoned jam might have been designed to either kill any one of the ladies or, if they gave that particular jar away, make the ladies look bad when someone else died."

Bessie frowned. "I can't imagine anyone hating a harmless bunch of old ladies that much," she said.

"You keep calling them harmless, but they seem to have upset and angered a lot of their own families."

"Families quarrel," Bessie said. "Murder goes far beyond that."

"Do any of the ladies get along with their children?" the inspector asked.

Bessie sighed. "Agnes did, but her son died. We talked about that before. The same is true for Elinor. Nancy didn't have a great relationship with her kids and her daughter doesn't have very nice things to say about the other ladies, either, but a bit of resentment is a long way from murder."

"Hmmm," John made a note. "What about Joan Carr and Margaret Gelling?"

"Joan was close to her two children that passed. I'm not sure how close she is to the one in prison, assuming he is still in there. Margaret's children are both across. I don't think she sees them."

"What about the two jam ladies that died? Any idea how close they were to their children before they passed away?"

"Oh, that reminds me," Bessie exclaimed. "I was told that Peggy's son is on the island at the moment. Apparently he's staying in one of the cottages down the beach from me. I must try to find out which one and stop and visit him."

John made a note. "Was he close to his mother?"

"Sorry, that was what you asked," Bessie flushed. "I think they got along quite well. He got transferred with his company, though, and rarely made it back to the island. I think he does something with computers, but I'm not sure. I certainly don't remember any trouble between him and his mother."

"And Elizabeth Porter's family?"

"The children were across when she died, but I know she used to visit them once in a while. I think they were as close as they could be under the circumstances," Bessie replied.

John nodded. "What about other family on the island? Do any of the ladies have brothers and sisters or cousins around?"

Bessie shook her head. "I'd really have to think about that one," she told him. "None of the ladies actually grew up in Laxey. I think that was part of what drew them all together, really. They may have other family around the island somewhere, but the ladies are in their seventies, so I don't think they'll be a lot of siblings around, anyway."

"I'd like you to spend some time trying to remember what other family there might be," John requested. "Maybe you could ring around and talk to a few old friends. See if anyone knows anything about the ladies that you don't."

Bessie nodded. "I can do that," she replied. "I want to feel as if I'm helping."

"Just make sure you limit yourself to phone calls," John said sternly. "I don't want you putting yourself in any danger."

"I shall be spending some time with the jam ladies," Bessie said. "I'm sure they'll have some sort of gathering so that we can all remember Agnes."

"I'd love to tell you to stay away from them," John said with a sigh. "But I know you wouldn't listen."

"You can't think they're dangerous?" Bessie demanded.

John shrugged. "At this point, they're definitely suspects."

"Why on earth would one of the ladies want to kill Nancy or Agnes?" Bessie asked.

"As we don't yet have any motive for anyone killing either lady, we have to keep all possibilities open," he told her.

"I can't imagine any of the ladies having anything to do with murder," Bessie said.

"I won't argue with you," John replied. "But I'm keeping them on my list."

Bessie nodded. "I suppose you have to do that."

"Anyway, be careful when you're with them. It looks as if someone might be targeting the group and I'd hate to see you get caught in the crossfire, as it were."

Bessie sighed. "What a horrible thought," she said.

"Let me know if you hear anything from your friends that might help," John reminded her as he rose to leave. "

"I definitely will," she assured him.

Once he was gone, Bessie set to work ringing her friends. She frowned as she flipped through the small address book she kept by the phone. Agnes and Nancy were both still listed in it and she hated to cross out their names. She hated to cross out any names, as it reminded her of the fragility of life.

By the time Doona returned, Bessie had spoken to nearly everyone she could think of to ask about the jam ladies.

"No one knows anything," she complained to Doona.

"I brought pizza," Doona told her. "And three bottles of wine."

Bessie laughed. "I don't think we need three bottles, but I could do with a glass of wine after the frustrating afternoon I've had."

Doona poured the wine while Bessie dug out plates for the pizza.

"How was your meeting with John?" Doona asked after they'd sat down.

"It was fine," Bessie said, staring at her friend. There was something in Doona's voice that worried her. "We just talked about Agnes and the other jam ladies, although he doesn't seem to want to really talk to me about it. He just wanted to pick my brains and tap into my connections."

"That sounds about right," Doona said with a sigh. "He's not talking to anyone about this case. But then, he's not talking to anyone about anything at the moment."

"What does that mean?" Bessie asked.

Doona sighed and took a big drink of her wine. "I don't know," she muttered. "I thought we were all getting to be good friends down at the station. Everyone likes and respects John and we all work hard at working together to provide the best possible service to the public, you know, all that sort of stuff we're supposed to do."

"But?"

"But lately John's been a lot less friendly. Ever since Nancy died, he hasn't been as much fun to be around. I know he got into some trouble with the Chief Constable about including you in interviews during the last case, but as you helped work it all out and the guilty party gave the police a full confession, John wasn't given more than a verbal warning. I don't know if it's this case that has him really worried, but I almost hate going into work at the moment and that hasn't happened since Pete Corkill was in charge."

"Inspector Corkill isn't that bad," Bessie said. "As for John, I'm really sorry if I got him into trouble. I'm not sure what's bothering him, but I suspect it may not have anything to do with Nancy's murder."

"What do you mean?"

"He mentioned that he's looking to buy a house or a flat in Laxey," Bessie told Doona.

"Yeah, he's been thinking about that for a while, so?"

"I don't know, I just got the feeling he was looking for a place for himself, rather than for a family."

Doona flushed. "You think he and Sue are having trouble?"

Bessie shrugged. "As I've never met Sue, I really can't say."

"I've never met her either," Doona said.

"Really? Doesn't she ever visit the station to see John?" Bessie asked.

"I don't know if she even knows where Laxey is," Doona said. "John used to talk about how miserable she was in Ramsey and how badly she wanted to move back to Manchester. He hasn't mentioned it lately, but maybe that's because she's decided to go."

"It's all very sad," Bessie said. "I would hate to see her go and take the children away from John, but I really hate the idea of him leaving even more."

Doona nodded. "I hate the thought of him leaving as well. Even as grumpy and impossible as he is at the moment, he's still my favourite boss."

The women settled in with their pizza and wine, deliberately talking about anything and everything other than the Raspberry Jam Ladies or John Rockwell. With the pizza and the first bottle of wine finished, Doona cleared the table and opened the bakery box she'd brought with her.

"Double chocolate brownies?" Bessie grinned. "You are feeling down."

Doona nodded. "Nothing like wine and chocolate to cheer a person up."

Bessie couldn't argue with that. After the first bite of brownie, she began to feel less miserable about her disappointing afternoon.

"I can't believe no one in Laxey knows anything," she said to Doona as she took a second brownie.

"Anything about what?" Doona asked.

Bessie laughed. "You weren't following my train of thought?" she teased.

"After half a bottle of wine, I'm not following my own train of thought," Doona told her with a giggle.

"No one seems to know anything about the Raspberry Jam Ladies," Bessie told her. "I mean everyone has heard things about them, there's tons of skeet, but no one knows anything for certain."

"Like what?"

"Well, everyone talks about their relationships with their kids. I was told by more than one source that Jonathan Gelling was abusive and that's why the kids don't really keep in touch with Margaret."

"Physically abusive?" Doona asked.

Bessie shrugged. "No one would come right out and say that, but it was definitely hinted at."

"Those poor kids."

"And poor Margaret. There weren't a lot of options for battered women in those days," Bessie said.

"What else did you learn?" Doona asked.

"Apparently Agnes had an older brother. They grew up in the south and he moved across before Agnes married. From what my source could tell me, he and Agnes were close when they were young, but the brother was gay and the family cut him out of their lives when they found out."

"Poor Agnes," Doona sighed.

"I was told that Agnes's son became friends with his uncle when he moved across and that Agnes got to see him when she visited with Matthew. He passed away last year, though."

"So he can't have murdered Nancy or Agnes, even if he'd had some motive that I can't begin to imagine."

"No," Bessie agreed. "And that's another part of the problem. Even when I find out about some relative or other that I didn't know about, he or she is usually long dead. Agnes's brother never married or had children, and no one seems to know anything about her husband's family either. He came over to the island in the thirties on some scheme to train up more electricians and just never left. Whatever family he had, though, is probably all in the UK."

"Did you learn anything else about anyone else?" Doona asked.

Bessie shrugged. "The ladies are all pretty private people, really," she told her friend. "What I'm finding most surprising about all of this is how little people actually do know about them. I've known them all for fifty years or so, so I probably know more than most, but it's all pretty superficial."

"What about fights between them? Did Elinor ever flirt with Margaret's husband or did Peggy steal a pie recipe from Agnes? Anything like that?"

Bessie shook her head. "You know, that might even be more surprising than the lack of solid information about them all. I didn't get a single hint that there were ever any arguments between the ladies. When I think back, I can't remember ever hearing about them not all getting along. Which is strange in itself."

"We've never had a fight," Doona pointed out, pouring herself another glass of wine.

"But there are only two of us and we're at rather different places in life. This was a group of seven women, all the same age, all bringing up children and dealing with husbands. I would think that they made a real effort to avoid disagreements or at least to avoid letting anyone else hear about any disagreements. There must have been some."

"How did they keep them quiet in a tiny village like Laxey?" Doona asked with a chuckle.

Bessie had to admit that she had no idea. "I wish I knew. There's plenty of gossip about me out there and if I knew how to keep it quiet, I would," she told her friend.

"People love to gossip," Doona said with a laugh. "Do you think they'll be talking about my spending the night here again?"

Bessie nodded. "Everyone seems to think I'm unwell or something," she replied. "Either unwell or under house arrest. One person actually said she'd heard I was the chief suspect in Nancy's death."

Doona laughed heartily. "Do you even know how to make jam?" she asked Bessie.

"Of course I do," Bessie said indignantly. "All girls were taught to make jam and preserves in my day. I haven't made it for years, but I could if I wanted to."

"Let's take a walk," Doona suggested suddenly. "It's a nice warm night and the beach is calling to me."

Bessie shrugged. "Why not?" she replied.

The pair cleared the table, leaving only their half-full wine glasses on it, and then made their way outside. Doona kicked off her shoes and headed straight for the water.

"Yikes," she exclaimed loudly as the first wave washed over her feet. "The water is freezing."

Bessie had left her own shoes at home. Now she followed Doona into the sea. "It's a little chilly," she said with a smile. "But it never gets warm, you know."

"I know," Doona replied. "But I forgot."

The pair walked slowly down the beach, nodding and smiling at the families that were still splashing in the sea and building sandcastles on the shore. At the stairs to Thie yn Traie, they turned around and headed back towards Bessie's cottage.

They were walking back slowly, enjoying the sunset, when Bessie heard the shouting.

"Hey, hey, Bessie Cubbon, is that you?"

She spun around and stared at the tall man who was hurrying down the beach towards her, waving a stick.

CHAPTER 8

Doona stepped in front of Bessie, ready to intercept the stranger.

"For goodness sake," Bessie hissed. "We're on a public beach in full sight of dozens of people. I'm fine."

Doona didn't answer. Her gaze was fixed on the man who had nearly reached them.

"Aunt Bessie? It is you, isn't it?" the man said, coming to an abrupt halt a few paces away from the women.

Bessie studied the man closely. He was over six feet tall, chubby and completely bald. His eyes were shaded behind those glasses that darken in the sunlight, even though the sun was rapidly setting. There was something quite familiar about him, but Bessie was distracted by the golf club in his hand.

"Spencer Cannon?" Bessie said. She didn't so much recognise him as assume it was him, based on circumstances.

The man flushed. "You remember me?" he asked. "I wasn't sure anyone would remember me."

Bessie nodded and stepped closer to him, ignoring Doona, who was still glaring at Spencer suspiciously.

"Of course I remember you," Bessie told the man. "From your

childhood, but also from when you came back for your mother's funeral."

Spencer nodded. "That was a bad time," he told Bessie. "I don't really remember much of that visit. That's one of the reasons I'm here now. I loved the island when I was younger and I was hoping to recapture that feeling that I sort of lost during that horrible time."

"Your mother was a very special lady," Bessie said softly. "Everyone who knew her still misses her."

"What's the golf club for?" Doona interrupted in a harsh tone.

Spencer looked at her and then looked at the club, as if unsure where it had come from. "Oh, I was just, that is, I was working on techniques for getting out of the sand behind my cottage when I saw you two walk past. I didn't want to miss the chance to say hello to Aunt Bessie."

"When did you take up golfing?" Bessie asked.

"Oh, I've been taking it up and then dropping it off and on for years," Spencer replied. "It's hard work and frustrating, but then I have a good round and I'm hooked all over again."

"Would you like to come back to the cottage for a cuppa?" Bessie asked.

"Oh, I'd love to, if you wouldn't mind," Spencer replied.

Doona gave Bessie a disapproving look, but Bessie ignored her and led the way back to her cottage. Inside she popped the kettle on and dug out a box of biscuits. She arranged them on a plate while Doona set out the tea things, then the threesome sat down at Bessie's kitchen table.

"Oh, this is my friend Doona Moore," Bessie told the man. "Doona, this is Spencer Cannon. His mother was one of the Raspberry Jam Ladies."

Doona nodded towards the man, but didn't speak.

"It's a real pleasure to meet you," Spencer told Doona. "Bessie always has interesting friends, but I don't remember her having such lovely ones."

Doona flushed. "Thanks," she muttered, grabbing a biscuit.

"So what's brought you back to the island this time?" Bessie asked.

"A little bit of nostalgia, mostly, I think. I had a bunch of holiday time to use up so I thought I would come over for Tynwald Day and then stay and get some golfing in. The island has some of the best courses I've ever played."

"You were here for Tynwald Day?" Doona asked.

"Yeah, I got here on the second and I'm booked through the end of next month. A nice long lazy stay, where the most ambitious thing I have to do is an odd round of golf."

"Did you see the Raspberry Jam Ladies at Tynwald Day?" Bessie asked.

"Yeah, I did. They all said how great it was to see me and all that," he shrugged. "They were mum's friends and I shouldn't say anything bad about them, but I never really liked any of them. Now they all seem like creepy old ladies, especially Mrs. Lewis."

"Did you hear about what happened to Nancy King?" Doona posed the question Bessie was about to ask.

"I did, and you know what? They tried to give me some of that jam, but I turned them down. My mum was terrible at making jam, and a little obsessed with it. She made hundreds of jars of the stuff every year and it was always unpleasant. I promised myself that once I was an adult, I would never eat raspberry jam again."

Doona and Bessie exchanged glances. "That promise might have saved your life," Bessie said.

Spencer nodded. "Don't think I haven't thought about that," he said emphatically. "I suppose mum's lack of cooking ability did me a favour after all."

Bessie poured out more tea. "Did you hear about Agnes Faragher?" she asked.

"No, don't tell me something's happened to Mrs. Faragher," he said. "She was always my favourite."

"The brakes on her car failed and she drove off the mountain road last night. She didn't survive the crash," Bessie said somberly.

"Oh, dear," Spencer said, looking shocked. "I hadn't heard. Wow, that's weird, isn't it? Two jam ladies dying in just a few days."

"You grew up around the ladies," Doona said. "Do you know anyone who might have had a grudge against them?"

Spencer laughed for a moment and then stopped suddenly. "Oh, you're serious?" he asked. "I mean, they were just a bunch of women who met to make jam and compare notes on childrearing. I can't imagine why anyone would want to kill them, especially now that they're all old. Surely none of them have much time left anyway?"

Bessie harrumphed loudly and Spencer flushed. "Oh, dear, I didn't mean, that is, I wasn't suggesting, I was, rather, that is, um…." He took a hasty sip of tea and looked helplessly at Doona, who laughed.

"Well, whatever you meant, never mind," Bessie said, waving his discomfort away with a hand that held a chocolate digestive. "Are you suggesting that anyone might have wanted to kill them years ago, then?"

Spencer shook his head. "Oh, no, or rather, not really."

"Which means what?" Bessie asked.

"Well, all the kids used to get forced to spend time together, especially on school holidays and the like. You know, all our mums would drag us to one of the other houses and the kids would be expected to play nicely together while the ladies drank tea and complained about our dads. Lots of us weren't very fond of the ladies as a group, but that was just kid stuff. We didn't want to kill them all or anything, we just didn't want them to keep meeting all the time and making us come along."

"Anyone in particular especially unhappy with the group?" Doona asked.

Spencer shrugged. "I don't really remember all that much," he said. "It was a long time ago. I suppose Ted Porter was the one that complained the most. He was one of the younger kids and I think he got rather bullied by the older King boys."

"Interesting," Bessie said.

"My biggest complaint was against Nathan Lewis, though," Spencer said, his eyes unfocussed as he remembered the past. "He was, well, slow, I think is the best way to put it. But he didn't seem to understand that, which I suppose makes sense. Anyway, he always wanted to do whatever Fred King and I were doing, and he just couldn't keep up. But if we didn't include him, he'd go off and cry to his mother and then Fred and I would be in trouble," Spencer sighed. "It was so many years ago now, I can't believe how miserable I still feel when I think about it."

"But it's all very interesting to me," Bessie said. "Someone seems to be targeting the jam ladies and it's important we work out who that someone is."

"But didn't you say Agnes's accident was, well, an accident?" Spencer asked, frowning.

"The police aren't sure," Bessie replied. "But I don't like coincidences."

Spencer nodded. "It does seem a big coincidence. But like I said earlier, I can't imagine anyone having anything against the ladies. Some of their husbands, maybe, but they're all long dead."

"What do you mean?" Doona asked.

"It was such a long time ago," Spencer said with a sigh. "But I still feel as if I shouldn't talk about such things. For instance, I promised the Gelling kids I would never tell anyone how their father used to treat them. In those days, there weren't shelters for battered wives or anything. Their mum had nowhere to go."

Bessie nodded. "That Jonathan Gelling was abusive is fairly widely known now," she assured the man. "You aren't giving up any secrets."

"He wasn't the only one, though," Spencer confided. "Matthew Faragher's father beat him to within an inch of his life once. He'd worked out that Matthew was gay and he thought he could beat him straight."

"I didn't know that," Bessie said in surprise.

"Yeah, obviously it didn't work, although Matthew did try. He went out with Hazel Gelling for a while, but they were really just friends. It got Matthew's dad off his back, though," Spencer recalled.

Bessie shook her head. "Please don't tell me you have any more stories like that," she replied.

Spencer shrugged. "Nathan used to say that his dad hit him, but we all thought he was making it up. He didn't always have a clear understanding of reality and fantasy."

Bessie nodded. "I never spent much time with him," she said. "Elinor didn't take him out much, but I do remember talking to him once and him being certain that there was a family of fairies living in their garden."

"The Jones-Windsors," Spencer laughed. "Oh my, I haven't thought about them for years. Nathan was always talking about the Jones-Windsor fairy family and what they got up to in his garden. We all had to pretend to believe him or else he'd cry to Mrs. Lewis and we'd all get in trouble."

"I'm almost afraid to ask if you can remember anything else," Doona said with a smile. "Your childhood sounds, um, unusual."

Spencer smiled at her. "It didn't seem so at the time," he replied. "It was just like everyone else's."

"If you think of anyone that might have any reason to kill the jam ladies, either all of them or any one of them, please ring the police and talk to them," Doona told the man. "They may well want to talk to you anyway."

"I'm happy to talk to them," Spencer told her. "But I really don't think I can help."

He finished his tea and grabbed one last biscuit. "I'll just take this one for the walk back to my cottage, if I may?"

Bessie smiled. "Of course," she replied.

"Oh, um, well, that is, um, Doona? I was wondering if maybe you'd like to have lunch with me one day next week?" the man said as he walked towards the door.

Doona smiled, but shook her head. "I'm really sorry, but I don't think I should. I work for the police here in Laxey and it's just remotely possible that you're tied into the Raspberry Jam Ladies case. Once they find the murderer, though, if you're still here, I'd love to have lunch with you."

"I most definitely am not tied to any murders," Spencer said angrily.

"I know that," Doona said in her most soothing voice. "But my boss is very particular about the company we keep outside of work. Anyone with any connection with a current case is strictly off-limits."

Spencer nodded, but he still looked angry. "Whatever," he muttered.

Doona grabbed her bag and dug out a scrap of paper. "Here," she said after she'd scribbled something on it. "My phone number. Ring me when the murderer is found and we'll get lunch, on me."

Spencer took the paper and looked at Doona, his frown slowly changing to something close to a grin. "That's a deal," he said, finally. With a last wave at Bessie, he headed back out, grabbing his golf club from beside the front door as he went.

"That was interesting," Bessie said as Doona sat back down.

"That's one word for it," Doona muttered, grabbing another biscuit.

"He didn't seem like your type," Bessie said in a deliberately casual tone.

"I don't have a type," Doona told her. "Right now, I'll go out with anyone who's breathing as long as they aren't drunk when they ask me out."

Bessie laughed. "It isn't that bad," she argued.

"Maybe, maybe not," Doona shrugged. "It hardly matters. I can't see the case being solved while the man is still on the island."

"You should have more faith in John," Bessie told her.

"Yeah, I probably should," Doona said quietly.

Doona helped Bessie tidy up and then the women headed for bed.

Sunday morning Bessie was up, ate a quick breakfast of cereal and tea, and was out for her walk before Doona was up. The sun was already coming up and the sky was clear as Bessie made her way along the beach.

Back at home, Doona had the kettle boiling and Bessie had a round of toast soldiers with soft-boiled eggs, since Doona had done all the cooking.

"Delicious," she sighed as she swallowed the last of her toast. "I should make eggs more often."

"You didn't make eggs this time," Doona laughed.

Bessie grinned at her. "You should make me eggs more often," she suggested.

"How about a trip into Douglas for some shopping?" Doona suggested as the pair washed up the breakfast dishes. "We could check out that new bookshop and have lunch somewhere."

"I was ready to go when you said new bookshop," Bessie laughed.

The drive into Douglas was uneventful and the friends spent an hour happily browsing through the many shops on the high street. The new bookshop was their final stop.

"The shop is lovely," Bessie told the woman who was ringing up her purchases an hour later. "If it were twice this size, it would be even better."

"We'd love to expand," the girl told her with a smile. "But high street rents are so expensive, we thought we'd better start small. We're hoping to extend the selling floor into the space upstairs if things go well. It's just storage at the moment."

Bessie took her two very full bags from the shop assistant. "Well, I'll certainly be back," she assured the girl.

Doona paid for her own much more modest collection of books and the pair headed back to Doona's car.

"I'm almost ready to skip lunch so that I can get home and start reading," Bessie said as they piled their shopping into Doona's boot.

"I'm never ready to skip a meal," Doona replied, laughing. "But if you really want to get home, we can just grab something quick."

"No," Bessie replied. "Let's have a proper lunch. I'm just excited because they had so many books I hadn't seen before. I do hope they don't hurt business for the bookshop in Ramsey where I usually shop, though."

"I would hope there are enough avid readers on the island to support two good bookshops," Doona replied.

They went to their favourite little Italian restaurant and stuffed themselves with salad, garlic bread, and spaghetti. They were both too full for pudding.

"How about if you each take a piece of tiramisu home with you," the waitress suggested.

"Sold," Doona laughed.

"Go ahead, make it two," Bessie added.

Back at Bessie's cottage, both women curled up with new books for a few hours.

"I'm ready for my tiramisu now," Doona said after a while.

"We should eat something healthy first," Bessie told her.

"I'm not hungry for something healthy, though," Doona replied.

Bessie laughed. "I'm not going to stop you, but I'm going to have a sandwich before I have mine. I think I'll have a short walk as well. As much as I love reading, some fresh air sounds good."

Doona sighed. "I hate when you're right," she complained. "Let's walk first," she suggested. "Then we won't have to feel at all guilty about the tiramisu."

The sun was shining, but the temperature was comfortable. They walked as far as Thie yn Traie and stood at the bottom of the stairs looking up at the wall of glass that was the back of the luxury home.

"I thought someone had made an offer on this place," Doona said.

"Doncan said it fell through at the last minute," Bessie told her. "Apparently the wife decided she'd rather have a summer home in Portugal."

"I'd have mine in Tuscany," Doona said with a sigh. "Or maybe the south of France. What about you?"

"If I were buying a summer home, I'd want something back in the US," Bessie replied.

"Really? You never talk about living there. Why would you want a house there?"

Bessie shrugged. "When I was growing up we lived near Lake Erie in Cleveland and there were some lovely old mansions right along the water. Matthew and I used to talk about buying one of them some day."

"Is that why you bought your cottage on the beach?"

"It was certainly part of the reason why," Bessie told her. "Treoghe Bwaane was as close as I could get to Matthew's and my shared dream."

They made their way back to Bessie's cottage where Bessie made sandwiches for both of them. They ate quickly and then enjoyed their long-awaited treat.

"This was so worth it," Doona said with a groan as she scraped her plate. "Next time we go there, I'm getting two of these to take home."

Bessie laughed. "It is really good," she agreed, finishing off her last bite only a moment behind Doona.

They quickly took care of the dishes and tidied the kitchen together.

"I need to pop home and grab some work clothes for tomorrow," Doona told Bessie after they'd finished.

"You don't have to stay here again tonight," Bessie replied. "I'm fine."

"I know you're fine, but I'm staying anyway," Doona said firmly.

Bessie sighed, but she didn't waste her time arguing. "You go and get what you need, then," she said.

"I thought maybe you could come with me," Doona replied.

"I think I can safely be left on my own for twenty minutes," Bessie said tartly.

Doona shook her head. "I'm sure you'd be fine, but I'd be worried. It will simplify both our lives if you come with me."

Bessie sighed, but she grabbed her handbag, tucking the book she had started earlier inside. "I'm just doing this to humour you," she told Doona.

"Thank you," Doona replied. "I really do appreciate it."

Bessie resisted the urge to stick her tongue out at her friend. Just because Doona was treating her like a child, didn't mean she should behave childishly.

Doona's small bungalow felt almost chilly, in spite of the sunshine that they'd enjoyed that day.

"I should have left some curtains open," Doona said as they stepped into the dark interior.

"It feels gloomy in here," Bessie said as she headed towards the small sitting room to the left of the door.

"It does, rather," Doona agreed. She swept open the sitting room curtains, which only helped a small amount, as the sun was beginning to set.

Bessie switched on a few lamps, which did rather more to dispel the gloom. "I'll just settle here with my book," she told Doona.

Doona nodded and then disappeared. Bessie could hear her footsteps as she walked through the house to the large master bedroom at the very back. The house was quiet and Bessie told herself it was cosy as she tried to find her place on the page. The doorbell interrupted her.

"Doona, someone's at the door," she called as she headed towards it.

Before she reached it, Doona came rushing up from the back of the house.

"Who is it?" she demanded of Bessie.

"How should I know?" Bessie said, shaking her head.

Doona glanced through the small window in the door and then sighed. She pulled the door open. "John, this is a nice surprise," Bessie heard her say. She quickly joined Doona in the doorway.

"Ah, Bessie, there you are," John said, with a smile. "I was just heading back to my little flat and I saw Doona's car. I wanted to check that everything was okay, because she'd mentioned she was staying with you for a while."

"Everything's fine," Doona assured him. "I needed some clean clothes, that's all. We'll be heading back to Bessie's soon."

"Great, well, I won't keep you," John said. "I don't suppose you have anything to tell me?" he asked Bessie.

"Why don't you come in and I'll fill you in on my visit with Spencer Cannon while Doona packs?" Bessie suggested.

John and Doona exchanged glances that Bessie couldn't read and then he shrugged. "Sure, but just for a minute."

"That's all it will take," Bessie told him.

Twenty minutes later, the inspector had heard every bit of skeet about the Raspberry Jam Ladies and their families that Bessie had managed to extract from her friends and Spencer.

"Lots of hints and innuendo, but nothing concrete," John said with a sigh.

"I have a few more people to ring tomorrow," Bessie said, trying to sound enthusiastic about a job she hadn't enjoyed thus far. "It's hard, poking around in these women's lives," she told the man. "They're my friends and I feel as if I'm prying."

"If we can stop the rest of them from getting murdered, surely it will be worth it?"

"But what if Nancy's death hasn't anything to do with the jam ladies and Agnes's death was just an accident?" Bessie asked.

"If you don't want to keep trying to find out more, then don't," John said. "I'm not forcing you to do it."

Bessie frowned at the words that sounded quite harsh. "I'll let you know if I hear anything," was her noncommittal reply.

John sighed deeply and then glanced towards the back of the house. "Bessie, I'm sorry," he said. "The random nature of Nancy's murder has everyone incredibly uptight. Have you seen the papers?"

Bessie nodded. The *Isle of Man Times* had run an entire ten-page section on serial killers and random mass murders and the like, speculating darkly that no one on the island was safe from the "Raspberry Jam Assassin."

"Doona's been fielding so many phone calls from terrified residents that we've had to add extra staff just to answer the phones and assure people that their food is safe. I've had at least fifty requests for lab tests on various foodstuffs that people have brought in, convinced they've been set up to be the next victim. The Chief Constable is seriously considering inviting Scotland Yard over to help with the investigation and…." He stopped and drew a deep breath. "Well, I'm having some personal issues as well," he said after a moment.

"I hope the kids are okay," Bessie said.

"The kids are great," Rockwell said, with a small smile. "But really, at this point, I'm hoping that the two incidents are connected. Someone with a grudge against the jam ladies should be easier to find than someone with a grudge against the entire island."

Bessie nodded. "I'm sorry, I wasn't thinking about how hard

this must be for you," she said, patting his arm. "Please, if you need someone to talk to, come and see me. Whether you want to talk about the case or about more personal matters, I'm always there for my friends and anything we discuss will never be repeated."

John smiled and then gave Bessie a hug. "Thank you," he whispered in her ear as he squeezed her tightly. "I'll probably take you up on that offer soon."

Bessie went back to her book while the inspector shouted a quick goodbye to Doona and let himself out. She'd only turned one page when the doorbell rang yet again.

"Are you always this popular?" she demanded of Doona when the woman rushed up from the back of the house again.

"Ha, I wish," Doona laughed, looking through the window. "I think this visitor is for you, anyway," she told Bessie.

Doona pulled the door open and Bessie walked over to see who was there. Elinor Lewis's smile looked tentative until she spotted Bessie.

"Ah, yes, there you are, Bessie," she said briskly. "I was hoping I might find you here, although I was sure Ms. Moore could get you a message if I didn't."

"Hello, Elinor," Bessie said. "I'm so very sorry about Agnes."

Elinor waved a hand. "Yes, thank you. That's why I was in the neighbourhood, actually. I've just been to her house to pick out a dress for her to be buried in."

"Oh, I hadn't thought about that," Bessie said in surprise.

"Well, she has no family here. Someone had to do it."

"Does that mean her sister's children aren't coming for the funeral?" Bessie asked.

"I'm not sure," Elinor replied with a shrug. "I just thought it might be helpful, that's all. They can always choose something else if they do come."

Bessie stared at her for a moment and then nodded. "Why did you want to see me?" she asked as the pause became awkward.

"Oh, yes, well, we, that is the Raspberry Jam Ladies, we're going to have a little remembrance for Agnes on Tuesday at our regular meeting. I thought you might like to come along as well."

"Oh, yes," Bessie said. "I'd very much like to come."

"Me, too," Doona interjected. "I can drive."

Bessie frowned at her friend's pushiness, but Elinor didn't seem to mind. "That's lovely, dear," she said almost absently. "We'll see you on Tuesday, then." She turned and headed back down the short path to the road without waiting for a reply.

Doona and Bessie watched her climb into her car and drive away before Doona pushed the door shut.

"I'm sorry I invited myself along," Doona told Bessie quickly. "But I think it's in everyone's best interests."

Bessie shook her head. "I'm getting very tired of you treating me like a small child," she told her friend. "I might be getting older, but I can look after myself."

"We're in the middle of a criminal investigation," Doona reminded her. "If there's any chance I might hear or see something that might help John work out who killed Nancy, it's worth inviting myself where I'm not especially wanted."

Bessie opened her mouth to argue, but after what John had told her about the investigation, it was just possible Doona was right. She sighed instead.

"I'm just going to go and finish packing," Doona told Bessie.

Bessie sat down with her book yet again. Within minutes, Doona was back and the pair set out for Bessie's cottage, the atmosphere between them still somewhat strained.

At the cottage, they both read for a while before Bessie made hot chocolate for them both. Using it to wash down some chocolate-covered biscuits improved both of their moods.

"I'm sorry if I'm mollycoddling you," Doona said as she washed up the dishes from their snack. "But you've become very important to me and I'm not sure what I'd do if anything ever happened to you."

"I know you mean well," Bessie said. "And I understand that you want to get this case solved as well. I'll try to stop taking everything so personally."

The pair hugged each other tightly before heading to bed. Bessie took her book upstairs with her and managed to finish the story before she got too tired. She closed it with a sigh. The fictional detective had solved everything in spite of his chaotic personal life.

As she snuggled down under the duvet, she wondered why so many fictional policemen drank too much and had difficult relationships with women. She rarely saw John Rockwell drink, although she did wonder about his relationship with his wife. She sighed. There was nothing she could do to help with the inspector's personal life, but she would do what she could to help sort out the case that was giving him so much trouble.

CHAPTER 9

Monday morning was dark and rainy and Bessie actually considered skipping her walk and just curling up with another book. As she ate her toast, she stared out at the relentlessly falling drops, frowning at their persistence.

"You aren't going for a walk in this, are you?" Doona asked from the kitchen doorway.

Bessie smiled at her friend, who was still wrapped in a bathrobe, wearing fuzzy slippers. "I was thinking about it," she said.

"But it's horrible out there," Doona said, checking that the kettle was still hot. She made herself a cup of tea while Bessie watched the weather a bit more.

"It might not get any better later," Bessie said eventually. "I think I'll just take a short stroll."

"As I'm trying very hard not to treat you like a child, I won't even argue with you," Doona told her. "But I will tell you I think you're crazy."

Bessie laughed. "I suspect a lot of people would agree with you."

She put on her raincoat and her Wellingtons and grabbed an umbrella. "It isn't windy, at least," she told Doona as she pulled open the back door to the cottage.

"I'm going to go and get a shower," Doona replied "I bet I come out of it drier than you'll be when you get back."

After a few steps, Bessie started to think Doona might be right. It wasn't terribly windy, but what breeze there was seemed to be blowing the rain in every direction at once. She made sure her coat was zipped to the very top and pulled the umbrella down as close to her head as possible. This was definitely going to be a short walk.

Bessie walked as far as the last of the rental cottages and then turned around. The beach was completely deserted and only a few of the cottages even had lights on in them as yet. Bessie was halfway back to her home when she noticed a man standing on the small patio behind his cottage.

"Hulloo, Miss Cubbon," he called.

Bessie waved at him. He was standing under the small awning that partially covered the patio, holding a small umbrella and frowning up at the sky.

"Hello, Spencer, how are you this morning?" Bessie called in reply.

"I had an early tee time for the course in Castletown," he told Bessie. "I've just rung and apparently it's just as bad down there as it is here. What can you recommend for me to do on a rainy Monday?"

"Have you been around the Manx Museum yet?" Bessie asked. "Or Castle Rushen? The House of Manannan in Peel is wonderful as well, and all three are indoors."

Spencer smiled brightly. "Those are all great ideas," he said. "I really should know more about the island's history. Maybe I'll try the Manx Museum. That's in Douglas, right?"

Bessie gave him directions. "Have a wonderful time," she told him as she headed towards home.

Back at her cottage, Doona was just climbing into her own Wellington boots. "I was just coming to look for you," she told Bessie. "I have to get to work and I was hoping you'd come with me."

Bessie sighed. "Really? As much as I love your company, the thought of spending the day at the police station really doesn't appeal to me."

Doona looked as if she wanted to argue, but she didn't. "Promise me you won't do anything I wouldn't approve of," she demanded of Bessie.

"Like what?" Bessie asked.

"Like let any suspects into the cottage or go for long walks on the beach by yourself or anything else that might put you in danger."

Bessie shook her head. "I'll be as careful as I can be," she told her friend. "But I'm not going to stop living my life. You go do your job and I'll make something nice for dinner for when you get home."

"That sounds good. I'll stop at the bakery on my way back and grab some pudding."

"Perfect."

With Doona out of the way, Bessie did some straightening and tidying of her cottage and then read for a while. After a simple lunch she was feeling restless. The rain had tapered off to a light but steady tempo, so she put her raincoat and boots back on and headed up the road behind the cottage.

At the top of the hill was a tiny shop that sold a little bit of everything. Bessie grabbed a few ingredients to help with dinner. The girl behind the counter was as surly as ever and Bessie quickly remembered why she hated shopping there. It took the girl three tries to get Bessie's change right as well, and Bessie spent the walk back home thinking seriously about ringing the shop's owner to complain. That the girl was his daughter was the only thing that stopped her.

At home, with a steak and kidney pie now bubbling away in the oven, Bessie rang a few more people to try to help the inspector. After only half an hour, she gave up. She hadn't learned anything new and she'd run out of people to ring. Perhaps she'd have better luck with the actual ladies the next day.

Now Bessie curled up with yet another book. An actor with a slight drinking problem stumbled across murder as Bessie turned the pages, engrossed. Having just been involved in her own theatrical murder mystery, she enjoyed it more than she might have otherwise.

Doona was back at the cottage before Bessie reached the last page, and Bessie was tempted to make her wait for her dinner until she'd finished. The delicious smell coming from the oven changed her mind.

The steak and kidney pie came out perfectly and the profiteroles that Doona had brought rounded out the meal nicely.

"That was delicious," Doona said, collecting plates for washing.

The friends curled up with books and had a quiet evening in. Tuesday morning, Doona headed for work as soon as Bessie got back from her walk.

"I'll pick you up at half one and we'll head over to the meeting," she told Bessie when she left.

Bessie did a load of laundry and then searched her wardrobe for something to wear. She found another black skirt and a different grey blouse. The outfit was similar to what she'd worn the last time she'd seen the ladies, but she was too old-fashioned to consider wearing anything other than black or grey for such an occasion.

Doona was right on time, which meant they were early when they pulled into the car park outside the community centre.

"It doesn't look as if anyone else is here yet," Doona said. The car park was completely empty.

"Maybe we should drive around for a short while," Bessie suggested.

Doona shrugged and pulled back out onto the narrow road. They drove through the streets of Laxey for a few minutes and then headed back to the centre. There were three cars in the car park now and Doona pulled into a space.

"That should be everyone, shouldn't it?" she asked Bessie.

"I recognise Elinor's car," Bessie replied. "But I'm not sure what Joan and Margaret currently drive. It's always possible Elinor invited a few other people as well."

Inside the building, the three remaining Raspberry Jam Ladies were sitting together on one long couch. Elinor jumped up as they entered.

"Ah, Bessie, we're so glad you're here," she said. "And your friend, of course."

"I'm glad we could come," Bessie replied. "Agnes was a lovely woman and I'm ever so sorry about her accident."

"We all are," Joan said from her spot on the couch. "It doesn't feel real, of course."

"No, of course not," Doona said in a soothing voice.

"I keep expecting her to come out of the kitchen and tell us the tea is ready," Joan said sadly. "But then, I keep looking for Nancy to arrive as well."

"Yes, well, the tea isn't going to make itself is it?" Elinor asked. "Perhaps someone would like to volunteer to get it ready?"

"I'll do it," Doona offered. "That way you can all share your memories and I won't be in the way."

"Oh, you wouldn't be in the way, my dear," Elinor answered. "But it would be very helpful of you to get the tea ready for us. We'd all be very grateful, I'm sure."

"Thanks, Doona," Bessie whispered to her friend before Doona headed across the hall to the small kitchen.

"I could help," Margaret said suddenly, starting to stand up.

"Oh, no," Elinor told her firmly. "You sit tight and join in remembering Agnes."

Margaret nodded uncertainly and sat back in her place. Elinor rejoined the other two on the couch, motioning Bessie into the chair opposite. Bessie sat down and smiled at the others.

"This is very difficult for me," she began. "I can't imagine how hard it must be for all of you. You were all so close for such a long time. I know I've said it already, but I am really sorry for your loss."

"We were all Agnes had," Margaret said softly.

"She had a sister," Elinor disagreed. "Not that that sister of hers was anything to brag about, but at least she had one."

"I had a sister once, too," Joan said. "She died when she was in her forties, though. She had the same cancer as my Mary."

Bessie leaned forward and patted Joan on the arm. "I'm sorry," she said quietly.

"You don't get to our age without losing people you love," Elinor said briskly. "Life goes on, nevertheless."

"Why didn't Agnes get along with her sister?" Bessie asked.

"She didn't approve of young Matthew's, well, shall we say, differences," Elinor told her. "She thought Agnes should have cut off all contact with him unless he changed his ways."

Bessie opened her mouth to argue, but Elinor held up a hand. "We all stood by Agnes, regardless of how we felt about her son," she reminded Bessie. "It's a shame her own sister couldn't do the same."

"It is at that," Joan agreed. "I don't know what the daughters are like, but I imagine we'll find out."

"Are they coming across then?" Bessie asked.

"They'll be here tomorrow," Elinor replied. "They've already had hours of conversation with young Doncan Quayle. No doubt they're eager to get their hands on their inheritance."

"I'm surprised she didn't leave everything to all of you," Bessie said. "You were essentially her family for much of her life."

"Yes, well, she made her own choices," Elinor said. "I can tell you that she just changed her will in the last month. I think the previous one was rather different."

"In what way?" Bessie couldn't stop herself from asking.

"I believe, in her previous will, she did just what you suggested," Elinor replied. "I believe she had arranged to leave her estate to the Raspberry Jam Ladies."

"Why did she change it?" Bessie pushed on, being nosy.

"We didn't know that she did change it," Joan whispered.

"So you were disappointed when you heard she'd left everything to her nieces," Bessie suggested.

"I would say surprised, rather than disappointed," Elinor said. "After everything we'd done for her over the years, it was surprising that she decided to leave her estate to strangers."

"Was she very wealthy?" Bessie asked, feeling certain that eventually Elinor would tell her she'd asked one question too many.

"She left a pretty fair amount, from what I understand," Elinor said. "You know her husband was an electrician, and I'm sure you remember how, let's say frugal, he was with his money. He left Agnes very comfortable and by the time he died, she had learned to be almost as careful with money as he'd been. Her only extravagance was trips across to see Matthew, and even then, he paid for most of it, as far as I know."

"Of course, the house will be worth some silly amount," Joan added. "Even though it's quite run-down and needs modernising, it'll fetch a ridiculous sum when they sell it."

"No doubt," Bessie agreed.

"Those two girls must be thrilled with their unexpected legacy," Elinor said crossly. "Not that any of us need the money, but after all we'd done for Agnes, well, as I said, it was disappointing."

"Who has a good memory of Agnes?" Margaret asked suddenly.

"I remember her bringing Matthew down to the beach by my cottage when he was young. He was always running as fast as he could up and down the shore. He also loved to hide and I remember Agnes going nearly crazy trying to find him one day when he'd found a particularly good hiding spot." Bessie laughed at the memory. "In the end, Agnes was sitting on the rock behind my house sobbing because she thought she'd lost him for good and he came running up. He was so sorry he'd upset her that he promised he'd never hide from her again."

"And did he?" Joan asked curiously.

"He did," Bessie replied. "But always in places that made him much easier to find."

The women all chuckled.

"I remember once, when my Michelle was so sick, Agnes came over and took Mary and Mark away for a few hours. I never did find out what they'd done that afternoon. They always just laughed and said it was their secret time with Auntie Agnes, but it gave me undivided time to be with Michelle during her final days, and I was ever so grateful for that," Joan said.

"She always wanted lots of children," Margaret said quietly. "But after Matthew she just never had any more. She didn't know why and she would never have asked her doctor about it, but it made her sad sometimes."

"I always thought one child was quite enough," Elinor said loudly.

"That way you can give that child all of you. I can't imagine trying to love a second child as much as you love the first one. My Nathan took up every inch of my heart."

"Nathan was very special," Joan said, patting her friend on the arm.

"Oh, but guess who I saw the other day," Bessie said. She told the ladies about her visit with Spencer. "He reminded me of so many things," she said. "He was reminiscing about the Jones-Windsor fairy family that Nathan used to talk about."

Unexpectedly, Elinor burst into tears. She jumped up and ran out of the room towards the loos.

Bessie looked at the others. "I didn't mean to upset her," she said helplessly.

Joan shook her head. "Nothing ever upsets Elinor," she said in a puzzled voice. "I'd better go and see if she's okay."

She was halfway across the room when Doona reappeared.

"The tea's ready," Doona announced, looking confused. "Did I miss something?"

"Elinor's just gone to the loo and Joan needs to go as well," Bessie explained. She'd tell Doona the whole story later, but the other ladies didn't need to know that.

"You go and get your tea," Joan said. "Elinor and I will catch up with you in a bit."

Margaret and Bessie followed Doona into the kitchen where Doona had set out plates of biscuits as well as the tea service. Bessie poured tea into mugs and the three women prepared their drinks. They settled in at the table and everyone helped themselves to a few biscuits.

"Do you have any special memories of Agnes?" Bessie asked Margaret.

Margaret flushed. "Oh, well, yes, of course," she said. "We were friends for a great many years. My kids used to stay over at her house once in a while to get a break, I mean, for a change of scenery, you know? She was very kind to the children and they were both devastated when I rang to tell them she'd passed on."

"How are your children, then?" Bessie asked.

"Oh, they're fine," Margaret said. "We didn't talk long. They're both so busy with their lives and their families. But I wanted them to know about Agnes. They were both glad I'd rung."

"I'm sure they were," Bessie said softly.

Joan walked back in the room and took a seat at the table. "Elinor will be here shortly," she said as she picked up a biscuit and broke it in half.

A moment later, Elinor came in and made herself a cup of tea. She sat down with it and then looked defiantly at everyone who was watching her. "I'm fine," she said sharply. "Bessie's comment just took me by surprise. I hadn't thought of young Spencer in many years. He was always a troublemaker, anyway. He used to make my Nathan cry all the time."

Bessie bit into a biscuit, rather than biting her tongue. The effect was the same: it kept her from arguing with Elinor.

Doona poured refills as cups emptied. The atmosphere was strained as everyone sat silently, presumably lost in her own thoughts.

"Well, that was pleasant," Elinor said after a while, her tone deliberately cheery. "Why don't we head back next door and we can share a few more memories of Agnes and Nancy."

"I'll take care of the washing up," Doona announced as everyone collected plates and mugs and piled them by the sink.

"Thank you, my dear," Elinor said, leading the others out of the room.

"Thank you," Bessie said, giving her friend a quick hug.

Back in the other room, everyone settled back into the same seats. Elinor looked around with an expectant look on her face.

"Right, who else would like to share a memory of Agnes, or indeed of Nancy?" she asked the others.

"I miss both of them," Margaret said sadly. "They were both always there for me and I don't think my life will be the same without them."

"At least you all still have each other," Bessie reminded her gently. "I know the police are doing their best to work out what's going on and to protect you all."

"Protect us?" Elinor said. "Why on earth would we need protecting?"

"I think they might be worried that someone is targeting you as a group, with Nancy's murder and Agnes's accident happening so close together," Bessie explained.

"Nonsense," Elinor said haughtily. "Nancy's murder was random and Agnes's accident was just that, an accident. We are as safe today as we ever were from the vagaries of life."

Bessie wasn't sure how to respond to that, so she simply nodded.

"Agnes was living on borrowed time anyway," Elinor said abruptly.

"Whatever do you mean?" Bessie asked as Margaret drew a sharp breath and looked away.

"I mean she had heart trouble," Elinor explained. "Her doctor told her to avoid any shocks or upsets. That's why we were all checking on her so much. We were worried that the stress of Nancy's death might kill her."

"I didn't know that," Joan said, her face pale. "Why didn't anyone tell me that?"

"Agnes told me in confidence," Elinor replied. "I wasn't going to go around telling other people her business."

"We aren't exactly 'other people,'" Joan argued. "We were her best friends, too."

"And if she'd wanted you to know, she would have told you," Elinor said complacently.

Joan flushed and then stood up. "I need some air. I'll be back in a minute."

The others silently watched her walk out of the room.

"I didn't mean to upset her," Elinor said defensively. "I thought it might make everyone feel better if they knew that Agnes probably wouldn't have been around much longer anyway."

"That's what you said about Nancy as well," Margaret said, getting to her feet. "It wasn't very nice then, either." She stomped out of the room, without looking back.

Elinor gave Bessie a helpless look. "Surely you can understand what I was trying to do?" she said imploringly.

Bessie nodded. "I do understand," she assured the woman. "But everyone's emotions are so close to the surface right now. It's difficult to know what might upset anyone."

A moment later Doona walked in. "Oh, dear, is everyone okay?" she asked.

"Margaret and Joan have stepped outside for some air," Bessie told her. "Perhaps you'd like to check on them?"

"Of course I can," Doona said cheerfully.

"She's a nice person," Elinor said. "Even if she is awfully young."

"I like having young friends," Bessie said with a laugh. "They keep me busy and active."

"I suppose," Elinor shrugged. "I've had the same friends for so long now that I think I've forgotten how to make new friends."

"It isn't hard," Bessie told her. "I'm sure you'd find it surprisingly easy if you tried."

"Perhaps I ought to start trying," Elinor said dryly. "The friends I have right now don't seem very happy with me."

Bessie shook her head. "Nothing can split up the Raspberry Jam Ladies," she told Elinor. "I'm sure you've all had little difficulties over the years. This too will pass."

"Little difficulties?" Elinor shook her head. "We've had screaming rows, that's what we've had."

"What could you possibly have had to argue about?" Bessie asked, trying to sound off-hand, but nearly bursting with curiosity.

"Oh, mostly when anyone argued it was over childrearing. We didn't all see eye-to-eye on the best ways to raise children. I have to say, some of us were more successful with our children than others as well, and that often caused little resentments."

Bessie nodded. "I can see that," she said. "Everyone wants to believe that their children are perfect and it must be difficult to have your parenting choices questioned, even by your dearest friends."

"There were odd disagreements about financial things once in a while," Elinor continued. "Some of the women were rather better off than others and that sometimes caused friction. Agnes, for instance, had to very careful with her money and she used to get quite upset when some of the other women would forget to pay their dues, week after week. Agnes always bought the supplies for the group, you see, and she'd end up having to spend her own money if people didn't pay, which caused no end of trouble with her husband."

"Poor Agnes," Bessie sighed. "I'm often glad I never married."

"I wish I'd been smart enough to stay single," Elinor said in a confiding tone. "Marriage never did suit me, although I suppose I must be grateful that I was able to get my Nathan out of it. He was worth all of the suffering, of course."

"I'm sure he was," Bessie agreed.

"Of course, there used to be odd arguments about husbands as well," Elinor added, seemingly warming to the topic.

"About how best to train them?" Bessie asked with a grin.

Elinor smiled grimly. "More like accusations over flirting and affairs," she told Bessie.

"Really? I don't believe it."

"Believe it," Elinor said tightly. "More than one of the ladies had little flirtations with my husband, for example, and I suspect that he might have done more than flirt with at least one them. As our marriage was pretty much over long before the Raspberry Jam Ladies began to meet regularly, it shouldn't have bothered me, but it was difficult being friendly with women who were quite possibly seeing my husband behind my back."

Bessie shook her head. "I'm so sorry," she said. "I can't imagine how difficult that must have been."

"It would have been harder, I suppose, if I'd been the only one, but one of the ladies flirted with all of the husbands and I think she slept with most of them."

"I won't ask which lady," Bessie said, although she was dying to know.

"I wouldn't tell you if you did ask," Elinor answered smugly. "It's ancient history now, anyway."

Bessie opened her mouth to ask another question, but she was interrupted when Doona and the others returned.

"Oh, good, everyone's back," Elinor said too brightly. "I've just been telling Bessie all about the great fun we always had when we were younger. Do you all remember the time we took the train into Douglas and then took the horse trams to the Sea Terminal for lunch? It was meant to be a special day out for everyone, but it poured with rain and the food was terrible and then one of the kids wandered off. Which one was it?"

"It was Spencer Cannon," Joan said, laughingly. "He got bored with waiting for pudding, so he went off to the kitchen to find out what was taking so long."

"I remember now," Margaret said. "On his way to the kitchen, he spotted the ferry and decided he wanted to go for a ride. When Peggy found him, he was trying to persuade the man taking the tickets that his parents had gone on board without him and he needed to find them."

"Peggy was so mad, she rang her husband right then and there and had him leave work and come and get him. She rode back to Laxey on the train with us while Spencer got driven home by his very angry father," Joan recalled.

"He always insisted that your Mark put him up to it," Elinor reminded Joan.

"It's just the sort of mischief that Mark would have tried to cause, as well," Joan said with a sigh. "I know I did a lot wrong with that boy, but I do think some kids are just born bad, and unfortunately my son is one of them."

"Where is Mark now?" Bessie asked tentatively.

"I have no idea," Joan said, her eyes filing with tears. "I haven't heard from him in years. I assume he's still in gaol, otherwise, he'd be writing or ringing and asking for money."

Margaret rubbed her friend's arm. "You poor thing," she whispered.

"Ouch, um, sorry, but could you not rub just there?" Joan asked her.

"What's wrong with your arm?" Doona asked.

"Oh, I spilled some hot water all over myself the other day," Joan told her. "I'm embarrassed to admit it, though. I was making myself a cup of tea and ended up with water everywhere."

"How did you do that?" Elinor demanded.

"My kettle isn't working, and I haven't had time to get into Ramsey to get a replacement. I wanted a cuppa, so I was boiling water in a mug in the microwave," Joan told her. "I'd never done that before and I didn't realise how hot the handle of the mug would be. When I pulled it out of the microwave, I pulled my hand back really quickly, letting go of the mug and splashing boiling hot water everywhere. The bulk of it burned my arm, though."

Joan pushed up her sleeve, showing the other ladies a sore-looking red patch.

"That looks painful," Doona said. "Have you seen your doctor?"

"Not yet," Joan shrugged. "I thought I'd see how it goes. I have a standing appointment every Friday anyway for all my other aches and pains, so if it isn't better by then, I'll have them take a look at it."

"Why don't you borrow the spare kettle in the kitchen here?" Margaret suggested. "I'll get it for you."

She disappeared into the kitchen before Joan could reply. Margaret was back a few moments later holding an old kettle.

"I'm sure no one will care if you borrow it," she said softly.

"What if someone needs it here?" Joan asked.

"The mums and tots group is on their summer break until September," Elinor told her. "We're the only group using the space at the moment. Surely you'll have a chance to replace your kettle before then."

"Oh, yes, I was planning to go into Ramsey on Saturday," Joan replied. "I need to do a big grocery shop and get some other things as well."

"In that case, you're more than welcome to use the spare from here," Elinor told her. "No one need ever know, not that anyone would mind."

"Thanks," Joan said with a sheepish grin. "Maybe I won't burn myself on my next cuppa, at least."

"Let's hope not," Elinor said with a smile.

The group broke up after that. Bessie felt peculiarly unsettled by the meeting, but she wasn't sure why. She had a lot of things she needed to discuss with the inspector that might give him some new ideas about his difficult case.

Doona took Bessie home by way of the nearest Chinese takeaway. They bought at least five containers more than they could ever possibly eat, but they both felt as if they needed to indulge themselves in some way.

Back at Bessie's, they spread the feast out on the counter and filled plates. Bessie hesitated and then opened a bottle of wine.

"Neither of us is driving tonight," Doona pointed out as Bessie poured.

They drank their wine and enjoyed their food, getting through the vast majority of it. Bessie put all of the leftovers in the fridge.

"That's lunch for tomorrow, anyway," she told Doona.

With the wine bottle nearly empty, Bessie was thinking longingly about her bed.

"We didn't have our fortune cookies," Doona said suddenly.

"I knew I still needed something sweet," Bessie said with a laugh. Bessie grabbed a cookie and broke it open. She nibbled at the crunchy treat as she unfolded her fortune.

"Danger comes from all sides," she read in a somber tone.

"Really?" Doona demanded. "That's a terrible fortune."

Bessie nodded and showed the slip to her friend. "I hope yours is better," she said.

"Here goes nothing," Doona laughed. She broke her cookie into pieces and popped the largest in her mouth before unfolding her fortune.

"Your happiness lies closer than you think," she read to Bessie.

"Well, that's certainly better than mine," Bessie said, washing down the last of her cookie with the last of the wine.

"I just hope mine is right and yours is wrong," Doona told her friend as she began to tidy up the kitchen.

Bessie quickly gave her a hand and then hugged her tight. "I hope you're already pretty happy," she told her friend.

"I am," Doona assured her. "At least I'm a lot happier now than I was when we met a few years ago. That was, without a doubt, the lowest point in my life. Things are much better now, even with John being grumpy all the time."

"Time for some sleep," Bessie suggested. "You have to go to work in the morning."

"So true," Doona laughed. "It feels like the weekend somehow, maybe because I had the afternoon off."

"Tell John I want to talk to him," Bessie told her. "I learned quite a lot today that he might be interested in."

CHAPTER 10

Bessie took a longer walk the next morning, as it was sunny and comfortably cool. By the time she got home, Doona had already left for work. Bessie grinned as she read the note her friend had left.

Since you aren't here, I can't drag you to the station with me. I hope you had a nice walk. I'll tell John you want to talk to him. He'll probably try to drop by some time today. I'm bringing pizza and ice cream to you tonight, unless you ring and request something else.

Pizza and ice cream sounded just about right, Bessie thought as she made herself a cup of tea. She'd had breakfast before her walk, but she was just considering another slice of toast when someone knocked on her door.

Bessie smiled at John Rockwell when she opened the door. "Doona said you'd probably come over, but I didn't expect you quite this early," she said as she let him in. "I thought you might get here just in time for lunch again." She stopped talking when she noticed the expression on his face.

"Please don't tell me someone else has died," she said, already anticipating his answer.

"I'm sorry, Bessie," he replied. He gave her a hug and then led her over to a chair. Once she was sitting down, he refilled her kettle and flipped in on.

"Who?" Bessie choked out.

"I thought maybe I should make some tea first," John prevaricated.

Bessie shook her head. "Please tell me."

"Joan Carr was found unresponsive at her residence this morning. An ambulance was rung for, but they were unable to revive her."

Bessie drew a deep breath, feeling tears flowing down her cheeks. "What happened?" she asked after a moment.

John handed her a mug of tea. Bessie took a tentative sip, feeling as if nothing would make her feel better, but grateful that he was trying.

"At this point, the investigation is in its very earliest stages," John began as he rummaged through Bessie's cupboards. "But it looks as if she was electrocuted when she turned on her kettle."

Bessie set her mug down on the table with shaking hands. "It wasn't her kettle," she gasped.

"That's what Elinor Lewis and Doona both told me," John replied. He'd found a box of biscuits and now he piled a few onto a plate. "Eat something," he suggested. "Your body needs the sugar."

Bessie took a biscuit and nibbled on it, her mind racing. "Doona told you about the kettle?" she asked after a while.

"She did, but I'd like you to walk me through exactly what happened as well. The more versions of the story I hear the better."

Bessie nodded. "We had tea with the jam ladies yesterday afternoon," she began.

The inspector held up a hand. "Could you please start with your morning and take me through your whole day?" he asked her.

Bessie sighed. "I forgot, you always do that," she said. She began again, telling the inspector everything she could remember from the previous day, including all of the startling revelations that Elinor had shared with her. He took several notes, but didn't interrupt. By the time she'd finished, she felt as if she was beginning to recover from the shocking news.

"Obviously, this last death changes the case rather dramatically," he told her when she'd finished.

"Could it have been an accident?" Bessie asked.

"Anything's possible, but it seems unlikely. Our crime scene team is going to go over that kettle at least a dozen times."

"It was pretty old," Bessie told him. "And it probably hadn't been used for years."

"We have detectives working on finding out exactly when it was used last," John told her. "There are only two groups that use the centre regularly, and Elinor says they never used that kettle as they never needed more hot water than a single kettle full."

"Poor Elinor, she must be devastated. And poor Margaret, she was the one who suggested that Joan borrow the kettle in the first place," Bessie shook her head. "I must ring them both."

"Right now they're both at the station. I took their statements and now they're going through them again with the head of Douglas CID. As far as I'm concerned, the longer they stay in police custody the better."

"To keep them safe? It really does seem as if someone is targeting them as a group."

"To keep them safe, maybe," John said. "And also because they're top of the suspect list."

"You can't be serious," Bessie said. "You can't possibly suspect Elinor or Margaret of anything."

"There are a limited number of people who had access to that kettle," John pointed out. "The mums that use the space probably don't even know the jam ladies, so they aren't likely to have any motive for killing them. If the kettle was tampered with, Elinor and Margaret certainly had the opportunity to do it."

"Maybe someone was trying to kill one of the mums from the other group," Bessie suggested.

"In some ways, that would be worse," John replied. "While I hate the thought of someone out there targeting your friends, I'd hate to think someone is targeting more than one group."

"But if you think it was deliberate, Margaret has to be your number one suspect, and there's no way you'll ever convince me she rewired a kettle to kill someone."

John shrugged. "The space is available for hire and has been used by dozens of groups over the last year or so. That blows the suspect list wide open, but it also makes it seem far more random, like the first murder. The fact that all the ladies who have died are part of the same group suggests that there is nothing random about these murders."

"But only the first one was definitely murder," Bessie said, thoughtfully. "Maybe Agnes and Joan both just had accidents."

"Maybe," John said. "But it seems unlikely."

Bessie sighed. "I hope Margaret is okay. She was very upset yesterday."

"She was very upset this morning. She found the body," John told her.

"Oh, no," Bessie gasped. "The poor woman."

"Apparently after Agnes's death, the group started a routine of ringing one another every morning. This morning it was Margaret's turn to ring Joan. When Joan didn't answer, she went to check on her. I understand all of the ladies have keys to all of their friends' homes. Anyway, she let herself in and found the body. It looks as if Joan decided to have a cup of tea before bed last night and, well, the kettle was faulty."

"Didn't anyone check on her last night?" Bessie asked.

"Elinor rang her at nine," John replied. "According to her, Joan was quite upset and Elinor said she actually suggested that she should have a cup of tea before bed."

Bessie shook her head. "Poor Elinor, she must be blaming herself," she said.

John frowned. "You need to understand," he told Bessie sternly, "we're looking very closely at Elinor, and at Margaret as well."

"Why would either of them want to kill their friends?" Bessie asked. "There's no motive for either of them to kill anyone."

John sighed. "So far, I can't find any motive for anyone to kill any of the women," he told Bessie. "And yes, at least two of the deaths could have been accidents, which is complicating things to say the least. This was a difficult case to begin with, and it's getting more and more complex every day."

"What about all the things that Elinor told me yesterday?" Bessie asked. "Is it possible that her husband had affairs with some of the other ladies, for example?"

John shrugged. "You never heard a whisper of it over the years, right? Could they possibly have kept something like that quiet in a village this small?"

Bessie sipped her tea while she gave the question some thought. "I simply don't know," she admitted finally. "I would have said no a few days ago, but the more I think about the ladies, the more I realise just how close-knit and secretive they actually were."

"And still are," John commented. "Elinor didn't tell me about any of this when we spoke. She insisted that no one could possibly have any motive for killing any of the ladies."

"Surely her husband's affairs don't give anyone a motive for murder," Bessie said.

"Except, perhaps, Elinor."

Bessie flushed. "You think she might be killing off the women her husband slept with thirty-odd years ago?"

"I'm saying it's possible," John countered. "It's the first motive I've heard for killing more than one of the ladies, at least."

"Elinor said they fought about other things as well," Bessie said.

"Anything that would give Margaret a motive?" John asked.

"I don't know. I suspect a lot of the arguing about childrearing could have been between Elinor and the others. I don't know that all of the ladies were as fond of Nathan as Elinor was."

"So we're back to Elinor having a motive for killing more than one of the ladies," John said.

"There must be people outside the group with motives," Bessie argued.

"There may be, but I'm having trouble finding them," John told her. "And then there's means and opportunity." He sighed. "I really can't discuss the case with you," he said. "You're too close to it and it's too big a case."

"I see," Bessie said sharply.

"No, you don't," John said sadly. "But that can't be helped. Can you walk me through the whole conversation about the kettle again? It doesn't make sense."

Bessie told him the whole story again. This time he interrupted frequently.

"Did you actually see the burn marks on Joan's arm?" he asked.

"I told you I did," Bessie answered. "Her arm was red and it looked very painful. There were a couple of large patches and lots of little marks, like you'd get if you splashed boiling water on your arm."

"How did the killer know her kettle was going to be broken?" John asked.

"Did you find a broken kettle at her house?" Bessie asked. "Other than the one that killed her, obviously."

"I don't know," John said. "But I'll find out." He pulled out his phone and made a quick phone call. Bessie got up and turned the kettle back on, feeling the need for another cup of tea. As she flipped the kettle's switch, she winced. Would she ever be able to turn on her kettle without thinking about poor Joan, she wondered.

"They're doing a complete inventory of her kitchen now," John told Bessie when he'd disconnected.

"Of course, if there isn't any broken kettle there, it won't prove anything. She might have just thrown it away."

"But if there's a working kettle there, that might tell us something," John replied.

"What?" Bessie asked.

"I don't know," John said shaking his head. "Nothing makes sense about this. If the kettle the ladies used at the centre had been tampered with and someone had been killed at a meeting, that might have made sense, but who tries to kill someone with a kettle kept in the back of a cupboard? It could have sat there for ten years before it was ever used."

"It seems more likely that Joan's death was just a tragic accident," Bessie said sadly.

"If it had happened in a month's time, maybe," John said. "Or if the kettle hadn't come from the centre where the ladies meet, maybe. Too many things just don't add up to accident for me."

"Well, you're the expert," Bessie said, a touch grumpily.

John chuckled. "That doesn't sound like a ringing endorsement," he said. "But at the moment I don't feel I deserve one, so fair enough."

"You know I think you're the most clever policeman on the island," Bessie told him. She'd made more tea and now she poured some into each of their cups.

"I don't feel very clever," he replied. "This case is like nothing I've ever dealt with before. It's totally random killings with very specific targets." He shook his head. "I'm sorry," he told Bessie. "I need to get back to the station. Inspector Corkill will be done with Elinor and Margaret by now. We need to compare notes and see what we can come up with."

"Tell Inspector Corkill I said hi," Bessie requested as he got up to leave. "In spite of all of our difficulties in May, I think he's pretty smart too. I'm sure the two of you will work this out."

"I just hope we can sort it out before anyone else dies," John replied gloomily.

He was gone before Bessie could reply. She shut the door behind him, frowning at his last words. She felt as if she were on autopilot as she tidied up the tea things, unable to make sense of Joan's death.

The phone rang a few minutes later.

"Bessie, are you okay?" Doona demanded as soon as Bessie answered.

"I'm fine," Bessie replied without thought.

"Yeah, but how are you really?" Doona asked.

Bessie thought for a moment. "I'm shocked and upset and scared for Margaret and Elinor," she told her friend. "I'm also confused and I really don't know what to think."

"Why don't you grab a taxi and come and spend the rest of the day at the station?" Doona suggested. "I'd come to you, but, as I'm sure you can imagine, things are crazy here. We've got Pete Corkill, the two remaining jam ladies and Spencer Cannon here and I've been fielding non-stop calls about Joan since I walked in this morning."

"And I'd just be in the way," Bessie added. "I'll be fine," she assured her friend. "I think I'll take a taxi into Douglas and work on some research. That should keep my brain busy for a while."

"I'll be at your place by six," Doona told her. "With pizza and ice cream."

"I'll be here," Bessie replied.

She put down the phone and sighed. Doona was right. She shouldn't sit at home. She rang for a taxi before she gave herself time to think, knowing if she thought too much about it, she'd change her mind and go back to bed.

When her favourite driver, Dave, arrived to take her, she forced herself to smile. "I'm glad it's you," she told him as she climbed into the cab.

"I am, too," Dave laughed. "I've always been glad to be me. Where are we headed?"

Dave kept up a non-stop stream of inane chatter all the way into Douglas, for which Bessie was hugely grateful. As he dropped her off near the shops, he handed her a card.

"My mobile number," he told her with a grin. "Don't ring the service when you're done; ring me direct. I'll come back for you."

"This isn't going to get you into trouble, is it?" Bessie asked.

"No, not at all," he said confidently.

Bessie wasn't convinced, but she was grateful. The service had several drivers and most were fine, but she wasn't sure she could stand riding with Mark Stone today.

Research at the museum suddenly held no appeal, so Bessie headed towards the shops. As she and Doona had just been in town, though, she quickly grew bored with window-shopping. It was nearly time for lunch, but she didn't feel hungry.

She strolled down to the promenade and sank down on a bench to watch the sea. The day was overcast but dry, and there appeared to be hundreds of families spread out across the sand, building castles and the like.

"I hate when there's someone sitting on my favourite bench," a voice said from behind Bessie.

Bessie flushed and spun around, smiling as she recognised the speaker. "Bahey Corett, what a nice surprise."

Bahey shook her head. "You always say that when you see me down here, but I live here, remember? I'm down here, sitting on this bench, just about every day."

Bessie chuckled. "I do remember. And I remember that you wanted to talk to me about something, but I never rang you to set up a meeting."

"Oh, aye, but you've had rather a lot going on, haven't you?" Bahey asked. "I remember them jam ladies from when I was little. So sad to see them dying off all sudden like. I hope you weren't too close to any of them."

Bessie shook her head. "I was friends with all of them, but not terribly close. Laxey's a small community, of course, and it's all very sad."

"Very sad," Bahey agreed. "And very strange. I mean, they didn't offer me any jam at Tynwald, but if they had, I would've taken it for sure. Did you get jam?"

"I did," Bessie admitted. "But I never opened it."

"Aye, and that's a lucky thing," Bahey replied. "I was telling Howard how I was sure you'd have been given a jar."

"How is Howard?" Bessie asked.

"Oh, he's okay," Bahey said, blushing. "I must say, it's different, this relationship thing. I never tried it when I was younger and I think that's a good thing. I'm having enough trouble getting the hang of it now."

Bessie chuckled. "He'd seemed like a very nice man, and he's rather handsome as well."

Bahey turned even redder. "Oh, aye, he's probably way too good-looking for the likes of me, but he doesn't seem to know it yet."

"Nonsense," Bessie said firmly. "You two made a lovely couple at Tynwald Day."

"Ah, thanks, but you should hear what the other women in the building have to say," Bahey told her. "There's a bunch of widowed women in my building and every one of them thinks she'd be better for Howard than me."

"Who cares what they think?" Bessie asked. "As long as Howard is happy, that's what matters."

"Oh, aye, and you know what? We seem to make each other happy."

Bessie smiled at the surprise she could hear in Bahey's voice. "I'm really pleased for you," she told her friend.

"Now we just have to find a nice man for you," Bahey suggested.

Bessie laughed and shook her head. "I'm too set in my ways to find a man now," she told Bahey. "I went out with my fair share of men when I was younger. Now I'm more than happy on my own with my little cottage, my research and my books. A man would just get in the way."

Bahey laughed. "I would have agreed with you a few months ago," she told Bessie. "But right now I'm not so sure. It's really nice to have someone to have meals with and watch telly with. He just makes me feel special, you know?"

Bessie nodded. "I remember how being in love felt," she told Bahey. "And there are times when I feel I've missed out. But then I see a couple on the beach arguing about whose turn it is to change their baby's nappy and I decide I'm better off on my own again."

Bahey laughed. "Well, at least I don't have to worry about having that particular argument with Howard," she said.

"But why did you want to talk to me?" Bessie asked again.

"Oh, well, there's something been going on in our building, but I don't know if it's really a problem or just my imagination, like. Howard says I'm seeing things that aren't there, but it worries me for some reason."

"What's going on?" Bessie asked.

"I'd rather not talk about it right now," Bahey answered. "There's some things I need to check out first. Besides, Howard is away, visiting his daughter, and I want him to be in on the conversation. Maybe we could have lunch when he gets back in early August."

"Are you sure?" Bessie asked. "In all my mystery books, the person who says that always ends up mysteriously disappearing or meeting with an unfortunate accident."

Bahey laughed. "It isn't anything like that," she assured Bessie. "And I don't want go saying things and then finding out it's nothing. Let's make plans for lunch, and even if I haven't worked things out by then, I'll tell you all about it, okay?"

Bessie checked her diary and the pair agreed on a date. "Where would you like to meet?" Bessie asked.

"Oh, come to mine," Bahey suggested. "I'll cook something simple for the three of us."

"That sounds good," Bessie agreed. "I'll enjoy getting to know Howard better, as well."

Bahey wrote down her flat number for Bessie. "You can see it from here," she said, pointing down a short alley that led up from the promenade.

Bessie smiled. "If I can't find it, I'll just come and sit on this bench and you can come and find me."

"I'll send Howard," Bahey told her with a laugh.

"Perfect."

Bessie was feeling better about life after her chat with Bahey, and Bahey's mysterious problem gave Bessie something else to think about as well.

Feeling suddenly as if life was too short to worry about silly things like proper nutrition, Bessie treated herself to fish and chips from a chippy on the promenade. She ate them while seated on another bench, still watching the sea and the holidaying families. After lunch, she dropped into a small convenience shop and bought herself a few of the sort of celebrity magazines she usually only read while waiting in her doctor's surgery. On impulse, she added an indulgent chocolate bar to her purchases.

Now feeling as if she was well stocked up for a quiet afternoon at home, she rang the number on Dave's card and was pleased when he told her he could pick her up in just a few minutes at the same place where he'd left her. She was only a short stroll away, and she arrived there only seconds before Dave pulled up.

Back at her cottage, she curled up in her favourite chair with a magazine and her bar of chocolate, ready to wallow in the comings and goings of the various celebrities who were happy to have their lives splashed across the tabloids. A couple of hours later she was tutting over the incredibly tacky wedding of some vapid-looking blonde soap actress whom Bessie had never heard of to some man who played football, a sport Bessie never followed. She was startled when she heard Doona's special knock.

"Would you get married in lime green?" she demanded of Doona after she'd opened the door.

"I don't plan on ever getting married again," her twice-divorced friend reminded her. "In any colour at all."

"But really, if you were young and beautiful, why would you get married in lime green?"

Doona set down the pizza box she was carrying and put the tubs of ice cream in the freezer before she looked at the magazine Bessie was waving around.

"I think it's one of her new husband's team colours or something," she answered after she'd taken a quick look. "But that's not what's interesting about that wedding," she added. "Did you see the photo on the next page?"

Bessie turned the page and then gasped. "That's Sienna Madison," she exclaimed. "What's she doing there?"

Bessie and Doona had met Sienna only a month earlier when the pretty young actress had been caught up in a murder investigation that began at Peel Castle.

Doona quickly skimmed the article while Bessie dug out plates.

"According to this, she was one of the bridesmaids," she told Bessie. "I suppose that's why she's wearing fuchsia."

Bessie shook her head. "I read that the bride was a soap actress, but I never made the connection with *Market Square*."

Doona handed Bessie the magazine back. "I can't believe you're reading this sort of rubbish anyway," she told her friend.

"I needed something mindless," Bessie replied.

"It's certainly that," Doona said with a laugh.

Bessie opened the pizza box and the pair grabbed their first slices. "Shall I open a bottle of wine?" Bessie asked.

"Can't hurt," Doona replied. "I've had a very long day."

Bessie stood up and then hesitated. "Red or white with pizza?"

Doona laughed. "Whichever you can get open fastest."

Bessie chuckled. "I bought a bottle of white zinfandel the other day," she told Doona. "The girl in the shop said it was very popular. It's sort of pink, so maybe it can go with everything."

She opened the bottle, poured some into wine glasses and then took a cautious sip. "It's good," she said.

Doona took a large drink from her glass. "It is good," she agreed. "Although after the day I had, I wouldn't complain if it tasted like paint thinner."

"Well, I would, and it definitely doesn't," Bessie replied.

"No, it definitely doesn't," Doona agreed.

The pair ate pizza and drank wine in companionable silence for a while. When the pizza was finished, Doona sat back with a sigh.

"I'm sorry I'm not more chatty," she said. "I spent the entire day dealing with crazy people, either on the phone or in person. The silence just now was lovely."

"It was busy at the station?"

"It was a madhouse. Pete Corkill was there; he's been called in to help John work out what's going on. Elinor and Margaret were there for much of the day, answering questions and, I don't know, being watched, I imagine. We had dozens of people ringing in to report seeing everything from Agnes's ghost to a mysterious man, dressed all in black, hanging around Joan's house." Doona shook her head. "Every tip has to be investigated, of course. Poor Hugh's been chasing ghosts all day."

"You should have invited him to join us," Bessie replied.

"He was going straight to Grace's after work. I'm sure he'd rather spend his time with her."

Bessie nodded. "I'm sure you're right about that."

"Anyway, in between all the tips were the calls from a bunch of very worried residents of Laxey who are now convinced there's a serial killer running around killing people entirely at random."

"At this point, it seems that only Margaret and Elinor need to be worried," Bessie suggested.

"Ah, but once the jam ladies are gone, who'll be next?" Doona asked dramatically. She shook her head. "There are lots of little groups in Laxey, like the jam ladies, and it seems at least one person in every one of them is convinced they're going to be the next group targeted. No one wants to listen to reason, and no one believes that any of the deaths were accidental, either."

"At least it's Wednesday," Bessie said. "The weekend is coming."

"Yeah, but if the two inspectors don't get things worked out quickly, I might have to work this weekend. They're sending a couple of desk staff from Douglas up tomorrow to help me field phone calls and visitors for the rest of the week. Come the weekend, though, there's no way our regular weekend constable can handle all this on his own."

"Oh, dear," Bessie said. "You need the time off."

"We all do," Doona told her. "I've never seen John so stressed and even Pete Corkill, after just a few hours up here, was looking incredibly grim."

"Think how awful it must be for Margaret and Elinor," Bessie said. "I must ring them both and make sure they're okay."

"They're fine," Doona said with a shake of her head. "Oh, Margaret's all timid and quivery, but neither one of them seems to think they're being targeted by a madman. They're both quite calm about the whole thing, really. Very sad about losing their friends, but not at all worried about being next, from what I've seen."

"I'll ring them both tomorrow," Bessie said. "Remember they're both tough women who were taught to keep a stiff upper lip and all that. They'll be working hard to make sure no one knows how they really feel."

"They'd be better off acting terrified," Doona told her. "Right now they're just making the inspectors even more suspicious of them."

Bessie sighed. "I can't imagine Margaret or Elinor suddenly

turning into a serial killer at seventy-odd," she said. "I've known these women for most of their adult lives."

"We need to have one of our gatherings where we go through motive, means and opportunity," Doona said. "But we need Hugh and John to do it right."

"What about tomorrow night?" Bessie asked. "See if Hugh is free and tell John what we're doing. He can join us or not, as he likes."

"Maybe we should invite Pete Corkill as well," Doona said after a moment. "He knows you and I think he knows how clever you are. If he comes, John might be more willing to come as well."

"Invite whomever you like," Bessie told her. "I'll make a blueberry crumble if you bring Indian or Chinese."

"I'll bring something," Doona promised, "other than pizza."

The women went to bed not long after, with Bessie curling up under her summer-weight duvet with another new book. She read the first three chapters and then put it to one side. It wasn't holding her interest. Her mind kept replaying the exchange between Margaret and Joan about the spare kettle.

After a while, she turned off her light and flopped down on her pillow. She tried to think about other things, any other things, but her brain refused to cooperate. She fell into a restless sleep with Joan's words echoing through her head. *"Maybe I won't burn myself on my next cuppa,"* indeed.

CHAPTER 11

Although the next day was only Thursday, Bessie was in need of a trip to the grocery shop. She rang her usual service and requested a taxi not long after she got home from her daily early morning walk. When the taxi beeped outside, she knew that her least favourite driver would be behind the wheel.

"Good morning, Mark," she said politely as she climbed into the car.

"Morning, Bessie, me love," he replied. "Ramsey today, is it?"

"Yes, please, I have guests coming over tonight and I need to make a pudding."

"Not jam roly poly, I reckon," he laughed loudly. "I won't be eating raspberry jam myself for a good long time, I can tell you. Not that those old dears shared any of their precious jam with me at Tynwald Day, anyway," he said with a frown. "I suppose my not being from Laxey kept me from getting poisoned, anyway."

Bessie stared out the window, choosing to ignore the man rather than tell him what she was thinking.

"I was telling the wife, just the other day, about one of them jam ladies," he rabbited on. "I used to take one of them back and forth to one of the other houses all regular like, but then I come to find out that it wasn't the other lady she was visiting, if you know what I mean?" He winked at Bessie, who was still trying to hide her surprise at the revelation that Mark was married.

I suppose there truly is someone for everyone, she thought as her mind processed the rest of his words. "You mean one of the ladies was having an affair with one of her friend's husbands?" Bessie asked.

"Oh, yeah, but a long time ago," Mark said with a chuckle. "Hard to believe it, but that sort of thing even went on back in the seventies, when I first started driving a taxi."

"You should tell the police about it," Bessie suggested. Although she was curious, she wasn't going to ask the man for any more details herself. He was talking out of turn and she wasn't going to encourage him to gossip about his customers.

"Tell the police? Why?"

"They're interested in anything and everything to do with the jam ladies," Bessie said. "They're trying to find a motive for three murders."

"Oh, but what difference does a long-ago love affair make? The husband died a long time ago," the man said. "I mean, the lady in question, her husband might have minded, but he's dead now too."

It took all of Bessie's willpower not to ask the man for the name of the woman he was talking about. Instead, she offered an alternative answer. "Perhaps the woman in question was visiting the children, rather than the husband?" she suggested.

"Whatever," Mark shrugged. "Anyway, here you are. You want me to collect you at a set time?"

Bessie shook her head. "I've several shops to stop in at. I'll ring the office when I'm done." And hopefully, get a different driver home, she added silently.

"Okay, see ya." He pulled away as soon as Bessie's feet touched the pavement. She frowned after him, wishing she'd reminded him to contact the police.

Her head was spinning now with this new piece of news, which was really more a confirmation of what Elinor had said. It seemed likely that at least one of the jam ladies had an affair with someone else's husband. While Bessie enjoyed hearing a bit of skeet now and again, this dredging up of what should have been long buried personal history made her miserable.

She did her usual Friday rounds a day early, visiting the bookshop and the charity shops, looking for more books to add to her already huge collection. This time, she'd finally remembered to bring a few books she no longer wanted to one of the charity shops so that they could be sold on to someone else.

"You've given me six books," the woman in the shop told her. "I suppose you'll buy at least that many to replace them with?"

Bessie laughed. "I probably will," she agreed. In the end, she bought four in that shop, adding another three during the rest of her travels.

Her last stop was the large ShopFast, where she did her weekly shop. As she wasn't sure how much longer Doona would be staying with her, she bought quite a bit of extra food, planning to freeze whatever she and Doona didn't eat over the next few days.

While she very much enjoyed her friend's company, Bessie was hoping that Doona would be leaving soon. It would be nice to have her own space back, and Bessie was really hoping that the Raspberry Jam murders would be solved quickly so that life could get back to normal.

Bessie ran into friends or acquaintances in just about every aisle, so the grocery shop visit took quite a bit longer than usual. Everyone wanted to talk about Nancy, Agnes and Joan as well as speculate on how Margaret and Elinor were coping. Bessie explained to everyone that she knew nothing beyond what was general knowledge and that she hadn't seen Margaret or Elinor since Joan's death, but she got the feeling that no one believed her. Since she was friends with a police inspector, everyone seemed to assume she knew a great deal more than she was willing to tell.

Maggie Shimmin was standing in front of the baking goods display when Bessie arrived there.

"Oh, fancy running into you here again," she said, giving Bessie a big hug. "I hope you aren't too miserable, what with losing another friend and all."

"I'm fine," Bessie replied. "Although it's all quite sad."

"Oh, it is, aye," Maggie said. "And Agnes and Nancy, that's three friends, isn't it, all this month. I can't imagine."

Bessie shook her head. "I'm trying not to think about it," she told the other woman.

"It's all I can think about," Maggie sighed. "I keep wondering who will be next? Like maybe the killer will change things up and kill someone else instead of a jam lady or something."

"Joan's death might have just been a tragic accident," Bessie pointed out as she picked up a bag of plain flour.

"Yeah, I know, and the same with Agnes's, but it does seem weird, doesn't it, the three of them dying so close together?"

"Tragically, such coincidences do happen," Bessie replied, trying to keep the conversation neutral.

"Yeah, I suppose they do," Maggie said with a shrug. "Oh, but I saw that Spencer Cannon the other day and he said he got to see you. He was ever so pleased that you remembered him."

"He came over for tea and we had a lovely time catching up," Bessie said with a smile.

"Yeah, he's done all right for himself, that one," Maggie replied. "But you'll never guess who I saw in Douglas the other day."

"If I won't guess, then you'll have to tell me," Bessie suggested, not in the mood for games.

Maggie frowned. "Yes, well, do you remember Ted Porter? He was Elizabeth's son."

Bessie thought for a moment. "I remember him a little bit," she said eventually. "Elizabeth died such a long time ago and the kids were both across when it happened. I only vaguely remember them. Don't tell me Ted's back on the island for some reason?"

"No, he's not, but I tell you I thought I was seeing a ghost. I was walking down the high street in Douglas and I swore it was Ted Porter standing in a shop doorway."

"But it wasn't?"

"Oh, no, well, I knew it wasn't because the lad in question was only about twenty-five, but he looked so much like Ted that I had to go over and speak to him. He looked well shocked, he did."

"I can imagine," Bessie commented wryly.

"Yes, well, anyway, after I explained that I'd grown up with Ted and whatnot, he introduced himself. Would you believe he's Ted's son? All grown up and everything."

"I didn't know Ted had children, but I never kept in touch with the family after Elizabeth's death. I'm sure Elinor and the other jam ladies know all about him."

"I don't know about that," Maggie said. "But he certainly knew all about them. He asked me straight away if I was one of them jam ladies, but I soon set him straight. I'm at least twenty years too young for that, I told him."

"What's his name?" Bessie asked.

"Jason, Jason Porter. He'd come across, he said, for Tynwald Day, but then he changed his mind about going and stayed in Douglas instead. He's just been hanging around and seeing a bit of the island. He said he'd never been here before but his father often talked about it."

"What did he know about the jam ladies?"

Maggie shrugged. "I suppose his father must have talked about them."

"Did he want to see the jam ladies or was he just asking about them?" Bessie asked.

"Don't know. Once I told him I wasn't a jam lady, he seemed to lose interest in talking to me, really. He was polite enough, but kinda uninterested. I think maybe he wanted to talk to people who knew his grandmother. Maybe he's interested in what sort of person she was and the like."

"I wonder if he rang any of the ladies. I'll have to ask Elinor if she's heard from him."

Maggie shrugged. "I better get going. Thomas had this stupid idea that we should offer some homemade puddings to our guests as well as the grocery shopping, so now I have to go home and bake pies for the rest of the day. He'd better be charging a ton for them. I hate baking pies."

Before Bessie could reply, the woman was gone, shoving her cart through the small crowd on a direct course for the closest till.

Bessie grabbed everything else she needed and headed for the tills herself. While she waited for her turn, she rang for a taxi. It was just pulling up as she emerged from ShopFast, feeling as if feeding Doona was getting to be rather expensive in spite of the fact that Doona kept bringing dinner home with her.

The driver was one that she barely knew, and Bessie was happy with the virtually silent ride back home. She made herself a quick lunch and then settled in with her phone to ring some friends.

"Margaret? It's Bessie Cubbon. How are you, my dear?"

"Oh, Bessie, I'm okay," the quiet voice came back down the phone. "I'm feeling terrible that I suggested that kettle to Joan, but Elinor keeps reminding me that I was just trying to help."

"You were," Bessie said in her most soothing voice. "You mustn't feel badly at all."

"I know you're right, but it was such a shock," Margaret told her.

"It was indeed."

"And coming right after Nancy's death and then Agnes's death, well, it's been a very sad July for us all." Bessie could hear tears in Margaret's voice.

"It has been very sad," she agreed. "Is there anything I can do to help?"

Margaret sighed. "I don't know," she said softly. "I mean, it does rather feel as if the police are somehow suspicious of me. I don't suppose you could talk to your friends in the police and tell them to leave me alone?"

"I wish I could," Bessie replied. "But they wouldn't listen to me, even if I asked. They're investigating everything and everyone. You mustn't take it personally."

"It's hard, though. They had me at the station for hours yesterday. I had to talk to two different inspectors and I don't think either of them believed anything I said."

"Perhaps you need a short holiday away," Bessie suggested. "Maybe you should go and visit one of your children."

"Oh, I couldn't bother them. They haven't time for me at the moment."

"Are you okay on your own?" Bessie asked.

"I suppose so," Margaret sounded so uncertain that Bessie felt a momentary pang of annoyance with the woman.

"Maybe Elinor could stay with you for a few days," Bessie suggested.

"Oh, I couldn't ask her to do that," Margaret replied. "We're ringing each other at least twice a day, just to check in, you know? I couldn't possibly ask her to do more than that. Elinor and I were never very close."

"I didn't realise that. I thought you were all very close friends."

"Oh, no, Elinor's never really liked me. Her husband was very kind to me, though."

Really? Bessie thought. That was interesting. "If there is anything I can do, please ask," she told the other woman. "I'm only a short distance away."

"Well, if you could, I mean, do you, would it be a huge bother…." Margaret sighed and Bessie heard her take a deep breath. "Would you come over for tea tomorrow? Only it's my birthday, you see, and I don't want to spend the whole day all alone."

"Of course I will," Bessie replied, almost without thought. It was appalling to think of the poor woman spending her birthday alone. "I might just bring my friend, Doona, if that's okay. She's the friend that came with me the other day to the meeting."

"That's fine," Margaret replied. "The more the merrier. I just thought I'd do a traditional tea, with scones and sandwiches and the like."

"I'll stop at a bakery and get you a cake," Bessie told her. "What's your favourite?"

"Oh, I don't, that is, I haven't had a birthday cake in years," Margaret said. "We never fussed when I was a child and obviously, once you have children of your own, well…."

"Well, nothing," Bessie said firmly. "I shall be bringing you a cake and if you don't care what sort, it will be chocolate sponge with chocolate icing. When I was a child in the US, that was what everyone had for their birthdays and it's the only thing that feels right to me, even if it isn't traditional here."

"Oh, Bessie, that sounds wonderful, thank you." Bessie could once more hear tears in the woman's voice.

"I'm happy to do it," Bessie told her. "I'll see you tomorrow, then."

"Oh, and Bessie, one more thing," Margaret said. "If you talk to Elinor, could you not mention that you're coming for tea tomorrow? She doesn't know it's my birthday and I'd rather she not feel as if she should make a fuss or anything."

"Of course," Bessie assured her, frowning at the phone. Clearly when Margaret said she and Elinor didn't really get along, she meant it. After fifty-plus years of friendship, Elinor didn't know it was Margaret's birthday? And Margaret didn't want her to know? Curious.

Bessie rang Doona next to check to see if her friend could fit the birthday tea into her schedule for the next day.

"I'll check with John and tell you tonight," was the best that Doona could do.

Bessie disconnected and tidied up her already spotless kitchen. She spent a few minutes refolding and fussing with the towels in the bathroom and then sighed. She really didn't feel up to ringing Elinor, but she knew she had to. Maybe she won't be home, she told herself encouragingly.

"Yes?"

"Oh, Elinor? It's Bessie Cubbon. How are you?"

"I'm fine, thanks."

"Oh, good, I just wanted to check on you and tell you how sorry I am about Joan's sudden passing."

"Yes, well, it was sudden, but those left behind must soldier on, mustn't they?"

"Well, yes, of course," Bessie replied.

"Was there anything else?"

"Well, no, I mean, I suppose not."

"Jolly good, well, as I said, I'm quite fine. Rather sad, of course. Always sad to lose a friend, but we've had rather a lot of that lately, haven't we? Anyway, I must dash as I'm in the middle of cleaning my kitchen and you know what a chore that is."

Elinor disconnected before Bessie had a chance to reply. She sat with the phone in her hand for a moment, rather stunned by the brief and impersonal conversation.

With her phone calls out of the way, no matter how unsatisfactorily, Bessie got on to making the blueberry crumble. She was just rinsing the container of blueberries she'd bought when someone knocked on her door. Quickly drying her hands, she opened the door.

"Grace? What a wonderful surprise," she said as her visitor smiled a bit sheepishly at her.

"I was in the neighbourhood," Grace told her. "And I thought maybe you'd like a visitor."

"I'm delighted to see you," Bessie assured her. "Do come in."

Grace crossed into the small kitchen. "Oh, but I'm interrupting something," she said.

"Not at all," Bessie replied. "I'm just putting together a crumble for later. Doona and Hugh are coming over, possibly with John and maybe even with Inspector Corkill. I promised them pudding."

Grace smiled. "Hugh told me there was a gathering tonight so that you could help them work out what's going on. I'm more concerned with how you're feeling, though."

Bessie smiled at her. "I'm fine, dear, really," she told the young woman.

"It must be very sad to have several friends all die so suddenly," Grace said. "Oh, that sounded rather rude somehow. I didn't mean it to be." Grace's fair skin flushed a deep red and she looked down at her hands.

"It wasn't rude," Bessie said, patting Grace's arm. "And it is rather sad, even if the ladies in question weren't exactly my friends, but as you get older you get somewhat more used to people passing away, especially people in their seventies."

Grace looked at Bessie and then stepped forward and gave her a hug. "I wish I knew what to say or do to make things better," she whispered to Bessie.

"Just being here, letting me know you care, helps a lot," Bessie told her. "Now sit down and I'll make you a cup of tea and we can chat about anything other than the Raspberry Jam Ladies."

"Deal," Grace said with a laugh.

Bessie switched the kettle on and then went back to her blueberries. "I hope you don't mind if I get this crumble in the oven," she told Grace. "Your Hugh will be very disappointed if there isn't any pudding later."

"Can I help?"

"Oh, no, crumble is quick and easy. Just forgive me for leaving you sitting there on your own for a bit."

Bessie quickly mixed up the butter, sugar and other topping ingredients together. She drained the blueberries and then patted them dry with a towel. By the time kettle boiled, she'd put them into a baking dish and covered them generously with topping.

With the crumble safely in the oven, Bessie sat down with Grace for tea and biscuits.

"It was kind of you to come," Bessie told the girl as they sipped their tea. "What brought you to Laxey?"

"Oh, I came up to look at a house," Grace said, blushing. "That is, I met Hugh on his lunch break so we could look at a house."

"What sort of house and where?" Bessie asked. "If that's not too nosy," she added, knowing perfectly well that it was terribly nosy.

"Oh, no, it's fine," Grace replied. "Just a little two-bedroomed semi-detached place on Baldhoon Road. It's nothing fancy, but it's in good condition and it's close to the primary school. I'm hoping to get a position there in the autumn so that I can move up to Laxey to be with Hugh."

"Oh, my," Bessie said. "That sounds serious. I do hope I hear wedding bells as well. I'm a bit old-fashioned that way."

Grace laughed. "You and my mum have a lot in common," she told

Bessie. "Poor Hugh is getting uptight about the whole thing, though," she added, in a more serious tone.

"Oh, I'm sure Hugh will do the right thing, eventually," Bessie said. "Maybe he just needs a little push in the right direction. I'll have a word with him."

"Oh, no, I mean, thank you, but, I don't know, that is…."

Bessie held up a hand. "Please don't worry," she said. "I'll be very careful. Quite frankly, though, I think he's very lucky to have found you."

"I think I'm quite lucky as well," Grace said, blushing again. "He's very handsome and quite clever."

"He's a good person as well, and that matters a lot," Bessie told her. "And we were just talking about hats and now I shall have to buy one. At least I assume I'll be invited to the wedding."

"Oh, of course," Grace replied. "Although I don't know that you'll need a hat. It's sure to be a very small event. Hugh and I can't afford a big lavish affair."

"No, well, big weddings don't improve the marriages that follow," Bessie said. "What's important is that you have your friends and family around you on your special day."

"Exactly," Grace said. "If Hugh ever asks, that is."

Bessie laughed. "He'll ask, one day, and probably sooner than you think. But we were talking about hats. Come on upstairs with me and let's see what we can find."

"Oh, I'd forgotten all about our conversation about hats," Grace told her. "I hope you don't think that I just stopped in to get a look at your collection."

Bessie laughed. "If I thought that, I wouldn't have offered to show them to you, although calling a few old hats a collection is a bit of a stretch. Come on, then."

Bessie led the way upstairs and into one of the spare bedrooms. "I think I shoved them all into the back of this wardrobe some years ago," she told Grace as she pulled open the doors on the front of the large furniture piece. She pushed aside several skirts and dresses that she never wore, searching behind them for the large hatboxes she was sure were around the cottage somewhere.

"Eureka," she exclaimed as she spotted four of them neatly stacked on the floor in the back of the wardrobe. She pulled them out one at a time and carefully set them on the bed.

"Let's have a look, shall we?" she suggested.

The first box had a large red and black hat. Bessie laughed as she took it out and tried it on. "I wore this to a friend's wedding in the sixties," she told Grace. "They were sort of, I don't know, I suppose you could call them hippy-type people, and they had a red and black colour scheme for their wedding. The bride wore a red dress and the groom wore all black and all the guests were meant to come in those colours as well. It was all very shocking in those days."

"It's lovely, though," Grace said in a slightly awed voice.

"Here, try it on," Bessie suggested, passing it over.

Grace set it gently on her head and turned to the mirror. "I wish people still wore hats," she said sadly as she studied her reflection.

"It looks much better on you than it ever did on me," Bessie said honestly. "Let's see what else I have."

The women went through the remaining boxes, with Bessie telling Grace about each hat and both women trying them all on.

"That was such good fun," Grace said as Bessie returned the last hat to its box. "Thank you for sharing your hats and their history with me."

"Now you must help me carry them downstairs," Bessie told her. "We'll get Hugh to load them into your car when he gets here, as he's due any minute."

"Oh, but I can't possibly take them," Grace objected.

"Well, then, help me carry them downstairs and I'll put them out for the bin men," Bessie told her.

Grace gasped. "You wouldn't."

"Of course I would," Bessie said. "No one wears hats anymore and they're all out of style anyway. You can have them if you like them, although I've no idea what you'll do with them."

"I don't know what I'll do with them, either," Grace admitted. "But I'd love to have them anyway, if you're sure."

"I'm very sure," Bessie said firmly.

Back downstairs, they carefully stacked the boxes on the kitchen counter and then Grace sat back down. Bessie checked on her crumble and then slid it out of the oven.

"It looks wonderful," Grace told her.

"You can have a little piece, if you'd like," Bessie replied. "No one will miss one little bit."

"I'd better not," Grace replied. "I haven't had dinner yet and besides, Hugh would miss it."

Bessie laughed. "You're probably right about that."

A few minutes later someone knocked on the door and Bessie opened it to admit Hugh. If he was surprised to find Grace there, he hid it well.

"Hello," he said, dropping a kiss on the top of Grace's head. "Have you enjoyed spending time with Bessie, then?"

"Yes, but she's gone and given me all these lovely hats, so I need you to put them in my car, please," Grace replied.

"No problem," Hugh took Grace's keys and made two quick trips back and forth with the hats. "You're all set," he told the girl as he handed her back her keys.

"I'll just get out of the way, then, before everyone else arrives," Grace said. "Bessie, I don't know how to thank you for the lovely hats," she said. "I'm so thrilled with them."

"They were just taking up space in my spare room," Bessie said. "I'm glad to see the back of them."

She gave Grace a hug and then walked her to the door. "Take care of yourself," she told the girl.

Hugh stood in the doorway with Bessie and they watched Grace pull away. As Bessie shut the door, Hugh sighed deeply.

"What's the matter?" Bessie asked the young man.

"She's really terrific," he replied. "And I know I should marry her quick, before she works out how much better she could do, but...." he trailed off.

Bessie narrowed her eyes at him. "But what?" she demanded. "Grace is lovely, she's smart and she puts up with your unpredictable job. What more do you want?"

"Nothing, that is, I know she's perfect. I think that's what scares me. I'm afraid she's going to realise how unperfect I am one of these days."

"Imperfect," Bessie corrected him.

"Exactly," Hugh said miserably.

Bessie smiled. "Look, Grace is terrific, but she isn't perfect," she began. "Right now, you're head over heels in love, but one day you'll start to notice little things about her that aren't so lovely and sweet and wonderful. If you think you can still love her in spite of those little things, then you should marry her. If she's willing to put up with your little things, she'll say yes."

"I'll love her no matter what," Hugh said. "What I don't get is why she cares about me."

Bessie shook her head. "If I could explain that, I'd be a billionaire in a huge mansion and you'd be having this conversation with one of my staff," she laughed. "Love isn't easy to explain or understand and there's little point in asking a spinster lady in her, um, late middle age to explain it."

"Doona's been married twice and divorced twice, Inspector Corkill's divorced, and I don't even think I want to know what's going on with Inspector Rockwell's marriage. Why should Grace and I be any different?" Hugh asked.

Bessie shrugged. "Do you want to be different? Are you ready to work hard? Because I've seen a lot of marriages, good, bad and indifferent ones, and the ones that work, they work because both people in the marriage work hard at it. It isn't usually the bad times or the good times that drive couples apart, either, it's the boring times in between when they start to forget how much they need each other and just start living their own lives. You and Grace are both young and you both have a lot to learn about life and about each other. But from what I've seen, I think you two have a better than average chance of making it as a couple in the long term. And that's more than I'd say to most couples these days."

Hugh stood up and gave Bessie a bear hug. He coughed a couple of times to clear his throat before he spoke. "Ah, thanks, I mean, I suppose, that is, ah, you know what I mean."

Bessie patted his arm. "You're welcome," she said.

A loud knock on the door announced the arrival of the rest of Bessie's guests.

CHAPTER 12

Bessie opened the door to let Doona in. She was followed by the two inspectors, each carrying a box full of containers of food.

"Nice to see you again, Inspector Corkill," Bessie said politely as the two men set their boxes on the counter.

"Nice to see you as well, Miss Cubbon," he replied formally.

"Please, do call me Bessie," she said as Doona and John began to unpack the boxes.

"Yes, well, you should call me Pete, then, at least when we're having dinner together."

Bessie grinned. "I'll try to remember," she told him.

The little group sat down to eat and Bessie kept the conversation light while they enjoyed the enormous feast the two senior policemen had brought. Bessie provided everyone with generous helpings of crumble when the food ran out, topping each with fresh custard.

"This is delicious," Hugh told Bessie. "Or rather, it was." He smiled at her as he scraped up the very last bite from his plate.

"It was good," Pete agreed. "I don't get homemade puddings very often."

Bessie smiled. "You're welcome here for pudding anytime," she told the man, wondering how his relationship with her friend Helen was going. She'd have to ring Helen and suggest that she do some baking, or better yet, maybe Helen and the inspector could do some baking together.

"As fun as this has been," Bessie said. "We have a lot to talk about."

"Before we go any further," Pete said, holding up a hand, "I think I need to make my position clear. I'm here because I know that Bessie knows the group of ladies involved and I also know that she's been instrumental in helping to solve various murders in the past. But this can't be a two-way street. Neither John nor I will be able to discuss anything that we've learned through our investigations. I hope that's clear."

Bessie nodded. "I don't want anyone in any trouble with the Chief Constable," she said. "What I want is to talk through the whole mess and see where we end up. I feel as if I've talked to just about everyone on the island about some part or other, but I can't seem to tie everything together."

"Motive, means and opportunity," Hugh said. "Those are always the key points, right?"

"For murder, sure," Bessie agreed. "But two of the women died in what could have been accidents. I'm afraid there's so much that's happened that it's muddying up the waters around the one case that we're certain was murder."

"So let's start with Nancy's death," Doona suggested. "I'll make some coffee. I need some, even if no one else does."

"Coffee sounds good," John told her. She smiled at him and then bustled around Bessie's kitchen for a short while, starting coffee and piling biscuits onto a plate.

"So, what do we know about motives for Nancy's death?" Hugh asked, a touch impatiently.

"From what I heard, she was dying anyway," Bessie said. "Why would anyone go to all the bother to kill her?"

"Unless she wasn't the intended victim," Hugh said. "We're back to the totally random nature of the first murder now. Maybe we should start with an easier one."

Bessie shook her head. "I can't help but think that Nancy's death is the most important one, somehow. If we assume she was the intended victim, though, I can't see any motive anywhere."

"What about her daughter?" Doona asked as she poured coffee into mugs. "Wasn't there something about Nancy changing her will?"

"That depends on who you ask," Bessie replied. "And I tried asking Doncan, but he wouldn't tell me anything. Of course, he shouldn't do, but I had to ask anyway."

Doona chuckled. "He's too good at his job. That man never gossips; I bet he doesn't even talk about clients with his wife."

"Anyway, aside from Nancy's daughter, Sarah, whose motive is questionable, I don't think there's anyone else who had any reason to kill Nancy," Bessie said with a sigh.

"What if the jam ladies told you the story the wrong way around?" Hugh asked. "What if Nancy had already made her will leaving everything to the jam ladies and now she was threatening to change it and leave it all to her kids? Maybe the jam ladies all got together and planned the poisoned jam so that they could get all of Nancy's money."

"It's possible," Doona said, excitedly. "And now, one of them is killing all of the others so she can get all of Nancy's money for herself."

"Except Nancy didn't have a ton of money," Bessie said. "And, as far as I know, all of the jam ladies are reasonably comfortable anyway. I don't think any of them need Nancy's money."

"If I had to pick a murderer out of the jam ladies, it would be Elinor," Doona said thoughtfully. "She's cold and calculating and I can see her scheming and plotting."

"What about opportunity, then? Agnes said the jam was already at the table when she arrived on Tynwald Day. Elinor didn't get there until later," Bessie reminded her friend.

"Maybe Elinor got there really early and left the jam and then snuck away, only to come back later and pretend she'd only just arrived," Doona said. "It would have been easy enough for her to give the poisoned jar to Nancy. If she did do it, she'd have marked the jar in some way. Knowing her, she passed out the jars to everyone and poor Nancy didn't have a chance."

"Where did she get the poison?" Bessie asked. "Do we know what poison was used?" She looked at John, who shook his head.

"We aren't releasing any details on that matter at the moment," Pete told her formally.

Bessie sighed. "I can't see Elinor killing anyone," she said with a catch in her voice. "I've known her forever, and while she isn't the friendliest person in the world, she was very close to the other jam ladies. I can't believe she'd do anything to hurt any of them."

"Even if they'd slept with her husband?" Doona demanded.

"We don't know that anyone slept with her husband," Bessie said with a sigh. "If she were going to get revenge for that, though, why wait this long? Her husband has been dead for twenty-some years. I can't see her suddenly feeling vengeful about what he got up to all those years ago."

"Maybe Agnes or Joan killed her and then had their accident," Hugh suggested.

"Agnes was Nancy's closest friend in the group," Bessie replied. "And she was devastated by Nancy's death. I won't even consider her as a possible murderer. As for Joan, well, I just don't see it."

Bessie shook her head. "This isn't helping," she complained. "I feel as if we're going around in circles and not getting anywhere. None of it makes sense."

"What about the jam?" Hugh asked. "Who could have made the jam? I mean, I know I couldn't, but could all the jam ladies make jam?"

Bessie nodded. "The only one that simply couldn't make good jam was Peggy Cannon, and she's been dead for years. But that doesn't really narrow things down all that much. Any woman on the island over the age of fifty could probably make jam if she needed to and anyone of any age who can follow a basic recipe could manage it. Jam making only sounds difficult; it's quite straightforward when you do it."

Hugh shook his head. "I'll take your word for it," he told Bessie.

"Grace has been teaching me cooking and baking, but I think jam making is beyond her talents."

"I shall have to have her around and teach her how," Bessie replied. "It can be great fun, done with friends, and homemade jam feels special every time you open the jar."

"And pretty much anyone at Tynwald Day could have dropped off the jam to the ladies' table," Doona mused. "At least anyone who got there nice and early."

"If they didn't care who got which jar, they didn't even need to stay," Bessie added.

"What about Agnes, then?" Hugh asked. "Do we know of anyone with a motive for killing Agnes?"

Bessie shook her head. "If anything, her case is worse than Nancy's. Agnes was more or less all alone in the world. I gather she's left her money to her nieces who live across, but from what I understand, they didn't know they were in line to inherit anything."

"So they could have a motive, but we've no evidence that they were on the island," Hugh said.

"I was told she had a weak heart," Bessie said. "Elinor was concerned that the shock of Nancy's death might kill her. Again, who kills someone who's dying anyway?"

"Someone who doesn't want to wait," John said quietly.

"But it could have been an accident," Doona said. "The *Isle of Man Times* report said that the police couldn't be sure whether the damage to the car's brake lines was accidental or intentional."

John and Pete exchanged glances. "A young constable in Douglas is on warning for leaking that information," Pete told them. "But yeah, the car was so old and there was so much wrong with it that the crime scene team couldn't be sure how or when the brake lines got damaged."

"In order to make it look accidental, though," Bessie speculated, "someone would have to know quite a bit about cars."

"Didn't you tell me that Elinor's husband worked with cars?" John asked her.

Bessie flushed. "He did, but that doesn't mean that Eliinor knows anything about them. Anyway, I can't see Elinor crawling under Agnes's car to tamper with brake lines."

Doona chuckled. "It's an interesting mental picture," she said. "But I'm with Bessie on this one. Elinor wouldn't get her hands dirty like that."

"So who would?" Pete asked quietly.

Bessie shrugged. "No one had any reason to kill Agnes. Of all the deaths, I think that one is most likely to have been an unfortunate accident. Does anyone know why she was on the mountain road that night?"

John shook his head. "If anyone does know why she was there, they haven't admitted it to us."

"So let's talk about Joan's death," Hugh suggested. "It could have been an accident, it could have been another random murder or it could have been targeted and well-planned by someone."

"Joan has a son," Bessie said. "Last I knew he was in gaol across, though. Even if he's out, I can't see why he'd want to kill his mother."

"Does he inherit her money?" Doona asked.

"I have no idea," Bessie replied. "I would think so, but I don't even know if he's still alive. Joan never spoke about him."

"He's alive," Pete said. "And he's still in gaol, but probably won't be for too much longer."

"Oh, dear, that doesn't sound good," Bessie said. "But if he's in gaol, he isn't over here rewiring kettles or poisoning jam."

"Could he have set it up to get his mother killed so that he could inherit?" Doona asked. "Or does that only happen on telly?"

"Anything's possible," Pete told her. "And you can be sure the police are pursuing every possible line of enquiry."

"How hard would it be to rewire a kettle?" Doona asked. "I mean to make it deadly but still look as if it could have been an accident?"

"Not that easy," Pete said. "The police are still examining what was left of the kettle, but whoever tampered with it, if it was indeed tampered with, knew what they were doing."

"Which should prove Elinor had nothing to do with it," Bessie said.

"I can't see her having any idea how to switch around wiring in a kettle."

"What about Margaret?" Doona asked suddenly. "We've been talking about Elinor, but Margaret must be just as much of a suspect, surely?"

"I'm pretty sure Margaret doesn't know anything about kettles either," Bessie replied. "Or cars, although she certainly can make jam."

"The three different methods confuse things," Hugh complained.

"Maybe we're seeing connections where there aren't any," Bessie said. "Or maybe at least one of the deaths was simply an accident and we're trying to tie them all together when it's impossible."

"Or maybe someone has a grudge against the whole group and they're picking them off, one by one," Doona suggested.

"But who?" Bessie demanded. "They're a bunch of older ladies who aren't doing anything interesting."

"What about Spencer Cannon? What's he doing back on the island?" Doona asked.

"You met him," Bessie replied. "Did he seem like a mass murderer with revenge on his mind?"

"Well, no," Doona admitted. "But he seems as likely as Elinor or Margaret or even Sarah whatshername, when it comes down to it."

"Sarah Combe," Bessie supplied.

"I suppose a man might know quite a bit about cars and kettles, though," Hugh suggested. "And maybe he got a friend to make the jam and then added the poison later."

"Or maybe he made the jam himself," Bessie said, giving Hugh a stern look.

"Oh, yes," Hugh said, flushing. "Maybe he made the jam himself."

"Did Spencer give you any reason to suspect that he has any resentment towards the jam ladies?" Pete asked.

"I don't think he liked them very much," Doona said, thoughtfully. "But it's a long way from vague dislike to multiple murders."

"I haven't seen any of you to tell you what Maggie Shimmin told me today," Bessie said as she suddenly remembered. "Apparently, one of Elizabeth Porter's grandsons is on the island at the moment."

John pulled out his notebook and looked at Bessie expectantly. "Go on," he said.

Bessie smiled. "The boy's name is Jason, and from what Maggie said, he's staying somewhere in Douglas. He told her he came over for Tynwald Day but skipped going to St. John's. He asked her if she was a jam lady, and then lost interest in talking to her when she said she wasn't."

Pete Corkill had perked up when Bessie mentioned Douglas and now he and John exchanged looks. "You take it," John said, nodding at his colleague.

"I'll let you know if anything comes of it," Pete said as he noted the details in his own small notebook.

"I suppose you won't let me know, though, will you?" Bessie asked.

Pete shook his head. "Once the murderer is safely behind bars, I'll answer any and all questions," he offered.

Bessie sighed. "Anyway, I can't see what sort of motive the boy could have. He's never even lived on the island or met the jam ladies."

"It's interesting timing, that's all," John told her.

"I suppose it is at that," Bessie said. "Anyway, tomorrow I'm having tea with Margaret for her birthday."

"I've cleared it with John so I can come along," Doona told her. "I'll pick you up."

"Can you stop at the bakery and pick up the cake as well?" Bessie asked. "I ordered it, and I was going to get it on my way to Margaret's."

"I can do that," Doona agreed. "Chocolate, I hope?"

"Indeed," Bessie smiled. "I got the feeling that Margaret's never had a birthday cake before."

"Let's hope it isn't her last," Hugh muttered darkly.

"Will Elinor be at this little party?" John asked her.

"No," Bessie replied. "In fact, Margaret specifically asked me not to mention it to Elinor if I spoke to her."

John frowned. "I thought they were all best friends," he said. "Surely Elinor will want to be there?"

"Margaret reckoned that Elinor doesn't even know it's her birthday," Bessie said sadly. "Apparently she and Elinor don't get along very well."

"Interesting," was John's response. He made a few notes in his notebook before putting it away.

"Have we worked out anything?" Hugh asked, sounding frustrated.

"I don't think so," Bessie said with a sigh. "We don't know if we have one murder or two or three. We don't know if one or two of them were random or targeted. It's all just a big jumbled mess."

"It seems to me that the jam ladies are at the centre of all of this," Hugh said. "And I talked to both Margaret Gelling and Elinor Lewis yesterday and neither one of them seemed especially scared of being next."

"Which is strange," Doona added. "Because it seems to me, from the phone calls we've been getting at the station, that half of the good citizens of Laxey are worried about being next."

"Perhaps they're just resigned to their fate," Bessie said. "I think Margaret has been afraid of everything for most of her life. Maybe she's just beyond caring."

"And maybe Elinor Lewis knows exactly what's going on," Hugh suggested.

Bessie sighed. "I know Elinor seems the most likely candidate in some ways, but she hasn't any real motive and I can't see her climbing under Agnes's car or rewiring a kettle."

"We're keeping a close eye on both of the remaining jam ladies," Pete told her.

"I'd really rather you stayed away from them," John added.

"I can't miss Margaret's birthday tea tomorrow," Bessie told him firmly. "She doesn't have anyone else to celebrate with and she deserves a celebration."

"I'll be going with her," Doona pointed out. "And Elinor won't be there."

"Not that I have anything to fear from Elinor," Bessie said. "I'm sure there's something or someone we're missing here."

"Maybe Margaret will have some ideas when you see her tomorrow," Pete said. "Maybe she knows of someone who dislikes the ladies or, perhaps, just dislikes some of them."

"That's a point," Bessie said. "Just because the three victims were all jam ladies, doesn't mean someone is trying to kill them all. Maybe there was something that connects Nancy and Agnes and Joan, but not the others."

"There are lots of possibilities," John said. "That's what worries me."

Bessie stood up. "Does anyone want more coffee or biscuits?" she asked.

"I wouldn't mind another cup," Doona said. "But you sit down and I'll make it."

"No, I need to stretch my legs," Bessie told her. She refilled the coffee maker and switched it on, and then she refilled the plate of biscuits.

"I know I've been caught up in several other murders lately," she commented. "But this one feels much more personal. I suppose all of the others involved folks from across that just happened to bring their problems with them. This one is local in every way."

"Moirrey Teare was local," Doona pointed out.

"She was, but her killer wasn't," Bessie replied. "And maybe the killer this time isn't local either."

"Like Spencer Cannon or Jason Porter?" Doona asked.

"Or someone we don't know anything about," Bessie said.

"Murder tends to be very personal," Pete told them. "There are always exceptions, but this feels personal. Poisoning someone's jam, especially when they belong to a group that is known for making jam? That's very close to home."

Bessie shivered. She stared at the coffee machine, watching the dark fluid drip slowly into the pot. The sound reminded her of a heartbeat and she felt sadder than she had in a very long time.

The conversation was stilted and awkward as everyone sipped more coffee and nibbled on biscuits.

"I feel as if you all think Elinor is the murderer," Bessie said finally.

"I don't think any such thing," Pete told her. "I think she's a possibility, but I also think there are others options that need investigating."

"If I seriously thought Mrs. Lewis did it, I'd have her at the station right now," John said. "I have my suspicions about her, but I can't prove anything and there are too many holes in my theory at the moment."

"I think she did it," Hugh said. "But I don't like her very much. She used to frighten me when I was a kid."

"I bet she still scares you," Doona teased.

"Maybe, a little bit," Hugh replied. "She's very unfriendly."

"She's had a difficult life," Bessie said quietly.

"Her son was scary, too," Hugh said. "She used to have him on the beach all the time and he used to want to make sandcastles with me. Whenever I did something he didn't like, he'd smash the whole thing. My mother used to try to explain to me why this big adult man was acting like a small child, but I didn't understand, of course."

"Like I said, Elinor has had a difficult life," Bessie repeated herself.

"I think we'd better call it a night," John said tiredly. "We have a few new leads to chase tomorrow and more ground to go back over as well."

"Thank you for your hospitality," Pete said as he stood up. "I enjoyed going over things with you. You've given me some different insights."

Bessie nodded. "It was nice of you to come," she said. "If I hear anything interesting tomorrow, I'll let you know."

"Thanks."

The two inspectors left and while Bessie was showing them out, Hugh and Doona got busy with the washing up.

"Thank you," Bessie said as she sank back down at the table. "I'm feeling quite worn out."

"Why don't you go up to bed?" Doona asked. "Hugh and I will finish here and then I'll be up in a little while."

"Actually," Bessie replied. "I think I'll take a short walk on the beach. I won't go far," she added when she saw the look on Doona's face. "I just need some fresh air to blow away a few cobwebs before I try to sleep."

Doona looked as if she might argue, but Bessie didn't give her a chance. "I'll be back in twenty minutes or so," she told her friend. "You probably won't even have the kitchen tidied by then."

Bessie went out the back door and walked down to the water's edge. She slipped off her shoes and touched the water with a tentative toe. The water was cold, but the sensation was welcome. She took a few steps into the sea, reveling in how alive the cold water splashing against her made her feel.

Turning away from her cottage, she began a slow stroll down the sand, leaving one foot in the sea and the other on the warmer sand. It was quite dark, but the moon was out and it gave enough light for Bessie to navigate by.

She walked slowly, thinking about the Raspberry Jam Ladies and everything that had happened since Tynwald Day. If she'd been expecting any great revelations, however, she was hugely disappointed. The fresh sea air helped to calm her spirit, however, and when she turned back towards home she was feeling slightly better for no real reason.

As she approached her cottage, she could just make out a figure sitting on the large rock behind her home. As she got closer, she recognised Doona, sitting alone watching the sea.

"Did you finish cleaning the kitchen, then?" she asked her friend when she arrived by Doona's side.

"We did, and I've sent Hugh home," Doona told her. "Do you feel any better?"

Bessie sat down on the rock next to Doona and joined her in watching the sea. "I don't know," she said eventually. "I'm really struggling with the idea that Elinor could possibly be behind all of this. It doesn't seem possible, but it seems likely at the same time."

"I'm sorry," Doona told her friend. "I wish I could say or do something that would make this all easier for you."

"Life isn't easy," Bessie told her. "But good friends are a big help. I'm just grateful that you're here."

The pair went back in the house and they both headed for bed.

"I'll see you in the morning," Doona said, hugging Bessie tightly. "Sleep well."

Bessie replied in kind before heading into her room. Now she lay in her bed, feeling wide-awake. She picked up the book she was halfway through reading and tried to lose herself in it. After several minutes she gave up. It was probably an excellent book, but she just wasn't in the mood. She turned off her light and tossed and turned for several minutes, seeking a comfortable position that would let her rest.

Exasperated, she pushed back the covers and got back out of bed. Back in the kitchen, she made herself a cup of milky tea as quietly as she possibly could. She sipped it in the dark while watching the sea through the window on the kitchen's back wall. Back in bed, she fell asleep quite quickly, but she had a restless night filled with bad dreams and long spells of sleeplessness.

CHAPTER 13

Bessie woke up at ten to six feeling groggy and miserable. She sat up in bed and looked out at a rainy, grey morning. For a moment she was tempted to simply hide under the duvet for the rest of the day, but as that wasn't an option, she slowly got herself out of bed.

The shower helped, at least a little bit, and she spent extra time patting on the rose-scented dusting powder that reminded her of Matthew. In spite of how painful his loss had been, the morning ritual always seemed to calm her and help settle her mind. She had lived through that loss and nothing else in her life would ever feel as traumatic.

Tea and toast helped her to feel even better and her morning walk, in raincoat and Wellington boots, carrying an umbrella, seemed to blow away the last remnants of her ugly mood. She returned to her cottage with her equilibrium mostly restored.

Doona was up and had set a pot of coffee going. Bessie poured herself a cup and smiled at her friend.

"I'm going to make my usual trip into Ramsey this morning and try to find an appropriate present for Margaret. Any suggestions?" she asked.

Doona shook her head. "I have no idea what women of a certain age like for their birthdays," she told Bessie. "You must have some ideas."

Bessie shrugged. "Not really. I don't really know Margaret all that well. I suppose I'll get her some bath salts or something like that. Maybe a box of chocolates as well."

"Everyone loves chocolates," Doona agreed.

Once Doona had left for work, Bessie tidied up a little bit and then got ready to go out. Dave arrived at the appointed time.

"I'll need picking up at the bookshop, not ShopFast," she told him as they went. "I did my grocery shopping yesterday. Today I'm gift shopping."

"You're the boss," Dave said cheerfully. "At the usual time or do you need to change that as well?"

"The usual time will do," Bessie said. "I can always spend some extra time looking at books if I finish early."

With the arrangements in place, Bessie climbed out of the taxi and made her way into the bookshop. She spent a long time looking around the section marked "Gift Books," but nothing struck her as a appropriate gift for Margaret. She didn't want to buy anything that might look extravagant to the shy woman on a limited income, but she wanted to give the woman something special.

Bessie wandered away from the bookshop down Ramsey's main shopping street. She saw many things she was tempted to buy, but they were all for herself rather than her friend. Shaking her head at herself as she studied an especially attractive pair of shoes, she turned resolutely towards a small boutique that might just have the perfect present.

An hour later she emerged with what the assistant had called a "custom gift basket." The large woven basket had been stuffed full of bath salts, scented powder, and candles on one end. The other end was filled with specialty chocolates, luxurious biscuits and a bottle of wine. The whole thing was filled with tissue paper and then enclosed in a clear plastic wrapper tied up with ribbons and a huge bow.

The package was unwieldy, but attractive, and Bessie was certain that Margaret would be thrilled by the numerous small luxuries. Bessie made her way back to the bookshop and was relieved to find Dave waiting for her. She didn't fancy standing around holding the heavy basket.

"What have you got there?" Dave asked as he jumped from the taxi. He took the basket from her and put it carefully in the boot.

"It's a gift basket," Bessie explained. "Full of all sort of the little specialty things that most women love."

"Really?" Dave asked. "Where did it come from? I might have to give them a try for my mother-in-law for Christmas. She's impossible to buy for."

Bessie laughed. She had a passing acquaintance with Dave's mother-in-law and she often wondered how he managed to deal with the demanding and critical woman. "I'm sure she'd love something from there," Bessie told him. "Although she'd never admit to it."

Dave laughed. A few moments later he dropped her off at home, insisting on carrying the basket into the house for her. "I hope your friend appreciates the gift," he told Bessie.

"I'm sure she will," Bessie replied.

She made herself a light lunch and then went up to her bedroom to look for just the right outfit for the afternoon tea party.

By the time Doona arrived, Bessie had tried on and rejected half a dozen outfits. For some reason, this party felt important to Bessie and she wanted to be sure she picked something that would reflect the significance of the occasion.

Doona was right on time and she was still dressed for work in a dark suit that Bessie felt was just about right. She herself had decided on a summery dress in a light shade of blue that reminded Bessie of the summer sky. A pair of low heels and a matching handbag finished her look. Bessie even took the time to put on a little bit of makeup, an effort she rarely made.

"You look lovely," Doona told her as she studied Bessie's outfit. "I don't think I've ever seen you so dressed up."

"Today's important for Margaret," Bessie said, trying to put into words how she was feeling about the day. "She deserves a very special day. She's had a difficult life."

"It's sad that her children won't be here to celebrate with her," Doona said as they climbed into the car, after Doona had carefully put the gift basket next to the cake box in her boot.

"It is," Bessie agreed. "But that's between her and her children. We can only do our best to make her happy."

Margaret lived near the others in a small two-storey house that looked tired to Bessie. They climbed a couple of stairs to the front door, with Doona carrying the basket and Bessie carrying the cake. Doona knocked. After a few minutes, the door opened slowly.

"Ah, Bessie, you came," Margaret sounded both pleased and surprised. "And you brought your young friend as well."

Margaret let them in and Bessie glanced around as she followed Margaret down the short hall. There was a tiny formal sitting room that was nearly empty of furniture and looked immaculately clean. Next came an equally clean dining room with a small table with two chairs on either side of it. They stopped in the kitchen, which was still original from when the house had been built in the forties.

Bessie set the cake down on the small counter and then gave Margaret a hug. "This is for you," she told the woman, gesturing to the basket that Doona was still holding. "Happy birthday."

Margaret flushed and then shook her head. "Oh, no, you shouldn't have. I mean, I didn't invite you because I expected you to bring presents. I can't possibly accept."

"Of course you can," Bessie said with a laugh. "It's been put together especially for you."

Margaret looked as if she wanted to argue further, but then it seemed curiosity got the better of her. She peeked into the basket.

"Oh, my goodness," she said as she studied the contents. "Bath salts and candles and chocolate and wine and, oh, my goodness, but I can't." She burst into tears.

Doona, still holding the basket, looked helplessly at Bessie, who pulled Margaret into a hug. "There, there," she said soothingly. "I just thought you deserved a small treat, that's all. It isn't much and I certainly didn't mean to make you cry."

It was several minutes before Margaret could speak. Doona eventually found a small space where she could put the basket down and then she found a tissue box and handed several to the sobbing woman.

"I am sorry," Margaret said once she'd stopped crying. "I never, that is, crying, I just don't, oh, dear."

"It's fine," Bessie assured her. "It's been a very difficult time lately, hasn't it?"

"It has," Margaret agreed. "And I don't know that it's going to get any better, at least not soon."

"Why ever not?" Bessie asked.

Margaret glanced at Doona and then looked back at Bessie. "The police seem to think I've had something to do with all these sudden deaths," she whispered. "As if I would want anything bad to happen to anyone."

"I'm sure the police don't suspect you," Bessie said soothingly. "They just have to question everyone that might know anything, that's all. Three sudden deaths from a very small group of people looks strange, even if some of the deaths were accidental."

Margaret nodded, but looked unconvinced. "Anyway, let's not talk about sad things," she said. "I want today to be a happy day."

"I hope it is," Bessie told her.

"Me, too," Doona added.

"So let's have some tea and scones," Margaret suggested. "I've everything all ready."

Bessie and Doona sat down at the tiny kitchen table while Margaret began to set out the food.

"We could eat in the dining room," she said. "But this is so much friendlier."

"This is lovely," Bessie assured her. "Dining rooms are too formal for birthday parties."

Margaret giggled. "I'm seventy-four and I'm having my very first ever birthday party," she told them. "It's silly."

"Surely your husband made a fuss on your birthday when your children were small," Doona said.

Margaret flushed and pressed her lips together for a moment before she replied. "Jonathan didn't think birthdays were for celebrating," she replied. "He didn't like to make a fuss over me, or the children for that matter."

"What a shame," Bessie said. "Didn't the Raspberry Jam Ladies celebrate birthdays?"

Margaret shook her head. "Elinor didn't feel they were something to celebrate, either. Well, she always made a huge fuss over Nathan's, but his was special, you see. We were adults and we weren't meant to care about such things."

"Didn't any of you do anything for one another?" Doona pressed the point.

"Oh, no, such things were against the bylaws," Margaret answered.

"Bylaws?" Doona asked.

Margaret flushed. "Here, there's tea and scones and everything."

Bessie and Doona joined her at the counter and filled plates from the bounty that Margaret had laid out.

"Everything looks delicious," Bessie said as she selected from scones, biscuits and finger sandwiches.

"You must have spent hours getting all of this ready," Doona said.

Margaret shrugged. "It's not a big deal," she said shyly.

The trio sat down with their food and Margaret poured the tea. They ate silently for a few minutes before Doona picked the conversation back up where it had left off.

"I'm sorry, but did you say something about bylaws?" she asked their hostess.

Margaret looked down at her plate and then chuckled. "It's silly, really. And I can't believe I'm hesitant to tell you as there's only me and Elinor left to care, but we always tried to keep everything that happened in the group private."

"As you say, though, it hardly matters now," Bessie told her.

"Indeed," Margaret smiled. "Yes, we had bylaws. You can probably imagine who drew them up."

"Elinor," both Bessie and Doona said at the same time.

Margaret laughed. "Yes, well, it's sad, really. She's such a clever woman and from what I've heard she was an excellent teacher, and then she met Nicholas. I don't know if you remember him, Bessie, but he was altogether wrong for Elinor. Unfortunately, by the time she realised that, they were married and it was too late."

"What was wrong with him?" Doona asked.

"Oh, he was charming and he certainly swept Elinor off her feet, but then he was very fond of that sort of thing. Elinor was probably the first woman to make him work hard for her affections, which made him determined to get her. Once he married her, he lost interest, of course, but then Nathan came along and she didn't much care what Nicholas got up to, anyway."

"What did he get up to?" Doona wondered.

"Oh, mostly he just flirted, but he was particularly cruel about it. He would deliberately flirt with Elinor's friends. I think he resented the fact that he'd worked so hard to win Elinor's heart and then she turned out to be merely human after all," Margaret replied.

"What a creep," Doona said, shaking her head. "Poor Elinor."

"Did he actually have affairs as well?" Bessie asked.

Margaret shrugged. "There were all sorts of rumours and I've no doubt that Elinor believed them, but I don't know anything for sure. I can't imagine Elinor minded if he did, though. She was only interested in Nathan."

"Presumably she was interested in the jam ladies as well, if she wrote bylaws for you," Doona suggested.

Margaret laughed. "Well, yes, I mean at least a little bit. Elinor loved organising all of us. My goodness, we had rotas for just about everything, from whose turn it was to buy biscuits to who was hosting the next play-date for the children. We weren't supposed to meet up with one another outside of the group and we were never ever to buy presents for one another for any occasion."

"Why on earth not?" Doona demanded.

"Fairness and equality were of the utmost importance. If I bought a little something for, say, Agnes, then all of the other women might feel left out. And Agnes might feel as if she had to reciprocate and maybe she couldn't afford to do so. Times were tough in those days, of course, and finances were a real concern for all of us, so the rules made sense, even if they were a bit strict," Margaret explained.

"And you never celebrated your birthdays," Bessie said sadly.

"No, although we all went out to dinner as a group the year the last one of us turned forty. After a couple of bottles of wine, though, a few things were said that shouldn't have been and we never repeated the experience."

"I can't believe you had bylaws," Doona said, shaking her head.

"We had bylaws and lists of rules and rotas for everything. We were all expected to take turns hosting everyone's children for many years, but that started to get difficult after a while," Margaret said, her expression thoughtful. "Young Nathan was quite a challenging child and he could be cruel when he didn't get his way. After a while some of us got together and told Elinor that we didn't want to keep having all of the children at once."

"I bet that didn't go over well," Doona said dryly.

"No, Elinor was very upset. Thinking back, I think his afternoons with the other jam ladies may have been the only break she really got from Nathan. And she really needed time away from him. He was very demanding. But my priority at the time was my own children and I wouldn't have Nathan making them miserable week after week."

"I never realised the group was so well organised," Bessie said. "You always just seemed like a group of good friends."

Margaret laughed. "And we were never that," she replied. "Peggy hated Joan, Elinor and I never got along, no one approved of how Nancy raised her kids. Oh, goodness, the list is endless. The only reason we stuck it out as long as we did is because Elinor wouldn't let anyone leave."

"What do you mean, she wouldn't let you leave?" Bessie asked.

"Oh, it wasn't anything formal. Elinor's too clever for that. But if you missed a meeting or two, she'd come over 'to check on you' and tell you how worried everyone was about you. It was subtle pressure, but the pressure was always there to make it to every meeting and be a good little group member."

"Emotional blackmail," Doona muttered.

"Remember that in the fifties and sixties life was very different," Margaret continued. "Once you got married, you were married for life, no matter how bad things were. The other women were a lifeline in a way, even if I didn't like all of them. Most of our husbands worked long hours and some of them travelled as well. There we all were, struggling to raise small children in a tiny village. As much as we grumbled about one another, at least we had each other."

"And the Raspberry Jam Ladies outlasted all of your marriages," Bessie pointed out.

"I hadn't thought of that, but you're right, of course," Margaret chuckled. "Of course, we also could never quit because we were always somewhere on some rota for something. I actually did plan to quit once, but it was my month for bringing biscuits. Once that month was over, it was my turn to have the kids for an afternoon. After that, Joan's little one got sick and we all rallied around her." Margaret shook her head. "So I just kept going along. All of us did."

She got up to clear away the dishes and Doona jumped up to help. They quickly cleared everything and then Doona brought over the cake box and opened it carefully. She slid the cake out of the box and set it in the middle of the table.

"Oh, you've had them write on it and everything," Margaret exclaimed when she looked at it. Her eyes filled with tears again. "'Happy Birthday, Margaret,' she read off the top of the cake. "I've never seen that on a cake before, well, not on one for me, anyway."

Bessie and Doona exchanged looks. "Never mind," Bessie told her. "It's pretty but it will taste better than it looks."

"Oh, but can I take a picture before we cut into it?" Margaret asked.

"Of course you can," Bessie told her.

Margaret rushed out and Bessie could hear her climbing up the creaky stairs. She was back a few minutes later, clutching an old camera. "I hope this still works," she said. "It's ever so old."

After she'd taken several photos, the others insisted that she be the one to cut into the cake. Margaret cut very generous slices, carefully putting them onto fancy china plates that she insisted were just right for a party.

"I never use them," she told Bessie and Doona. "They were a wedding present from my mother-in-law and I've been saving them for something special ever since." She shook her head. "What a waste. I should have used them every day and if they got broken or damaged, too bad. Life's too short to save things for special. Every day is special."

The cake was delicious and very much enjoyed. Bessie and Doona insisted on taking care of the washing up, while Margaret spent a few minutes looking through the goodies in her basket.

"My goodness, I think I shall have truffles and biscuits instead of dinner tonight," she announced as she studied each small container. "I can soak in the bath with them and have a glass of wine and then have another piece of cake for pudding."

"That sounds like the perfect evening to me," Doona told her.

With the kitchen tidied and the rest of the cake back in its box, Bessie sat down next to Margaret.

"I know everything that's happened has been upsetting," she began. "But do you have any idea what's going on?"

"You mean everyone dying?" Margaret asked.

"Yes, I mean everyone dying," Bessie answered patiently.

"Well, we all have to die sometime," Margaret said with a shrug. "After the lovely time I've had today, I think I should be quite content to go any time now."

"But you don't want anyone to get away with murder," Doona suggested.

"I suppose," Margaret said. "But Joan and Agnes both had accidents, Elinor said so. Only poor Nancy was murdered and that was probably an accident in a way, too."

"In what way?" Bessie asked.

"Well, Elinor said that someone was probably trying to kill someone and poor Nancy got the wrong jar of jam." She glanced around and then leaned towards Bessie to whisper. "I think it was that Joe Robinson what did it. He had the booth next to ours and everyone knows he's having an affair with his wife's sister. I reckon he brought the jam and put it on our table while he was setting up and then Nancy and Agnes got there and found it and he was stuck."

"Do you think he was trying to kill his wife or her sister?" Doona asked.

"Maybe he didn't much care," Margaret shrugged. "Maybe he just wants rid of one or the other of them."

"It's an interesting theory," Doona said. "I hope you've passed it along to the police."

"Oh, no," Margaret said, looking surprised. "I'd hate to cause trouble for Mr. Robinson. He just lives down the street and he's ever so helpful. He cuts my grass for me all summer long and won't take a penny for it, either."

"If it wasn't him, who else might have poisoned the jam?" Bessie asked.

"Well," Margaret giggled. "I did tell Agnes that I reckoned it was one of us trying to finally get rid of Elinor after all our years of complaining about her."

"Really?" Doona asked. "Which one of you?"

"Oh, I couldn't say," Margaret replied. "It's in the bylaws. We aren't allowed to say anything critical of one another to anyone. Even if I knew who did it, I couldn't tell you or the police. The rules are very clear."

"You have rules that require you to shield murderers?" Doona asked incredulously.

"Well, they weren't designed for that, obviously, but Elinor wanted to make sure that we weren't gossiping about each other, so she made it a rule that we can't talk about one another, especially in a bad way."

"Surely she never intended it to extend to murder," Bessie said softly.

"Knowing Elinor, she considered it," Margaret replied. "There are rules for everything and I swear Elinor planned for every single thing that could ever happen." Again, she glanced around and then lowered her voice. "There are even rules for what to do if a third world war were to break out," she told the others.

Doona laughed, but Bessie nodded. "I'm sure that seemed like a real possibility in the aftermath of the Second World War," she said.

"Perhaps," Margaret said. "But I think Elinor just enjoyed sitting around planning for disasters. We had drills, too, you know."

"What sort of drills?" Doona asked.

"Emergency evacuation drills from wherever the group was meeting," Margaret replied. "We used to meet in the meeting room of the church and it was up a flight of stairs. Elinor used to have us practice climbing out the window in case of emergency."

"Oh, good heavens," Doona exclaimed. "That just isn't normal."

"She wanted us to be safe," Margaret said. "At least now we meet on the ground floor, so when we have our drills we just have to hobble outside and back again. I can't imagine going out a window now, at my age."

"Why didn't the group ever let in any new members?" Bessie asked. It was a question she'd wondered about for many years. She'd known more than one young mum in the area who'd wanted to find a similar group where she could make friends.

"We talked about it in the beginning," Margaret told her. "Especially when some of the others had more children and met more mums. Elinor didn't like the idea. She didn't want the group to get too big and unmanageable. We did have one or two mums come to a few meetings over the years, but none of them ever stayed for long. I think we all knew each other too well and the group was too, well, insular, for anyone else to feel welcome."

"I don't suppose any of the mums that only came once or twice are still around and harbouring resentment towards the group?" Doona asked.

"I shouldn't think so," Margaret answered. "I mean, it wasn't like we didn't let them in. They came for a few meetings and then just stopped coming. And we're talking about something that happened maybe forty years ago. I can't believe any of them even remember the group."

Just to be on the safe side, Doona got the few names of the women that Margaret could remember.

"As lovely as this has been," Bessie said, "we really should be getting out of your way. You've entertained us all afternoon."

"Yes, I suppose all good things must come to an end," Margaret said with a bright smile. "Once you've gone I'm going to start my bath and open my wine," she told them. "I really can't thank you enough for everything."

"It was nothing," Bessie told her. "I was happy to do it, and if I'd known how much it was going to mean to you, I'd have done it years ago."

"But then today wouldn't have been as special," Margaret told her. "I wouldn't want to change one thing about today."

She walked Bessie and Doona to the door, still talking about her bath and the lovely treats she'd enjoy in it. At the door, she stopped, staring out the small window next to it.

"Oh, no, Elinor is here," she said, her voice shaky. "I don't want to see her."

Bessie glanced out the window and saw Elinor making her way up the short path from the road to the door. She was carrying a brightly wrapped box.

"Can we hide?" Margaret asked, looking around the small hallway.

"I don't think so," Doona said.

Margaret opened her mouth, and then clamped it shut. "Never mind," she muttered.

When the knock on the door came, Margaret opened the door, a huge smile in place. "Elinor, what a lovely surprise," she said brightly.

"Margaret, happy birthday, my dear," Elinor said. She moved forward as if to enter the house and then stopped short, as Bessie and Doona left little room in the small foyer.

"Oh, I didn't realise you had guests," Elinor said, her tone chilly.

"Bessie and Doona found out it was my birthday and they brought me a cake," Margaret said gleefully. "And a present as well."

"Really?" Elinor asked coolly. "That was kind of them. I brought you a present as well, of course." She handed Margaret the box she was holding.

"You did? What a surprise," Margaret said, clearly somewhat flustered. "I mean, I never expected, that is, thank you," she stammered out.

"What sort of friend would I be if I didn't bring you a little something for your birthday?" Elinor asked. "Perhaps you could spare a small piece of birthday cake for your old friend? If there's any left."

"Oh, of course, there's plenty," Margaret said. "Do come in, that is, Bessie and her friend were just leaving."

"I don't want to chase them away," Elinor said.

"Oh, no, we have to be going," Bessie assured her. "Thank you again," she told Margaret. "It was lovely to see you, and happy birthday again, as well."

Margaret flushed. "Thank you so much for everything," she said, giving Bessie a big hug. "I wish, well, I wish we could have had a chance to be better friends all these years."

Bessie wasn't sure how to respond to that. Mindful that Elinor was listening closely, she replied carefully. "I enjoyed today. We should do it again soon."

"Yes, lets," Margaret said, smiling at Bessie. Margaret gave Doona a quick hug and then Bessie and Doona made their way back down the path to Doona's car. Neither spoke until they were well underway.

"That was weird," Doona said, breaking the silence.

"Which part?" Bessie asked, wryly.

"Every part," Doona said with a laugh. "But I really meant Eliinor showing up and with a present as well. I thought you said she didn't know it was Margaret's birthday?"

"Margaret told me that she didn't think Elinor knew. Apparently she did, though. It's strange that she brought her a present after Margaret said they never did such things"

"Maybe there are different rules when there are only two ladies left?" Doona suggested.

"Anything's possible with Elinor," Bessie said with a laugh. "Even though I don't think Elinor is the killer, I am a bit worried about what's in that box."

"Maybe I should ring John," Doona said. "What if it's a bomb?"

"I doubt very much that Elinor could make a bomb, even if she wanted to," Bessie said. "But I do think you should ring John, and I'm going to ring Margaret and ask her what Elinor gave her, as well."

Back at Bessie's cottage, Doona rang John. "He's going to send someone over to check on Margaret," she told Bessie once she'd disconnected. "He's sending one of the best female constables. Hopefully she'll be able to find out what was in the box."

Bessie waited an hour and then rang Margaret. "Just checking in on you, love," she said when Margaret answered.

"You and everyone else," Margaret laughed. "I'd only just chased Elinor away when a police constable turned up. She said she was checking in on me, but I still think the police think I had something to do with Nancy's death. Anyway, she's gone now and I was just getting ready to run my bath, finally."

"It was kind of Elinor to bring you a birthday present," Bessie said.

"Kind of strange, you mean," Margaret said with a laugh. "But as it was just a few old books that I'm sure she wanted to get rid of, I'm happy."

"Old books?"

"Oh, yes, Elinor is a great reader and she always used to share her books with the group once she'd read them. We had a book exchange for years, but Elinor used to get cross because she'd bring in dozens of books and the rest of us would bring one or two. Eventually she just started bringing in the books she'd finished, letting us all take what we wanted. We used to trade them as we finished them, as well."

"I see," Bessie said slowly.

"Anyway, at least now I have something to read while I take my bath," Margaret continued cheerfully. "I get awfully bored in the tub if I don't have a book or a magazine and it would be a shame to take a short bath with all the lovely bath salts in there."

"I hope you enjoy your evening, then," Bessie told her.

"I'm sure I will."

Bessie and Doona spent their evening going back over everything that was said at the birthday tea. When Bessie went to bed, she didn't feel as if they were any closer to finding out what was happening to the Raspberry Jam Ladies. She had another restless night, filled with old memories and unpleasant dreams.

CHAPTER 14

When Bessie woke up the next morning, she expected the weather to match her mood, grey and stormy, but when she pulled the curtains back, the sun was rising and the skies were clear. Hoping a walk in the sunshine would improve her mood, she took a quick shower and headed out, careful not to wake Doona. As ever, the sea air calmed her and she returned home feeling more at ease.

Doona was up and had started a pot of coffee. "I hope you don't mind," she told Bessie. "But I felt like coffee to start the day."

"I think I'll join you," Bessie replied. "I had a cup of tea before I went out, but I think I need a jolt of caffeine."

Bessie made toast while Doona dug a box of cereal out of the cupboard. They ate in a friendly silence, both lost in their own thoughts.

"So, what do you want to do today?" Doona asked as she started to run the washing-up water.

"I thought you had to go into work for a while," Bessie said.

"Not today, but maybe tomorrow," Doona replied. "They've added an extra constable from Douglas to the usual Saturday staff, so they should manage. Tomorrow is a different matter, though."

"I fancy a complete change," Bessie said after a moment's thought. "Let's head down to Castletown and have a walk around the castle or something. I haven't been down there for ages."

"Sounds good to me," Doona agreed. "Just let me get a shower and we'll get going."

Bessie curled up with a book, something else she'd hadn't been doing as much as usual, and lost herself in early American history. She didn't feel up to reading her usual murder mysteries today. She was just marveling over the incredible life of Aaron Burr, as he committed both murder and mayhem, when someone knocked on her door.

As soon as Bessie opened the door, she knew what John Rockwell was going to say. The look on his face spoke volumes.

"I'm going to guess it's Margaret," she said sadly.

"It is," John told her, his voice gentle. "I'm very sorry."

Bessie nodded and then invited the inspector in. She sank down at the kitchen table and breathed out slowly as her tears began to fall. Doona, wrapped in a bathrobe with her hair in a towel, came rushing down when John called up to her.

"Margaret? But she was fine yesterday," she said, staring at him as if the words made no sense.

Bessie wiped her eyes and hugged her friend. "What happened?" she asked John after a moment.

"She fell down her stairs and broke her neck," John replied.

Doona gasped.

"Was it an accident?" Bessie asked.

John shrugged. "It certainly looks as if it was an accident," he told her. "She'd had a couple of glasses of wine, and from what I've been told, that was unusual for her. There's no sign of anything that might have tripped her at the top of the stairs and no reason to believe that there was anyone else in the house with her, either."

"What does Elinor say?"

"She found the body," John replied. "She's obviously shaken up, but we've no reason to suppose she had anything to do with it, at least not at this point."

"So, another accident," Bessie said with a sigh. "Elinor is the only one left. I need to talk to her."

"I'd rather you stayed well away from her," John said. "She's the key to the whole puzzle, one way or another."

"She's not a murderer," Bessie said. "But she could be the next victim."

"She's in police custody at the station," John replied. "Although she's complaining bitterly about it."

Bessie nodded. "How long can you keep her there?" she asked.

"I don't know. We've suggested to her that she's safer in protective custody, but she doesn't agree. She wants to go home. I think we'll have to let her go this afternoon unless we come up with something to charge her with."

"If she isn't the killer, she must know who's behind all of this," Doona said.

"Well, she isn't telling us anything," John said tiredly.

"I want to talk to her," Bessie said. "Maybe I can persuade her to tell me something, at least."

"I'll tell her you'd like to see her," John said. "Maybe she'll ring you when we let her go. I want you to take Doona with you when you see her, though, and I want you to ring me just before you go in and as soon as you come out."

"Sure," Bessie agreed. Her mind was racing. Talking to Elinor was the only thing she could think to do.

"In the meantime, we've checked out the names you gave us from your talk with Margaret yesterday and they all come back clear, or as clear as we can tell from an initial check. But I have to tell you, the more we investigate, the more likely it seems that Elinor is behind what's happening."

"I know you think I'm being stubborn, and I know anyone can commit murder if driven to it, but this isn't like that at all. This is something different, I just don't understand what," Bessie said, feeling tears coming on again.

"I don't know what, either, but I intend to find out," John said, angrily.

When he'd gone, Doona looked at Bessie. "Do you still want to go down south?" she asked.

Bessie shook her head. "I just want to sit here and wait for Elinor to ring," she told her. "I think she will. I'm sure she needs to talk to someone. No matter what she felt about Margaret, her death must be a shock."

"Unless she killed her," Doona muttered.

Bessie didn't have long to wait. Elinor rang only a short time later.

"Bessie? I understand you'd like to see me," she said when Bessie answered.

"I'm so sorry about Margaret," Bessie began. "I'd like to have a chance to express my sympathies in person."

"That suits me, as I'd like to see you as well. I'm still at the police station, but I expect to be home this afternoon. How about two o'clock?"

"I can do that," Bessie said.

"And before you ask, of course you may bring your friend Mrs. Moore. I assume her job is to protect you," Elinor laughed. "I'm either a serial killer or a serial killer's next victim, surely? I must be the most dangerous person in all of Laxey."

"I'd like to bring Doona," Bessie told her. "But not for protection. She's a good friend and it helps to have friends around in difficult times."

"As it seems all of my friends are dead, I'll just have to take your word for that," Elinor said, laughing again.

Bessie put down the phone and frowned at Doona. "I think she's losing her mind," she said slowly.

"I suppose that isn't surprising under the circumstances," Doona replied.

The rest of the morning dragged for Bessie. She tried reading a dozen different books, but nothing could hold her interest. Doona insisted that they go out for lunch, more to kill time than to avoid cooking. They went to the closest chippy and ate their food sitting on a bench, watching the sea.

"I'm not very hungry," Bessie said, picking at her chips.

"Margaret's death is very sad," Doona said.

"I feel as if I should have had her come and stay with me or something," Bessie said. "Maybe I could have saved her life."

"You can't start thinking like that," Doona told her. "You'll make yourself crazy. She didn't seem worried when we saw her yesterday. And at least we gave her a happy birthday."

Bessie didn't argue. She had a sick feeling in the pit of her stomach and she really didn't want to go and talk to Elinor. The more she thought about everything that had happened, the more likely it seemed that Elinor had murdered all of her friends. If she was planning to confess to Bessie, Bessie didn't want to hear it.

The modern building where Elinor lived looked nothing like the little forties bungalow she had shared with her son for so many years. Bessie studied the blocky building that was full of flats as Doona parked.

"It's pretty ugly," she commented.

"But they'll all have sea views," Doona pointed out. "If you can watch the sea all day, who cares what the outside of the building looks like?"

Elinor was on the second floor, and the lift took them up quickly and quietly. Bessie checked the numbers as they walked down the carpeted hall.

"It feels like a hotel," she said.

"Is that a good thing or a bad thing?" Doona asked.

"I'm not sure," Bessie answered.

Outside Elinor's flat, Bessie took a deep breath before she knocked. The door opened quickly and Elinor gave them a strange smile.

"Ah, there you are," she said. "Do come in."

The inside of the flat felt clean and cold. Bessie and Doona followed Elinor slowly down the short corridor that had a couple of doors leading off it, and into a large reception room with windows that looked out over the beach.

"What a wonderful view," Bessie said.

"It is nice," Elinor agreed. "Although I usually forget to look at it. Anyway, please sit down."

Bessie sat on a long couch that was angled towards the windows. Doona joined her and Elinor perched on a chair next to Bessie's end of the couch.

"I'd offer you tea, but I suspect you wouldn't want to drink it, would you?" Elinor asked.

"We just had lunch," Bessie told her. "I couldn't possibly manage even a cup of tea right now."

Elinor laughed. "Very politely done," she told Bessie. "But really, I'm sure by now you all think I killed my friends." She sighed deeply. "I planned this conversation in my head a million times. It was always going to happen, you know, but it wasn't supposed to happen just like this."

"If you're going to confess to anything, I have to remind you that I work for the Isle of Man Constabulary," Doona interrupted. "I shall have to report everything you say to the police."

"My dear girl, I'm counting on that," Elinor told her. "And now I'm going to do something I rarely do. I'm going to ask you to indulge me for a moment. I want to start this story at the beginning, if I may."

"Elinor, I don't really want to hear this," Bessie said. "We can get the police and get you someone to talk who can help."

Elinor laughed lightly. "My dear Bessie, you really do want to hear this, I can assure you. I didn't kill all of my friends, and you need to understand the whole story so you can tell the police. I would hate for anyone to misunderstand what happened."

"Go ahead, then, tell your story; however you like," Bessie said grudgingly. She looked out at the sea, wishing she were walking on the beach, far away from what she was about to hear.

"Did you know that Margaret and I went to school together?" Elinor asked.

"No," Bessie said. "You didn't grow up in Laxey."

"No, we didn't. We grew up in Ramsey and were friendly, if not exactly friends, when we were children. I went away and did teacher training, of course, and then came back and started teaching in Laxey.

I ran into Margaret one day in a shop and she invited me to lunch so that I could meet her boyfriend. She was so happy. She was sure he was about to propose." Elinor stopped and shook her head.

"I hated her, you know," she said conversationally. "My dear Mrs. Moore, would you be so good as to get me a glass of water?"

Doona jumped up and headed into the small kitchen that was open to the rest of the room in one corner. The cupboards had glass fronts, so she was able to find a glass quickly and fill it from the tap. She handed it to Elinor, who thanked her.

"I expect I'll need to keep drinking so that I can keep talking," Elinor said after she'd taken a sip. "I've ever so much to tell you."

"You were telling us why you hated Margaret," Bessie reminded her.

"Oh, yes," Elinor smirked. "That fateful lunch, that awful day, I remember it like yesterday. We met at Margaret's mother's house, just me and Margaret and her boyfriend, and my life was ruined."

She looked from Bessie to Doona and back again. "I'm sure you can guess where the story is going? No? Margaret's wonderful boyfriend, the man she thought she was going to marry, was Nicholas Lewis."

Bessie nodded; it was obvious, now that Elinor had said it.

"For whatever reason, he decided that he wanted me instead of Margaret. There were ugly scenes and Margaret and I didn't speak for a time, but I didn't care. Nicholas swept me off my feet. I'd never gone out with a man. I'd been focussed on having a career, and suddenly the only thing that mattered was being with Nicholas." She laughed bitterly.

"Once he'd married me, he lost interest, of course, but my life was over by that time." She shook her head. "I got my revenge by introducing Margaret to Jonathan. He was a nasty, horrid little man and he made Margaret's life miserable for many, many years, which went some way towards making up for the mess she made of my life."

Doona made a disgusted sound, but Bessie caught her eye and shook her head. Now was not the time to argue with Elinor. The woman was clearly insane and they needed to humour her and see what else she had to say.

"Did Margaret know that you disliked her?" Bessie asked.

"Oh, no, I was too clever to let her know. She thought we were all the best of friends, all of the Raspberry Jam Ladies, always there for each other, always supporting one another." Elinor shook her head. "It wasn't just Margaret and I that didn't get along, of course. There were all sorts of disagreements in the group. But it didn't matter as long as the group kept going strong."

"And you made sure of that," Bessie said.

"I did," Elinor laughed. "The group was all I had, really. My marriage was pretty much over within months of the ceremony. I was actually planning to leave after the first year. I had my bags packed and a plan in place. It was all arranged."

"What happened?" Doona asked.

"I found out I was pregnant, of course," Elinor replied. "And when I headed off to see the midwife for the first time, guess who I found there. Margaret, of course, all glowing and excited to be expecting her first child. I almost slapped her."

"And that's where the jam ladies began?" Doona asked.

"Exactly. Margaret was further along than I was, so she was already friends with the others when I started going. Once I joined in, we started getting organised and it just grew from there. It was hard for those months, though, as they were all so excited about their babies and all I could think was how much I hated my baby's father."

Doona's eyes flashed, but Bessie patted her arm. "How difficult for you," Bessie murmured, hiding her own feelings.

"It was better when Nathan arrived. In spite of everything, I actually came to love him. He was a gorgeous baby," Elinor said. "Wait, I'll show you." She walked slowly out of the room, leaving Bessie and Doona to talk in hurried whispers.

"She's crazy. We need to ring John and get out of here," Doona hissed.

"We need to hear her out," Bessie argued. "This could be our only chance to hear her side of the story. It isn't like she going to suddenly pull out a knife or anything."

"But she's…."

"Now, now, no talking behind my back," Elinor said with a chuckle. "I'm sure you think I'm insane, but I'm not, really, and I'm not even the littlest bit dangerous. Anyway, look at this."

She held up an old black-and-white studio photograph of an infant. He was looking solemnly at the camera, a small cuddly toy clutched in his hand.

"He's gorgeous," Bessie said.

"He really was," Elinor replied. She put the photo down on the coffee table next to a small closed box that was already there and sat back down. After a sip of water, she sighed.

"But where was I? Oh, yes, Nathan was a gorgeous baby and the jam ladies were meeting regularly and I was pretty much resigned to being stuck in my miserable marriage forever. Nicholas was cheating on me, of course, but I had Nathan, so I didn't much care what Nicholas was doing. But slowly, over time, it became apparent that Nathan was, well, different. He didn't meet his milestones like he should have. I didn't say anything to Nicholas for the longest time. It wasn't until the doctors told me that we should consider sending Nathan away that I finally told Nicholas what was going on." Elinor shuddered and then took a deep breath.

"He wanted to send Nathan away, of course. He said it would be best for all of us. Of course, I refused. Not long after that, Nicholas took a job in the UK. That was certainly best for all of us. I suppose those were the happiest years of my life, really, when Nathan was small and Nicholas was gone. If I had to be stuck in time somewhere, that's where I'd go, back to those days."

She stopped for another drink of water, her eyes unfocussed as she looked out towards the sea. Bessie and Doona exchanged glances.

"So what went wrong?" Doona asked after a moment.

"Pardon?" Elinor shook her head. "I'm sorry, I was lost in the past. What went wrong? We all got older, of course. I didn't mind. While all the other ladies complained about their children and their grandchildren, I still had my Nathan. He was gentle and kind and he could just about look after himself for a few hours once in a while so I could get to the jam ladies' meetings or do the shopping. I never thought anything would change, and then one day, it did."

Elinor's eyes filled with tears. Bessie spotted a box of tissues on a side table and quickly brought them to Elinor. She took one and pressed it to her eyes.

"Thank you," she said eventually. "I keep thinking that I've run out of tears for my poor Nathan, but they never seem to stop."

"I'm sorry," Bessie said, patting Elinor's hand. "I can't imagine what you've been through."

Elinor looked up at her, her eyes shiny with unshed tears. "My life ended," she said softly. "That day, when I got home and Nathan wasn't there to greet me, my life ended. I found him in the bath. He'd slipped and hit his head and drowned. That was when I decided I wanted to die."

Doona gasped, but Elinor didn't seem to notice.

"For the longest time, I just kept going out of habit," she continued. "I sold the house immediately. I couldn't even go back inside. The other jam ladies rallied around and packed all my things for me. It was six or seven months before I finally started thinking again. And that's when I decided to kill myself."

Bessie patted her hand again. "You should have rung someone," she said. "There are people that can help you."

Elinor shook her head. "I don't want help," she said. "I simply want to die. I've nothing left to live for. Nathan was all I had and he's gone. It's not a great tragedy or anything; I've just decided that I've had enough. Life's been hard and soon it will be all over. It's a relief, really."

"But what about the others?" Doona asked quietly.

"About three months ago, at one of our regular meetings, I told the others what I was planning to do. Actually, I asked for their help. I wanted to get enough sleeping pills together so that I could take an overdose and I was hoping they might all have some to add to the bottle that I'd managed to get from my doctor." She sighed and sat back in her seat, looking out at the sea again.

"And what happened?" Bessie asked.

Elinor laughed lightly. "I thought they'd try to talk me out of it or something," she said. "Agnes was the first to respond. She said she wished she were brave enough to kill herself. She'd just been told that her heart was weak and she must avoid anything upsetting. She said she'd spent the last week watching scary movies, hoping one of them might do the trick."

"Oh, my," Bessie murmured.

"Nancy knew her cancer was back, even though the doctors hadn't told her yet. She didn't want to face more treatments. Joan was so tired of all the pain that her arthritis gave her. And dear Margaret was getting forgetful. She knew her mind was starting to go and she wanted out before she forgot who she was and how to function. Oh, we were a group of miserable old ladies and we all wanted to die." Elinor stopped for another drink.

"So you decided to kill them before you killed yourself," Doona said.

"Oh, no," Elinor laughed. "My dear girl, we made a rota."

Bessie and Doona exchanged looks while Elinor laughed until tears began to flow again. After she wiped her eyes, she looked at them both.

"It was all so simple," she said. "And the police can't work it out. But now I have to tell you, so that no one ends up getting blamed for something they didn't do."

"Go ahead," Bessie said.

"It was a couple of weeks after that meeting where we all talked about wanting to die. I couldn't stop thinking about what everyone had said. They all wished they could die quietly in their sleep or something. None of them was brave enough to kill themselves. After a lot of thought, I came up with an idea and I brought it up at a meeting. Maybe we could murder one another."

"Wanting to die is one thing," Bessie said, shaking her head. "But murder is another."

"Yes," Elinor agreed. "And it took them all some time to think it through. Is it really murder, though, if the other person wants to die? That was the key to the whole thing. We all wanted to be dead. We were really doing one another a favour. Our last chance to help out our fellow jam ladies, if you like."

"It's insane," Doona said.

Elinor smiled at her. "When you get to my age, life becomes a burden rather than a blessing," she said sadly. "And the step from life to death gets so much shorter. Helping my friends to make that step seemed like the right thing to do, and eventually they all came to agree with me."

"So you planned to murder each other?" Bessie asked. "I don't understand."

"If there's one thing I learned over the years with the jam ladies, it was that we all had different talents. Now we pooled our abilities with a new goal in mind. Everyone was tasked with figuring out two different ways that someone could be murdered where it would look like an accident. Not everyone managed to come up with two, but we ended up with seven or eight ideas. After that, we just put them all in a hat and we each drew one. And that was how we had to kill our victim. We drew the victims from a hat as well."

Bessie sat back in her seat, stunned. "You drew names from a hat?" she asked after a minute, almost too shocked to speak.

Elinor nodded. "Each of us had an intended victim and a method and then I drew the numbers for the order in which we were to die," she said, talking as calmly as if she were explaining how she's arranged for a bake sale.

"So no one knew that they were next?" Doona asked.

"No, well, except for poor Margaret, because I had to be last, as I'm the only one willing to kill myself, you see," Elinor explained.

"Maybe you could just walk us through the whole thing from the beginning?" Doona asked.

"It was simple," she said, talking slowly as if explaining things to a not-very-bright child. "I drew Nancy's name first, so she was the first to die. Agnes had drawn her name and she'd drawn poison as the method." Elinor sighed deeply. "Of course, everything went wrong with Nancy's death, but I suppose I mustn't blame Agnes. It was really Sarah Combe's fault."

"Why?" Bessie couldn't help but ask.

"The poison idea was too complicated, anyway," Elinor continued, ignoring the question. "But that was Joan for you, always full of crazy ideas. Oh, the plan was splendid, but asking Agnes to execute it?" She shook her head. "I should have insisted that she draw a different method, but she was quite excited about making jam and I couldn't persuade her to change."

"So Joan came up with the plan, but Agnes carried it out?" Bessie asked, feeling confused.

"That was all part of it. No one could know the order of the deaths or indeed how they were going to die. If you knew it was your turn to die and that your brakes were going to fail, you simply wouldn't drive your car. This way the accidents were as much a surprise to the victim as to everyone else."

"So what did Agnes do wrong?" Bessie asked.

"I suppose I should blame Joan as much as Agnes," Elinor replied. "She had the idea about passing out jars of jam at Tynwald Day. She thought if we gave away dozens of jars, no one would suspect that one of them was poisoned. Agnes was meant to be at Nancy's first thing the next morning. She was supposed to switch the poisoned jam for a good jar and then leave the box of rat poison on Nancy's shelf, next to the sugar. The hope was the police would think that Nancy had accidently added rat poison to her breakfast tea instead of sugar."

"The police would have worked out otherwise," Doona said.

"Maybe, but maybe not," Elinor answered. "We thought they might decide that it wasn't an accident, but no one would suspect murder. And how hard would they even look at it? An old woman like that? The police aren't that interested."

"That's not fair," Bessie said. "The police work hard no matter who dies."

"Rather harder than I might like," Elinor said dryly. "But anyway, Sarah turned up to see her mother for the first time in years at just the wrong time, and that almost ruined everything. I had a very difficult time persuading everyone that we should press on in spite of everything."

"Maybe you should have stopped," Doona said.

"There was a very real chance that Agnes might get arrested," Elinor said. "She had the box of poison, after all."

"Where did it come from? And where is it now?" Doona asked.

"Joan's husband was a gardener. He used to use rat poison, many years ago, and after such things were banned, he kept some in their shed. Joan had actually been thinking about using it to kill herself, so she offered it to the group for our plan," Elinor answered.

"And where is it now?" Doona repeated herself.

"In that box," Elinor said, pointing to the box on the table. "Don't touch it, not yet," she snapped as Doona leaned forward towards it. "You have to let me finish. The box of poison isn't the only thing in the box."

"So what happened next?" Bessie asked, feeling numb.

"Well, clearly Agnes had to go. The poor woman was falling apart. She felt guilty about killing her best friend, in spite of the fact that Nancy wanted to die. Anyway, I'd drawn up the plans for tampering with her brakes. Joan carried them out, but not without a lot of complaining. Apparently she had a terrible time getting under the car, what with her arthritis and all." Elinor shrugged. "Anyway, Agnes's death went much more closely to plan, and if Joan followed my instructions exactly, the police will never prove the brakes were tampered with deliberately."

"Your husband worked with cars," Doona recalled.

"Yes, and when we were first married, he showed me some of the most important bits and pieces. He also left a bunch of books and manuals about car repair with me when he moved across. It was lucky that Agnes drove such an old car. More modern cars are more complicated."

"So Joan tampered with Agnes's brakes and that got rid of her," Doona said. "What about Joan?"

"Agnes's husband was an electrician," Elinor told her. "She wired an old kettle so that it would give someone a powerful shock when they switched it on. It might not have killed a younger person, but we're all old. Anyway, she doctored the kettle and left it with me. When it was Margaret's turn to kill Joan, I gave Margaret the kettle. She was supposed to have Joan over for tea and ask her to make the drinks. It was a bit of serendipity that the same afternoon that I gave the kettle to Margaret, Joan mentioned that hers was broken. Margaret just had to pop out to her car and get the kettle to give Joan."

"So it wasn't the spare one from the community building?" Bessie asked.

"No. After everyone left for the day, I took the actual spare kettle and hid it, so if the police looked they wouldn't find it. It's in a box marked 'napkins and paper plates' in the bottom left cupboard in the kitchen," Elinor replied.

"So then you just had to push Margaret down her stairs and that would be the end of that," Doona concluded.

"Oh, dear, how inelegant," Elinor said, shaking her head. "I did not push Margaret down the stairs. Last night I went to visit her again and I helped her run her bath and poured her a glass of wine. Once she was settled in the tub, I ran a piece of cord across the landing at the top of the stairs. I let myself out, went home, making sure to wave to the lovely policeman who was watching my flat, and then, several hours later, I rang Margaret."

"She only had the one phone, in her kitchen, right?" Bessie checked.

"Exactly, and she couldn't simply let the phone ring. All those years married to an abusive husband who would smack her if she didn't answer fast enough? She always rushed to grab the phone. She may well have fallen on her own, without the cord," Elinor said.

"But the police didn't find any cord," Doona said.

"No, hours later, well after midnight, I snuck out of here and walked over to Margaret's. I let myself in the back door and climbed up and removed the cord. It's in the box as well," she said, gesturing towards it.

"But you'd have had to climb over Margaret's body," Doona said with a shudder.

"I did," Elinor replied. "But as she was dead, she didn't mind." Elinor dissolved into giggles that turned into tears. Bessie sat staring at her, uncertain as to what to say next.

"I think that's the whole story," Elinor said once she'd calmed down and sipped at her water. "So you see, I didn't kill all of my friends, just one of them. And I was ever so pleased to draw her name. I've been wanting to kill Margaret for years."

"You'll have to come down to the police station now," Doona said, standing up. "You'll need to tell Inspector Rockwell everything you just told us."

"I'd really rather not," Elinor said, yawning. "You can take the box, though. It has all of the details of every plan, and a letter, signed by all of us, agreeing to it. Tell your inspector friend that he can come and get me in about an hour, or maybe ninety minutes would be better."

"Elinor, you can't kill yourself," Bessie said firmly. "Come along with us and we'll get you someone to talk to."

"I don't want to talk any more," she said, closing her eyes. "I'm very tired, though. Maybe you could let yourselves out quietly? I'll just take a little nap."

"Elinor, have you taken an overdose of sleeping pills?" Bessie asked, as the last puzzle piece slid into place.

"Don't send the police yet," Elinor said to Bessie, staring hard into her eyes. "Let me die in peace first. If you could, maybe you could sit with me? I'm not sure I want to die alone."

Bessie and Doona exchanged glances and then Doona headed for the door, grabbing the box of evidence on her way out. Bessie hurried to catch up.

"I'm ringing John," Doona said, punching buttons on her mobile as she walked. "You don't think we should just let her die, do you?"

Bessie shook her head. "She might not mind having the deaths of four of her friends on her conscience, but I'm not having hers on mine."

CHAPTER 15

Several days later, in the late afternoon, Bessie sat on the rock behind her house and stared out at the sea. When Doona sat down beside her and put her arm around her, she forced herself to smile.

"Hello," she said softly.

"Hello," Doona echoed. "How are you tonight?"

Bessie shrugged. "I think I'm starting to feel better," she said with a sigh.

"Are you ready to hear what the police found in the box?" Doona asked.

"I suppose," Bessie glanced at Doona and then looked away. Ever since their meeting with Elinor, Bessie had refused to discuss anything to do with the Raspberry Jam Ladies. Doona insisted on telling her that Elinor had died in the ambulance on the way to hospital, but beyond that nothing had been said.

"We don't have to talk about it if you don't want to," Doona said, looking anxiously at her friend.

"I'm a strong woman," Bessie replied, still looking out at the sea. "And I've lived through a lot. Something about this, these deaths, has really shaken me. I'm older than they were and I still feel as if I have so much to live for. Or at least I did, before all of this happened."

Doona gave her a hug. "You do have a lot to live for," she said firmly. "And you have friends who love you. John was explaining to me about how groups can be led in different directions depending on their leaders. Elinor wanted to die and she managed to convince the others that they wanted to die as well. With a different leader, the jam ladies would all still be around, complaining about their aches and pains, but carrying on like normal."

Bessie shrugged. "Does the evidence support her story?" she asked.

"It does," Doona told her. "Everything she said was there, is there. The ladies all signed a letter detailing their plans. There are sheets with each plan carefully laid out, including several that were never used. It's scary."

"I can see why Elinor wanted to die," Bessie said sadly. "Nathan was her whole life and she felt lost without him. But I don't really understand the others."

"Nancy's doctor has confirmed that she had six months, at best, and that they would have been painful ones at that," Doona told her. "As far as Agnes is concerned, her doctor told her in March that she could go any time. He was surprised she made it to July."

"Poor Agnes," Bessie said. "She was a sweet woman who lived a very hard life."

"They were all good people, except for Elinor," Doona said.

Bessie shook her head. "Elinor was smart and ambitious in a time when women weren't supposed to be either," she told Doona. "I think the strain of raising Nathan and the circumstances around his death drove her slightly crazy."

"She was more than slightly crazy," Doona responded.

"What about Joan and Margaret?" Bessie asked. "What did their doctors have to say?"

"Joan was in a lot of pain and her doctor did say that she spoke to him more than once about wishing it was all over. She didn't feel she had much to live for, apparently."

"I never thought she recovered properly from when her little one died," Bessie said. "I suppose you never do get over such a thing."

"She also told her doctor that she'd heard from her son and he's planning on coming back to the island when he gets out of prison. Apparently, she wasn't pleased about that."

"I wonder why," Bessie said. "I never did get the whole story with what happened to him. I suppose he won't bother coming now that his mum is gone."

Doona shrugged. "He's actually due out soon, from what I understand. John's keeping a close eye on him."

"And Margaret?"

"Margaret was diagnosed with dementia about a year ago. Apparently she was very concerned about being on her own as it got worse. Her doctor was trying to persuade her to move into a care home where she could be looked after, but she didn't want to leave the home she loved." Doona shook her head. "Dementia can cause depression and impaired judgment," she told Bessie.

"I think I was right to not want to talk about this," Bessie replied. "It's all very sad."

"It is sad," Doona agreed. "Perhaps you're right not to think about it."

The sound of a car arriving had both women turning to see who was there. Bessie recognised Hugh's car as it pulled up in front of her cottage. Both front doors opened and Bessie smiled as Hugh and Grace climbed out of the car. Hugh was carrying several pizza boxes and Grace had a bakery box in her hand.

"Hullo, Bessie," Hugh called. "We brought dinner."

Bessie laughed in spite of her mood. She and Doona made their way back up the beach and Bessie opened the cottage door for her guests.

"John should be here any minute," Hugh said as Bessie found plates and glasses. "He's bringing the champagne."

"What are we celebrating?" Bessie asked, looking hard at Hugh.

"Just life," Hugh told her with a grin. He looked over at Grace and then smiled at Bessie. "Grace and I have been talking and we aren't quite ready for marriage yet. We've only been together for a few months, after all."

"Oh?" Bessie said, looking at Grace for confirmation.

Grace smiled. "Hugh's right," she said. "We both only want to get married once and make it for life, so we have to be absolutely sure we're marrying the right person. I'm still going to try for that job up here so that we can spend more time together, but if I get it, I'll be looking for my own little place, rather than moving in with Hugh. We were kind of rushing things."

Bessie nodded and replied carefully. "You two have clearly given this a lot of thought," she said. "Just keep in mind that marriage is a huge leap of faith as well, no matter how well you know one another."

Hugh nodded. "Maybe we should start eating while we wait for John?" he suggested.

Everyone laughed and Bessie passed around the plates. John was only a few minutes late and he brought a bottle of champagne and a bottle of sparkling apple juice.

"For the people who are driving," he explained.

Everyone ate pizza and then enjoyed the jam roly-poly that Grace had brought for pudding.

"I'm glad it's strawberry jam," Bessie commented after she'd eaten her first bite. "I'm not sure I'll ever eat raspberry jam again."

Grace flushed. "Oh, dear, I never even thought about that," she admitted. "I'm so sorry."

"It's fine," Bessie said. "I was mostly teasing." She sighed. "I really do appreciate you all coming over tonight to cheer me up. I needed it."

"It's always fun to come and see you," Hugh told her. "Whether you need cheering up or not."

Bessie smiled at him. He was turning into a lovely young man and he and Grace had a good chance of having a happy life together, assuming he worked that out before she got away.

"I'm so lucky to have you all as my friends," Bessie said, thoughtfully. "In good times and in bad."

"To Aunt Bessie," Hugh said, holding up his glass for a toast.

"To Aunt Bessie," everyone echoed.

GLOSSARY OF TERMS

MANX LANGUAGE TO ENGLISH

- **fastyr mie** — good afternoon
- **kys t'ou** — How are you?
- **ta mee braew** — I'm fine
- **Thie yn Traie** — Beach House
- **Treoghe Bwaane** — Widow's Cottage (Bessie's home)

ENGLISH/MANX TO AMERICAN TERMS

- **advocate** — Manx title for a lawyer (solicitor)
- **aye** — yes
- **bank holiday** — public holiday
- **bin** — garbage can
- **biscuits** — cookies
- **boot** — trunk (of a car)
- **car park** — parking lot
- **chippy** — a fish and chips take-out restaurant

GLOSSARY OF TERMS

- **chips** — french fries
- **comeover** — a person who moved to the island from elsewhere
- **crisps** — potato chips
- **cuddly toy** — stuffed animal
- **cuppa** — cup of tea (informal)
- **flat** — apartment
- **gaol** — jail
- **holiday** — vacation
- **journal** — diary
- **lift** — elevator
- **loo** — restroom
- **midday** — noon
- **nappy** — diaper
- **pavement** — sidewalk
- **peckish** — hungry
- **plait** — braid (in hair)
- **pudding** — dessert
- **queue** — line
- **rota** — schedule or list of who is to do what job or task
- **shopping trolley** — shopping cart
- **skeet** — gossip
- **starters** — appetizers
- **telly** — television
- **till** — check-out (in a grocery store, for example)
- **trainers** — sneakers

OTHER NOTES

If someone "wouldn't say boo to a goose," they are shy and try to stay out of the way.

A "car boot sale" is like a garage sale or yard sale, where, traditionally, the goods for sale are loaded into the boot (trunk) of the car and cars are parked in neat rows so that people can walk around and see what's on offer. Now they are often held in church halls or schools where the goods are displayed on tables.

CID is the Criminal Investigation Department of the Isle of Man Constabulary (Police Force).

"Noble's" is Noble's Hospital, the main hospital on the Isle of Man. It is located in Douglas, the island's capital.

When talking about time, the English say, for example, "half-seven" to mean "seven-thirty."

A charity shop is a shop run by a charitable (non-profit) organisation that sells donated second-hand merchandise in order to raise funds

OTHER NOTES

for their particular cause. They are great places to find books, games and puzzles, as well as clothing, knick-knacks and furniture.

When island residents talk about someone being from "across," or moving "across," they mean somewhere in the United Kingdom (across the water).

The emergency number in the UK is 999, rather than 911, as used in the US.

Hospitals in the UK have "Accident and Emergency" departments (A&E) rather than Emergency Rooms.

Coronation Chicken is a cold chicken salad made with curry powder in a mayonnaise base. It was originally served at Queen Elizabeth II's coronation banquet.

Toast soldiers are simply slices of toast cut lengthwise so they can easily be dipped into the runny yokes of soft-boiled eggs.

Bessie's story continues in

Aunt Bessie Finds

An Isle of Man Cozy Mystery

By Diana Xarissa

Aunt Bessie finds herself in need of a change of scenery.

Bessie Cubbon, Laxey Village's "Aunt Bessie" is feeling overwhelmed by the twists and turns her life has taken recently. When a friend suggests that she look at a flat in Douglas, Bessie is seriously tempted to try relocating to the Island's beautiful capital.

Aunt Bessie finds another body.

This one is still breathing at least, but no one seems to know anything about the man. Could he be tied to the strange things that are happening in Bessie's friend's building?

Aunt Bessie finds that doing a friend a favour isn't as easy as it appears.

Moving to Douglas turns out to be the easy part. Figuring out what's going on in the building on Seaside Terrace is far more complicated. With John and Hugh both on their summer holidays and Doona working hard in Laxey, Bessie finds herself calling on other acquaintances for help this time around. The question is, can she trust them the way she knows she can rely on her friends from Laxey?

ALSO BY DIANA XARISSA

The Isle of Man Cozy Mystery Series

Aunt Bessie Assumes

Aunt Bessie Believes

Aunt Bessie Considers

Aunt Bessie Decides

Aunt Bessie Enjoys

Aunt Bessie Finds

Aunt Bessie Goes

Aunt Bessie's Holiday

Aunt Bessie Invites

Aunt Bessie Joins

Aunt Bessie Knows

Aunt Bessie Likes

Aunt Bessie Meets

Aunt Bessie Needs

The Isle of Man Ghostly Cozy Mysteries

Arrivals and Arrests

Boats and Bad Guys

Cars and Cold Cases

Dogs and Danger

The Markham Sisters Cozy Mystery Novellas

The Appleton Case

The Bennett Case

The Chalmers Case
The Donaldson Case
The Ellsworth Case
The Fenton Case
The Green Case
The Hampton Case
The Irwin Case

The Isle of Man Romance Series
Island Escape
Island Inheritance
Island Heritage
Island Christmas

ABOUT THE AUTHOR

Diana Xarissa lived on the Isle of Man for more than ten years before returning to the United States with her family. Now living near Buffalo, New York, she enjoys having the opportunity to write about the island that she loves so much. It truly is a special place.

Diana also writes mystery/thrillers set in the not-too-distant future under the pen name "Diana X. Dunn" and fantasy/adventure books for middle grade readers under the pen name "D.X. Dunn."

She would be delighted to know what you think of her work and can be contacted through snail mail at:

Diana Xarissa Dunn
PO Box 72
Clarence, NY 14031.

Find Diana at:
www.dianaxarissa.com
diana@dianaxarissa.com